ACCEL·WORLD

THE RED CREST

REKI KAWAHARA
ILLUSTRATION BY **HIMA**
DESIGN BY **bee-pee**

"You ask whether this chocolate color is real? Nearly every Burst Linker who meets me says the same thing."

CHOCOLAT PUPPETEER

A small female-type duel avatar with chocolate armor. Out of nowhere, she attacks Silver Crow...

KUROYUKIHIME
Vice president of the Umesato Junior High student council. Controls the "Black King," Black Lotus.

"...Haruyuki. Is it all right if I come sit next to you?"

"No matter what happens, I'll always be right by your side..."

HARUYUKI
Boy in the lowest school caste. Member of the new Nega Nebulus, led by Kuroyukihime. Duel avatar: Silver Crow.

"I'm looking
forward.
To the festival.
And I'm sure.
My brother
is, too."

RIN

A Burst Linker girl who
goes to an expensive
girls' school. She has fond
feelings for Haruyuki.
During duels, ownership of
her consciousness shifts to
Ash Roller, her older brother.

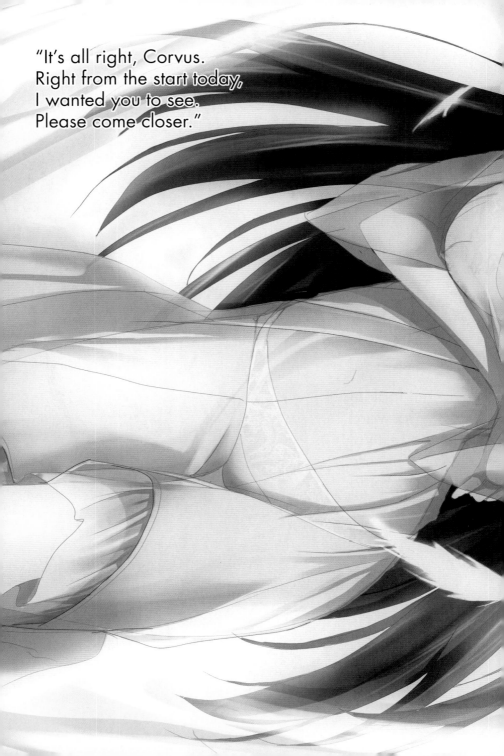

"It's all right, Corvus.
Right from the start today,
I wanted you to see.
Please come closer."

FUKO

Sky Raker, a Burst Linker in Nega Nebulus. The master who initiated Haruyuki into the Incarnate system.

MAIN DUEL AVATARS
List of Abilities

■ Nega Nebulus

Silver Crow
Aviation
?

Cyan Pile
Perforation

Lime Bell
Acoustic Summon

Black Lotus
Terminate Sword

Prominence

Cherry Rook
Wire Hook

Blood Leopard
Vital Bite
Mental Bite

Scarlet Rain
Vision Extension

Leonids

Frost Horn
Icy Slide

Tourmaline Shell
Piezo Armor

Blue Knight
Pain Killer
Limit Surpass

■ Crypt Cosmic Circus

Yellow Radio
Equilibrium
Acrobatics

Great Wall

Bush Utan
Longer Hanger

Olive Grab
Oil Coat

Ash Roller
Vertical Climb

Green Grandé
Double Payback

■ Oscillatory Universe

Ivory Tower
Undercover

Acceleration Research Society

Argon Array
Transcend Ray

Black Vise
Shadow Lurker

Others

Magnesium Drake
Flame Breath

Orchid Oracle
Hallucination

Mirror Masker
Theoretical Mirror

Wolfram Cerberus
Physical Immunity
?
?

▶▶▶ACCEL·WORLD 12

THE RED CREST

Reki Kawahara

Illustrations: HIMA

Design: bee-pee

YEN ON

NEW YORK

■ **Kuroyukihime** = Umesato Junior High School student council vice president. Trim and clever girl who has it all. Her background is shrouded in mystery. Her in-school avatar is a spangle butterfly she programmed herself. Her duel avatar is the Black King, Black Lotus (level nine).

■ **Haruyuki** = Haruyuki Arita. Eighth grader at Umesato Junior High School. Bullied, on the pudgy side. He's good at games, but shy. His in-school avatar is a pink pig. His duel avatar is Silver Crow (level five).

■ **Chiyuri** = Chiyuri Kurashima. Haruyuki's childhood friend. Meddling energetic girl. Her in-school avatar is a silver cat. Her duel avatar is Lime Bell (level four).

■ **Takumu** = Takumu Mayuzumi. A boy Haruyuki and Chiyuri have known since childhood. Good at kendo. His duel avatar is Cyan Pile (level five).

■ **Fuko** = Fuko Kurasaki. Burst Linker belonging to the old Nega Nebulus. One of the Four Elements. Lived as a recluse due to certain circumstances, but was persuaded by Kuroyukihime and Haruyuki to come back to the battlefront. Taught Haruyuki about the Incarnate System. Her duel avatar is Sky Raker (level eight).

■ **Uiui** = Utai Shinomiya. Burst Linker belonging to the old Nega Nebulus. One of the Four Elements. Fourth grader in the elementary division of Matsunogi Academy. Not only can she use the advanced curse removal command "Purify," she is also skilled at long-range attacks. Her duel avatar is Ardor Maiden (level seven).

■ **Neurolinker** = A portable Internet terminal that connects with the brain via a wireless quantum connection and enhances all five senses with images, sounds, and other stimuli.

■ **Brain Burst** = Neurolinker application sent to Haruyuki by Kuroyukihime.

■ **Duel avatar** = Player's virtual self, operated when fighting in Brain Burst.

■ **Legion** = Groups composed of many duel avatars with the objective of expanding occupied areas and securing rights. There are seven main Legions, each led by one of the Seven Kings of Pure Color.

■ **Normal Duel Field** = The field where normal Brain Burst battles (one-on-one) are carried out. Although the specs do possess elements of reality, the system is essentially on the level of an old-school fighting game.

■ **Unlimited Neutral Field** = Field for high-level players where only duel avatars at levels four and up are allowed. The game system is of a wholly different order than that of the Normal Duel Field, and the level of freedom in this field beats e t s e the next generation VRMMO.

■ Movement Control System = System in charge of avatar control. Normally, this system handles all avatar movement.

■ Image Control System = System in which the player creates a strong image in their mind to operate the avatar. The mechanism is very different from the normal Movement Control System, and very few players can use it. Key component of the Incarnate System.

■ Incarnate System = Technique allowing players to interfere with the Brain Burst program's Image Control System to bring about a reality outside of the game's framework. Also referred to as "overwriting" game phenomena.

■ Acceleration Research Society = Mysterious Burst Linker group. They do not think of Brain Burst as a simple fighting game and are planning something. Black Vise and Rust Jigsaw are members.

■ Armor of Catastrophe = An Enhanced Armament also called "Chrome Disaster." Equipped with this, an avatar can use powerful abilities such as Drain, which absorbs the HP of the enemy avatar, and Divination, which calculates enemy attacks in advance to evade them. However, the spirit of the wearer is polluted by Chrome Disaster, which comes to rule the wearer completely.

■ Star Caster = The longsword carried by Chrome Disaster. Although it now has a sinister form, it was originally a famous and solemn sword that shone like a star, just as the name suggests.

■ ISS kit = Abbreviation for "IS mode study kit." ("IS mode" is "Incarnate System mode.") The kit allows any duel avatar who uses it to make use of the Incarnate System. While using it, a red "eye" is attached to some part of the avatar, and a black aura overlay—the staple of Incarnate attacks— is emitted from the eye.

■ Seven Arcs = The seven strongest Enhanced Armaments in the Accelerated World. They are the greatsword Impulse, the staff Tempest, the large shield Strife, the Luminary (form unknown), the straight sword Infinity, the full-body armor Destiny, and the Fluctuating Light (form unknown).

■ Mental-Scar Shell = The emotional scars that are the foundation of a duel avatar (mental scars created from trauma in early childhood)—this is the shell enveloping them. Children with exceptionally hard and thick "shells" are said to produce metal-color duel avatars.

▶▶▶ *ACCEL·WORLD*

1

"…So it's finally my turn…"

Haruyuki gaped as the pounding rain of the Storm stage beat down on him.

The owner of the voice was a relatively small duel avatar on the ground in front of him. His four limbs were splayed out, his body half-buried in the surface of the road, cracks radiating out around him. His full armor was heavy metal, a matte gray tinged with brown.

After school the day before, Haruyuki had been completely and utterly trounced by this metal-color avatar. He had been so badly beaten that immediately after the duel, tears of regret had flowed down his face. But overnight, he had managed to pull himself to his feet again and now, after a little special training, had returned to challenge his victor to a revenge match.

This duel ended up being the flip side of their first: Haruyuki had slashed his opponent's health gauge down to a mere 10 percent by taking in his attacks and using them to slam his foe into the ground. But then something baffling occurred: His duel opponent, still prone on the concrete, had made this pronouncement about his turn, but in a voice and tone that were completely different from before.

Duel avatars—the virtual armor the Brain Burst program gave

to the boys and girls who became Burst Linkers—lacked mouth and nose structures, except for a few female types. As far as eye lenses go, Takumu's Cyan Pile and Kuroyukihime's Black Lotus just had faint, shining spots. In the case of Haruyuki's Silver Crow, the entire face was covered by a smooth mirrored visor.

Wolfram Cerberus, the mysterious metal-color avatar referred to as "the genius newb" by many, and his current duel opponent also followed this design line. His face was enveloped from above and below in a metal visor reminiscent of a wolf's jaws, and the goggles inside could only be glimpsed through a gap of mere centimeters.

So Haruyuki couldn't quite pin down where these words of Cerberus's were coming from, lying as he was in a puddle of water on the road. Normally, this was when he assumed there was a mouth hidden under the visor, but Haruyuki felt a peculiar truth in his gut:

What had spoken had not been Cerberus's head. It had been his left shoulder.

He hadn't really been aware of it up to that point, but when he looked with this in mind, the shape of Cerberus's shoulder armor closely resembled the helmet that encased his head. A form with a straight line popping up sharply like a wolf's head, then a zig-zagging line cut across the center like fangs.

Although the zigzag on his actual head had revealed the goggles inside until a few seconds before, it was now completely closed. Instead, the line on the left shoulder had opened about a centimeter, and a dark light radiated from within. This red glow colored several lines of water trailing along the armor surface, making them look like drops of blood spilling from the maw of a beast.

"Who are you?" Haruyuki asked hoarsely of the Burst Linker he'd driven to only 10 percent health via his specialized Guard Reversal technique.

"Heh-heh-heh." The chuckle he got in reply was like metal creaking. "Who am I? It's a little late for that, isn't it? You just mercilessly beat me into the ground, Crow. And I know aaaaaaall about you."

"Know? We just dueled for the first time yesterday," Haruyuki responded reflexively, and then he shook his head slightly. "N-no, wait. Are you really the Cerberus who was fighting me until just a minute ago? It's kinda like…like you're a totally different person."

"Heh-heh-heh, well, yeah. We were born like that, right from the start. You already know the meaning of *Cerberus*, right?" the left shoulder armor said, red light blinking.

Haruyuki gasped. In the back of his mind, the memory of the Wolfram Cerberus vs. Frost Horn duel the previous evening came back to life. His eyes had opened wide in astonishment when Cerberus had closed in with alarming speed and armor strength on Frost Horn, who was four levels higher, so Manganese Blade, an executive member of the Blue Legion, had explained the name to him.

"Wolfram" was tungsten, the heavy metal with the greatest hardness. And "Cerberus" was a creature from Greek mythology. Given that Haruyuki had played countless fantasy RPGs since he was very little, this monster was familiar to him: a massive dog with three heads, said to be the watchdog of Hell.

Three. Heads.

The instant his brain made it to this point, Haruyuki finally understood. Cerberus's shoulder armor didn't *resemble* a head; it *was* a head. He couldn't even begin to imagine what kind of logic would give rise to a phenomenon like this, but at any rate, it was a fact that the duel avatar Wolfram Cerberus had been born with three heads. That was why he had been crowned with the name of that three-headed watchdog.

Most likely, the cheerful, polite boy Haruyuki had been dueling until a few minutes earlier was what would be called Cerberus's primary personality. And the one with the rough tone conversing with Haruyuki now was the second.

"…Kerberos…" The Greek name slipped out of him.

"Heh-heh-heh." The second head on Cerberus's left shoulder laughed for the third time. "That's right, Crow. Although it took you a little while to realize it. I'll give you this, though: Your technique's something else. You're the first one who's ever dragged me out in the middle of a duel. Such a thrill. Now I can finally fight, too."

Hearing this, Haruyuki finally remembered that this was

Nakano Area No. 2—that this was a duel stage. And that Silver
Crow and Wolfram Cerberus were in the middle of a battle, with
a large Gallery watching.

"...I know you have all kinds of secrets. But right now, none
of that matters," Haruyuki said resolutely, banishing his own
amazement from his body. "Once you dive into the battlefield, all
that's left is to focus on the duel. Let's continue this chat the next
time we're in the Gallery together or something."

He glanced up at the health gauges in the upper part of his field
of view. While Crow's was practically damage-free, Cerberus had
been thrown and slammed into the ground with Guard Reversal
any number of times; he had barely anything left in his red gauge.

And the special-attack gauge displayed below his health was
completely drained. Which meant that the effective time of Cerberus's dreadful high-performance ability Physical Immune had
ended. Haruyuki had already confirmed in the duel the previous
day that given this situation, he could do damage if he aimed for
a gap in the armor.

"If you're not going to stand up, then I'll finish things like this,"
he said, looking down at Cerberus, who was splayed on the road.
He straightened out the fingers of his right hand sharply like a
sword and then readied them above his shoulder.

Even seeing this attack motion, Cerberus didn't so much as
twitch. He might have said, "I finally get to fight," but it appeared
he was ready to throw in the towel.

Or perhaps he was going to come challenge Haruyuki again once
this duel was over. In which case, this would be a proud blow to welcome the next fight. A fundamental rule of Brain Burst was that a
player could challenge the same opponent only once a day. The rule
wasn't *duel* the same opponent, because the system recognized the
right of the loser to immediately petition for a revenge match.

"...Sheh!!"

With a sharp battle cry, Haruyuki took aim at the throat of the
fallen Cerberus and drove his hand straight downward at top
speed. A silver light raced forward faster than the falling rain.

In that instant, the centimeter gap in the zigzag line of Cerberus's left shoulder suddenly opened wide, and Haruyuki realized with a shock that what he had thought was an eye was actually a mouth. The metal halves of the visor flew away from each other, and in the void of the darkness where they hid, a crimson light jetted upward like flames from deep, deep within.

The light scattered, coloring the raindrops, and touched Haruyuki's hand, attacking on its propulsive downward trajectory.

"Nggh...!" He involuntarily cried out. It wasn't that he had taken damage or that he had repelled it. His right hand was in fact being irresistibly pulled toward Cerberus's left shoulder. Forced off course from the target of his attack—Cerberus's unarmored neck—his hand was jerked toward the gaping maw of his enemy's shoulder.

Then I just have to punch right through his shoulder! Haruyuki shouted to himself, and he put everything he had into piercing the red darkness shining deep within the armor.

But he felt nothing; there was no impact. First, his fingers, his wrist, then his arm almost up to the elbow were plunged into the dark opening, but his senses communicated nothing: no response, no sensation of touch. But that was impossible. Cerberus's shoulder armor was exactly the same size as his head, twenty centimeters deep at best. Which meant that if Haruyuki's arm was in there up to the elbow, then his fingers should have long broken through the other side and pushed outward already.

Haruyuki felt something cold and extremely unpleasant in his arm, through his shoulder, and up his spine. He fiercely yanked back his plunging arm to stop the charge, and his arm began to emerge from the darkness filling this strange mouth.

And then the fangs closed.

Clank! A bizarre metallic sound echoed through the stage. The members of the Gallery, watching the events unfold from the roofs on either side of Nakano Street, stirred so loudly they drowned out the din of the pounding rain.

But Haruyuki wasn't conscious of this—nor even of Lime Bell's scream from somewhere in the Gallery. A burning pain shot up from his forearm to the center of his brain. The sensation of pain in the normal duel field was restricted to half that of the Unlimited Neutral Field, but even still, a low cry slipped out from beneath his helmet. *"Ghk...!"*

He held his breath and opened his eyes wide. The sharp, tapered edge of Cerberus's left shoulder armor had bitten deep into his right arm from both above and below. The fangs had dug down two centimeters into Crow's metallic armor and were trying to burrow even farther in, making a disturbing creaking sound as they did so. In sync with this, Haruyuki's health gauge was being carved away at a steady pace.

Tungsten, Wolfram Cerberus's armor color, had the greatest hardness of all the metal colors. Up until then, that hardness had basically been used for defense, but in the real world, tungsten's main use was in tools—particularly drills and saw blades. Put another way, this was exactly the kind of situation where tungsten demonstrated its real value.

Haruyuki decided his armor could withstand the attack, and as he endured the excruciating pain, he tightened his left hand into a fist. He took aim at the dark-gray body exposed at the base of Cerberus's left shoulder and launched a series of short punches. His enemy's health gauge was below 10 percent; Haruyuki should have been able to eat away the last of it with three hits.

But an instant before the first punch could land, Cerberus's right arm moved to cover the weak point at the base of his neck.

Nonetheless, Haruyuki beat down with his fist but, hindered by the hard tungsten of Cerberus's forearm, he was basically unable to do damage.

The reason Haruyuki had been able to unilaterally back Cerberus into a corner in this revenge match was because of the way he had broadly applied throwing techniques; taking his opponent's blows and beating him against the ground had rendered Cerberus's Physical Immune ability useless. In which case, all he had to do now was throw the already downed Cerberus down farther. But with one arm held fast in his opponent's mouth, that would be difficult. If he forcibly pulled Cerberus up off the ground, the damage to his right arm might grow in scale, and he would be the one injured by the move.

What am I going to do?! What should I do?! Haruyuki frantically racked his brain as he vainly launched strikes with his left hand.

It had been eight months since he had become a Burst Linker the previous fall, but this was the first time he had been caught in a biting attack with enough force to dig into his metal armor. But if he couldn't handle the technique just because he hadn't seen it before, he'd never seriously be able to make his way through the world of level-six and -seven high rankers. No matter what the attack, there was always a way to counter it. Even in a situation like this, with one arm held fast and the other hand guarded against, there was always some secret trick to turning it all around.

Haruyuki. He heard the voice from the deepest depths of his head. *Against simple hitting techniques, your Way of the Flexible will be an effective weapon. But you must not think you can win with that alone. Your opponent is not an Enemy that merely repeats the same attack patterns; he is a Burst Linker with knowledge and courage. Once he knows his blows will be repelled, he will immediately counter that. For instance, with a throwing technique, a hold technique, some kind of flying tool...*

The owner of the voice was, of course, Haruyuki's parent—the Black King, Black Lotus, aka Kuroyukihime. But it wasn't as though she had dived into this battlefield; even if she had been there, the heavy rain would have prevented her murmured words from reaching him. Instead, this was Haruyuki's memory. As much as he could, he had carved all the lessons from his sword-master into the deepest parts of his spirit: an archive for all eternity. The voice came from this place.

And of those techniques, although it may appear staid, the hold is actually the most difficult to respond to. Because there is a great deal of diversity in the technique logic. In addition to simple physical restraint, there are many attacks that hinder movement with electricity, magnetism, vacuum, and viscous liquids. It is difficult for even a veteran Burst Linker to respond appropriately to all of these the first time they see them.

However, Haruyuki—in the Accelerated World, you alone have a seemingly effective method of dealing with more than half of the hold techniques. Remember the time when you were sucked in by the magnet avatar of the Yellow Legion? If, rather than a hold fixing an opponent to the terrain, the hold affixes you to the enemy himself...then fly! Fly with your opponent still attached to you. If you reach an altitude high enough to definitively kill your enemy with drop damage alone, then you at least will not lose. As far as I know, there is basically no one who has been able to crash into the most impenetrable object—the ground—and walk away uninjured.

"...!!"

His master's words played back within him as a flash of light less than one-tenth of a second long. And the instant that light reached the end of his nervous system, Haruyuki shifted to action.

He brandished his left fist in the same motion as his previous useless punches. His opponent Cerberus's second personality—maybe he could call him Cerberus II—continued to guard the sensitive area at his neck with his right arm. Haruyuki's fist, which came down toward it regardless, this time opened up halfway down and tightly grabbed ahold of his opponent's wrist.

"*Unh...Aaah!*" Howling, Haruyuki threw his upper body up. His special-attack gauge was nearly fully charged from the battle thus far. He poured all of that shining blue light into the metallic fins on his back.

Chak! The silver wings deployed. The high-speed vibration of the blade fins pulverized the drops of rain as soon as they hit them, turning the water into a fine mist.

"*Grar...*" Unable to speak, because his mouth was clamped down on Crow's right arm, Cerberus II groaned like an animal. But he apparently decided not to release his biting lock. It seemed that II had not inherited the brilliant fighting instincts of the polite first boy—Cerberus I.

Once he had built up plenty of flight energy, Haruyuki stared at the black clouds above his head and kicked hard off the ground. A sudden fierce shock slammed into him as his left hand gripped his enemy's right wrist and his imprisoned right arm stretched out below him. Given the relative weight of tungsten, Cerberus was fairly heavy for his small size, but not so heavy that Crow's propulsive force couldn't yank him up into the air.

"Aaah...!" Haruyuki cried out once more and flapped his wings with everything he had. Cerberus peeled away from the dent in the road surface where he'd been half-buried moments before. They ascended rapidly, slicing through the pouring rain. Haruyuki flew at full speed, charging upstream along Nakano Sun Plaza, redeveloped and reborn as a skyscraper some ten years earlier, and windows shattered one after another from the shock wave.

He flew up past the 180-meter-tall building, and after ascending another 50 meters, Haruyuki shifted into hovering mode. The very little remaining in Cerberus's gauge would definitely be knocked out if he were dropped from this altitude.

Out of the corner of his eye, he caught sight of the members of the Gallery—which had shifted to automatic Battle Follow mode—appearing on the roof of Sun Plaza as Haruyuki released his left hand. Cerberus II lurched to one side; now the only thing keeping his significant mass in midair was Haruyuki's right arm, still caught in his mouth.

"The previous you would have blocked my chance to fly at first glance. I was surprised that your insides changed as well, but I can't really say you're stronger than the other one."

"...Grrr..." Cerberus's left shoulder growled at Haruyuki again, still biting down on his arm. The viselike pressure had stopped, fixing the distance between upper and lower fangs; the pain wasn't so great that he couldn't stand it.

As for Cerberus, he couldn't exactly bite off the arm in his mouth (although more precisely, it was in his left shoulder). The instant he did that, he would fall helplessly downward from an altitude of 230 meters. He might crash into the roof of a tall building rather than into the ground, and with the Physical Immune ability active, the terrain objects might have acted as a cushion, allowing him to live with 1 percent or so of his gauge. But Cerberus II, the personality in control now, did not appear to have that ability.

Although the whole thing had sent a serious chill up his spine at first—the second personality in the shoulder armor, the force of the tungsten fangs' biting attack—Haruyuki meant what he'd said. When he assessed the situation coolly, pre-switch Cerberus I was more troublesome than this II. Cerberus I was one of the least-compatible enemies Silver Crow had come across, but Crow was actually the natural enemy of Cerberus II, whose main weapon was a biting-hold technique. When II was yanked up from the ground to a high altitude the instant he bit down, the best he could hope for was a draw.

Having finally gotten this far in his analysis and regaining a little mental leeway, Haruyuki turned toward the avatar dangling from his right arm, not even trying to move, and spoke once more: "…Who's your parent?" He didn't expect Cerberus to obediently offer up an answer, but he still had to ask.

That day at lunch, during the special anti-Cerberus training session, Kuroyukihime and Fuko had told Haruyuki about two unfamiliar—and fearsome—ideas. The first was the "Mental-Scar Shell theory," a mechanism for the birth of metal-color avatars espoused by the Quad Eyes Analyst, aka Argon Array, at the dawn of the Accelerated World.

And the other was the "Artificial Metal-Color plan," a plan to push the Mental-Scar Shell theory forward by intentionally producing metal colors…apparently. It wasn't clear whether it had been implemented or not. But Kuroyukihime and Fuko seemed to think that Cerberus's too-sudden appearance and his battle power, almost impossibly ferocious for a level one, was something other than coincidence. That was someone's will at work.

"Fight him and watch carefully," Kuroyukihime had told Haruyuki.

He had drawn one new characteristic out of Cerberus, but it

wasn't enough to be certain. Thus, he asked for the name of his parent. But, naturally, he got no verbal response.

Instead, the mysterious metal color exerted a pressure several times anything he'd displayed so far on the tungsten fangs eating into Haruyuki's arm.

"*Nngh…!*" Haruyuki groaned again at the lancing pain.

A disagreeable *snap* echoing in the air, Cerberus's left shoulder closed completely. Silver Crow's right arm was severed a little below the elbow, and the crimson damage effect dyed the raindrops around them the color of blood.

Taking damage from losing a part, the health gauge on the upper left dropped dramatically. But with this, the duel was Haruyuki's victory. Rather than be peppered with questions while dangling in space, Cerberus II had chosen to fall and drop the curtain on this fight.

Haruyuki intended to watch his opponent's resignation right to the end, and he shifted his gaze down from his gauge—

"—?!"

—and then gasped in amazement.

Cerberus was not falling.

To be more precise, he had dropped about two meters in altitude the moment he bit off Crow's arm, but for some reason, he stopped there without falling any farther. Haruyuki wondered if Cerberus had hooked on to him with an ultrafine thread or something when he wasn't looking, but if that were the case, Cerberus would have to have been directly below him. But his hovering enemy was off ahead of him by at least a meter.

Haruyuki's eyes, opened wide in shock, could not discern any reason why his enemy failed to fall. Instead, his ears caught an uncomfortable sound.

Krrk. Rrk. Skrk. It was the sound of something hard being forcibly pulverized by something else. When he looked very, very carefully, the armor of Cerberus's left shoulder was moving slightly up and down. That was the source of the sound—it was the grinding. He was chewing Silver Crow's torn-off right arm.

The dreadful sound stopped after mere seconds. But the next phenomenon was even more chilling.

From Wolfram Cerberus's back, ten thin, sharp protrusions—wings—started to slowly stretch out on both sides. They had the same shape as Silver Crow's silver wings. But they were basically transparent, and the buildings around Nakano Station were hazily visible through them. It wasn't that they were made of a glass-like material; they seemed to not actually be real, because the ceaseless pelting rain didn't bounce off them.

But even if they were phantom wings, they were generating definite thrust. As the transparent fins vibrated, Cerberus floated upward and ascended to the same altitude as Haruyuki before settling into a hover again. The cries of the Gallery, ensconced on the roof of the Nakano Sun Plaza building fifty meters below, reached them as if chasing after them.

"H-he's not falling! He's floating!"

"Cerberus can't be a complete flying type, too, can he?!"

"No way! He has that power on top of Physical Immune?!"

These sounded very much like the cries Haruyuki had heard when he first flew in the Suginami area eight months earlier. He was frozen, unable to say anything.

"Relax," Cerberus said curtly, offhandedly. "My ability's not stealing. *Unlike him.*"

This statement contained some critical information, but his brain could not process this in the moment, and Haruyuki simply parroted back, "Not...stealing?"

"Yeah. It's Reproduction. Although even if it was stealing, you don't really have the right to grumble about it. I mean, you took something important from me."

"You're saying I took something from you?" Haruyuki asked, hoarsely, his mind finally 70 percent back online. The answer was something even more unexpected.

"I can't answer your earlier question about who my parent is, but I'll answer this one. I suppose you could call what you took from me my reason for existing."

"Reason...for existing...?"

"Exactly. More than half my basic potential's sealed away. I only have the one power, the Wolf Down I used before. Because I was tuned for a certain purpose."

"Tuned? ...What's this 'purpose'?"

"Simple. Equip that thing you sealed off somewhere. I say any more than that, and I'll get yelled at. And we're out of time anyway. I only ate half an arm, after all."

As Cerberus spoke, the wings on his back grew even more transparent. They lost form as if melting in the rain and turned into a hazy warping of space before finally disappearing. The gray avatar lurched forward. In the instant before he went into free fall, he tossed out his quiet final words.

"We'll meet again, Silver Crow. I'll finish up here today...And a message from Number One. He says, 'It was fun to duel with you. Honestly.'"

And then the super-hard metal color, the source of many mysteries, fell to the ground, curtained by large drops of rain. A few seconds later, the thunderous roar of impact sounded, and the health gauge in the upper right dropped to zero.

You win!!

The flaming text burned brightly in the center of his field of view before the results screen was displayed, but Haruyuki remained frozen in midair, unable to move. In the depths of his ears, Cerberus's speech from moments ago continued to play on repeat.

Equip that thing you sealed off somewhere.

That thing *you sealed off.*

Haruyuki had an extremely clear gut feeling about what this signifier meant. But even in his head, he seriously hesitated to give it form.

When the duel ended, the pounding rain of the stage turned into a drizzle, and the members of the Gallery applauded and cheered from the roof of Nakano Sun Plaza to send him off (although some of the voices sounded a little bewildered). But for a while, he wasn't even aware of that.

2

Even after the acceleration was released and he returned to the back seat of the EV bus racing down Oume Highway, Haruyuki simply stared at his own right hand for a while. He had succeeded in getting his revenge, but any exhilaration at his victory had been blown off somewhere.

Abruptly, he saw an index finger stretch out from his right and push the global-net disconnect button on the side of his Neurolinker. After the dialog box that popped up in his view to announce the loss of connection had disappeared, he saw Chiyuri's face through his virtual desktop, eyebrows furrowed together.

"Hey, Haru, what're you all spaced out for? This is Nakano, y'know? If you don't disconnect right after the duel, you'll get challenged again."

"O-oh...Sorry, thanks...," Haruyuki muttered, and his childhood friend changed the angle of her eyebrows, slightly cocking her head.

"...What's up? I mean, seriously. You won, but you look like you ate pickled eggplant or something."

His other childhood friend, Takumu, popped his face into Haruyuki's view from around Chiyuri's far side. "Once you pushed him to ten percent remaining, things seemed to take a fairly surprising turn," he whispered. "Is that why, Haru?"

And then Utai Shinomiya, sitting to Haruyuki's left, tapped at her holo keyboard in midair. UI> IT LOOKED TO ME AS THOUGH YOUR DUEL OPPONENT CHANGED MIDWAY. SYSTEM-WISE, THAT'S NOT POSSIBLE, BUT...

Haruyuki stared at the cherry-colored text in the ad hoc chat window sitting in the bottom of his field of view and then nodded deeply. Just loud enough for his friends in the back of the bus to hear, he offered, "It's just like Shinomiya says. That's what happened...I think. Cerberus also said he'd go home for today, so I'll tell you the details once we get back to Suginami. Let's change buses first."

They got off at the next stop, crossed the street at a nearby light, and got on a bus going the opposite way that came minutes later. Soon, they had crossed the border between Nakano and Suginami, and once the four had reconnected their Neurolinkers to the global net, they got off the bus at the Koenjirikkyo intersection. It was still raining, so they quickly opened their umbrellas.

"So what are we doing?" Chiyuri asked. "Are we going to Haru's?"

Haruyuki thought for a minute. If they were going to talk about Brain Burst, then the usual spot of the Arita living room was without a doubt the safest, but his condo was on the other side of the Chuo Line elevated bridge, in the exact opposite direction from Utai's house. He couldn't bring himself to make a fourth-grade girl walk two kilometers round-trip in this rain. Even if she was wearing those adorable red boots. "Um, maybe if there's somewhere around here we can talk first..."

Once he had gotten that far, Chiyuri grinned. "Then it's obviously Enjiya. The tatami rooms there are pretty secure, and Haru also promised to treat me and Taku."

"Gah! Treating you at Enjiya is a matter of national politics—"

"Ah-ha-ha! Kidding! Kidding! Hold on a sec, I'll just check." After laughing for a moment, Chiyuri ran a finger across her virtual desktop. She was connecting with the shop online and getting information on the customer seating in real time. "Oh! We're in luck! The inside room's empty. I'll reserve it."

She pushed a button that only she could see and swiped away the window. Bouncing up and down behind him, she shouted, "Hurry! Come on! The quick reservation there gets canceled after five minutes!"

Enjiya was a café with Japanese-style sweets set up in a small storefront a little north of Oume Highway. The short *noren* curtains across the doorway were a deep red—*enji*—so it seemed natural to assume this was where the name came from. But it was actually a shortening of Koenji, a fact that only longtime regulars knew.

The café was run by the owner, a man in his thirties or forties or fifties—in other words, a man of indeterminate age—and a woman who was probably in her twenties. While they did have traditional sweets, like the sweat bean paste of *anmitsu* and the jelly of *mamekan*, they also had over a dozen other types of treats, from gelato and waffles to homemade cheesecake and even enormous parfaits, so it was hard to decide whether to stick with the basics or go all out. Last fall, when Takumu and Haruyuki had gone to apologize for the backdoor hacking incident, Chiyuri had insisted on all the parfaits she could eat at this café as a condition of peace and had nearly broken both of their banks, a memory that was both sad and sweet now.

Perhaps she herself had long forgotten this—or perhaps she was merely pretending to have forgotten, for their sakes—but the instant she set herself down on a floor cushion in their reserved tatami room in back, she cried out, utterly carefree and without so much as glancing at the holo menu, "Let's see! I'm having the *kinako* parfait with rice dumplings topped with sweet bean paste!"

"Are you sure you wanna eat something like that right before supper?" Haruyuki remarked unthinkingly, and he got a chuckle in return.

"I'll thank you not to look down on athletes. My metabolism's different from yours, you know."

"I-I'm sorry. Um, I'm gonna have fresh chocolate gelato with nuts on top."

"Whenever we come here, that's all you ever order, Haru." This time, it was Takumu who chuckled at him. "I'll go with...*mamekan.*"

Haruyuki turned his face away—"Whatever, I like it"—and locked eyes with Utai, who was grinning at this little back-and-forth among the three childhood friends. The instant he saw her sitting in the *seiza* position on her own cushion—back straight, knees tucked under her—memories of the day before flashed through his mind.

After they had finished their club work, Utai had invited him to the Shinomiya house, where she had sat in the same formal position and told him about the world of Noh she had been born into and about the sad fate of Mirror Masker, the Burst Linker who had been her older brother and also her parent.

Perhaps intuiting his thoughts from the momentary look on his face, Utai smiled broadly and quickly typed, UI> I'VE NEVER BEEN TO THIS CAFÉ BEFORE. DO YOU HAVE ANY RECOMMENDATIONS?

Looking at the text displayed in the chat window, Haruyuki was more concerned with Utai's self-possession, which was so unlike a fourth grader, than the content of her question. When he really thought about it, a rich girls' school like Matsunogi likely prohibited its students from stopping to eat or drink on their way home. And yet Utai was calm and relaxed in this café, a place she was visiting for the first time, probably because even at that age, she was used to getting food and groceries by herself.

He had only learned of Utai's home environment for the first time the previous day, and the details started to resurface in the back of his mind, but he pushed them away for now and grinned. "Um. If it's your first time, then I guess maybe the *anmitsu*?"

Chiyuri was quick to agree. "*Anmitsu*'s the foundation of a Japanese-style sweetshop!"

UI> Foundations are important. Well then, I'll have this fruit *anmitsu*. Utai touched the holo menu with a small finger and pushed the COMPLETE ORDER button.

A female employee appeared in Japanese-style clothing with a tray of waters and hand towels. She greeted Haruyuki and his friends amiably (they had been frequenting the place for more than five years now) and then welcomed the newcomer Utai more formally before returning to the kitchen.

The students in the neighborhood whispered that the Japanese-style desserts were prepared by the owner, while the Western-style ones were made by the female employee—they also whispered the converse. But the truth of it was unknown. There were also rumors that a robot pâtissier had been spotted in the kitchen and that the café's sweets were all lies delivered to their brains via Neurolinker, but these were clearly jokes.

What was certain was that the uniform of the woman—a deep-red kimono with a snowy white apron—and her twenties-ish appearance had not changed in the slightest.

Once they had placed their orders and had all taken a drink of water, the eyes of the other three focused on Haruyuki.

"...So, Haru, what exactly happened? And why?" Inside the café, there were only two older customers at the counter and a group of three women who looked to be housewives at a table near the door. Age-wise, they couldn't have been Burst Linkers, but just in case, Chiyuri lowered her voice.

"Ummm..." Haruyuki reflected on the earlier duel. "Until ninety percent of his health gauge was carved away, it was just like you guys saw. But...a little after he went down...the visor on his original head closed, and the armor on his left shoulder opened instead. And then...maybe you won't believe this, but the left shoulder talked. It said, 'So it's finally my turn.'"

It took about five minutes to explain how it all had gone down, and just as Haruyuki finished, their orders arrived with perfect timing. The woman had no sooner placed the dishes on the table and urged them to take their time than the four Burst Linkers were reaching for their spoons.

Simultaneously scooping up rice dumplings and cream and *anko* beans in a miraculous balance on her spoon, Chiyuri opened her mouth and filled her cheeks. Pure bliss overtook her for about five seconds before she could get herself together again. "Mmm, mmmmm...It's like, the more I hear, the more this is, like, for serious, you know? If he's switching between personality extremes, I guess we have Niko for precedent."

"No matter how you look at it, Niko's angel mode is a performance." Haruyuki grinned wryly around a mouthful of chocolaty gelato. "The way Cerberus switched was definitely not on that level. And the way he talked—he's Cerberus because there are three of him. I mean, he was named after that mythological dog, so it's kinda like that, I guess? And actually, when it was his left shoulder, the abilities he used changed, too."

"So then, on top of the Cerberus I that you fought first and the Cerberus II of the left shoulder, there's a III, too?" Takumu asked as he scooped up *mamekan* with a lacquerware spoon.

Haruyuki thought a minute and then nodded. "When you think about it, the right shoulder's probably Cerberus III, huh? Cerberus I talks politely, II is rougher. No clue what III will sound like."

"My vote's for old-school style," Chiyuri remarked.

"L-like a grandpa character? That'll be hard to fight."

"So then his ability'll definitely be Drunken Fists," Takumu asserted. "The traditions of the fighting game."

The three of them kept talking, wandering further off track, and Utai followed along, eating her fruit *anmitsu* with a serious look on her face until she carefully set down her spoon before typing on her holo keyboard. UI> IT IS INDEED SURPRISING TO HEAR ABOUT A SINGLE DUEL AVATAR HAVING THREE PERSONALITIES, BUT THERE'S SOMETHING ELSE THAT IS OF MORE CONCERN TO ME.

She turned wide eyes on Haruyuki and his friends as she continued. UI> THAT CERBERUS REFERRED TO SOMETHING C HAD

SEALED AWAY. I BELIEVE THERE IS ONLY ONE THING THAT FITS THAT DESCRIPTION.

"…Yeah, I think so, too…," Haruyuki said, looking at the slightly dark silver of the spoon he held in his right hand. "…The Armor of Catastrophe…The Disaster. If what Cerberus II said is true, then he was born to equip that armor."

"Just thinking about what would happen if he were able to do that sends chills up my spine," Takumu said. "If he had the multiple defensive capabilities of the Armor on top of his own hard tungsten armor, it would be a bigger deal than just Physical Immune."

"It was a giga GJ you guys did in purifying the armor, Ui, Haru," Chiyuri said, mixing Ash-speak with Pard-speak, and the other three laughed involuntarily.

Haruyuki was getting absolutely nowhere with obtaining the Theoretical Mirror ability, the key to the attack on the Legend-class enemy Archangel Metatron guarding the Tokyo Midtown Tower, but the reason he could deal with all this without getting too serious, even as the situation grew more chaotic, was that he had his Legion comrades by his side. Haruyuki was silently grateful.

However, immediately after this, he thought that maybe that wasn't the whole story. The way his mysterious and powerful enemy had managed to reproduce his flight ability, albeit for a short time, was very much like when the "marauder" Dusk Taker had appeared three months earlier. But this time, Haruyuki hadn't felt that same heavy pressure crushing him, like he couldn't breathe. The reason for that had to be…

"…I think Cerberus is definitely an opponent to be on guard against, given that he switches personalities and knows about the Armor and stuff. But…I dunno. I don't hate him. Not Cerberus I…and probably not II either."

"Even though he ate one of your arms?" Chiyuri blinked rapidly. "It looked like that seriously hurt, though?"

"Well, it *did* hurt, but I mean…it's a proper ability. It's not like he has a BIC, like Dusk Taker or Rust Jigsaw. When he destroyed me yesterday, I hated it so much, I wanted to cry. But I didn't hate *him*. And I'm sure Cerberus feels the same after losing to me today. I mean, at the end, he said it was fun."

While Haruyuki earnestly searched for the right words as he spoke, his chocolate gelato got fairly soft, so he hurriedly scraped the rest of it together with his spoon.

Chiyuri abruptly slapped him on the back.

"*Pwah!* Wh-what're you doing?! You made a piece of almond go flying!"

"I'm giving you a compliment, so don't be so stingy!"

"Normally, you don't compliment people by slapping them on the back."

"Then you want me to bop you on the head?"

"N-no thanks!"

Listening to their exchange, Takumu and Utai erupted simultaneously in laughter. Soon enough, Chiyuri and Haruyuki got on board, too, and the back room at Enjiya was filled with gentle merriment.

I just know that Wolfram Cerberus has more secrets. And I still can't decide if he's the artificial metal color Kuroyukihime was talking about. But if I just keep fighting. If I go up against him in duel after duel where we smash up against each other, whatever plan he has'll burn up into nothing. I mean, above all else, we're Burst Linkers, after all.

Haruyuki digested this thought together with the last bite of gelato. Just as the last of the bittersweet flavor was disappearing, he turned toward his friends and announced, "At the very least, it seems like the Metatron operation is not moving this week. I'm going to go to Nakano Area Number Two after school tomorrow, too. Whether he challenges me or I go and challenge him, I'm fighting Cerberus again. I probably won't be able to win again like I did today, though. But I'm fine with losing. Winning and losing—that's the nature of the duel, after all."

Chiyuri and Takumu grinned and nodded, while Utai alone

had a slightly worried look on her face as she set her fingers into motion across the tabletop.

UI> I ADMIRE YOUR MINDSET, ARITA. BUT ARE YOU SURE? CON-SIDERING THE LEVEL DIFFERENCE, THE SAME NUMBER OF WINS AND LOSSES WILL MEAN A SERIOUS EXPENDITURE OF POINTS.

"Ugh!" When she put it like that, it really hit home. Haruyuki realized that the basic rules of Brain Burst had completely flown out of his head, and he stiffened up.

Chiyuri slapped his back one more time. "...Just let us know when you're going to go hunting Enemies to replenish your points. If we're free and full of energy, we'll come along with you, 'kay?"

"If it's a day when my kendo practice ends early," Takumu said.

UI> ME TOO. IF YOU'RE OKAY WITH GOING AFTER I'VE DONE MY HOMEWORK.

"...Thanks, guys."

This was all that was left to Haruyuki to say.

After they departed Enjiya with Utai, Haruyuki left Takumu in the entrance hall of their condo and got on the high-speed elevator with Chiyuri.

"That reminds me. What's going on with the Theoretical Mirror?"

Suddenly faced with the question, Haruyuki unconsciously let his gaze drift. "Y-yeah...I guess I've gotten a hint, if you could call it that. Or maybe I haven't quite gotten it..."

"What? You're not making sense. I know you're concerned about Cerberus, but, like, isn't the Mirror a higher priority for you, Haru?"

"...I mean, when you say priority, it's, like, *a* priority," he mumbled, and two fingers stretched out from beside him to yank on his right cheek. "H-hut're you hooin'?"

"I hate leaving a bunch of conditions to pile up unresolved," she said. "When I get more than five items on my to-do list or something like that, I get really annoyed."

"Really...? I basically never get it under ten items."

As he spoke, Haruyuki casually opened the to-do list app on his virtual desktop and found twelve items clearly listed. Items one through three were the homework they had been given that day, but number four—request tickets, if needed, for guests to the school festival—had been languishing there since the previous week. But, well, it was precisely because he hadn't immediately replied that he lacked guests to invite that he had been able to invite Rin Kusakabe the previous day—

"...What're you getting all dreamy about?" Chiyuri yanked even harder on his right cheek.

Haruyuki hurriedly shook his head back and forth. "N-nohhing!"

Fortunately, the elevator had reached the twenty-first floor at that point, and the door in front of them slid open.

"'K-kay, Chiyu, see you tomorr—"

"We're not done talking," she said with a frown as she stepped out into the hall, Haruyuki's cheek still pinched between her fingers. He was forced to follow her.

"H-hey, I'm on twenty-thr—"

"I know that! Another thing I hate is ending a conversation in the middle of it. We'll finish up in my room."

"Wh-what?!"

Haruyuki reeled as the elevator door closed behind him.

Since the hands of the clock had moved around to six PM, the instant they set foot in the entryway of the Kurashima home, captivating sounds and smells crashed into his senses.

And what makes this mellow and yet invigorating sour smell is—yeah, sweet-and-sour pork! he guessed, when the door on the left side of the hallway opened and Chiyuri's mother, Momoe, popped her head out.

"Welcome hom— Oh! Haru!" she cried, clutching a ladle in her hands.

"Th-thanks for having me." Haruyuki bowed his head.

A smile split her face in half, and her words came fast and

furious, like machine-gun fire. "Thank goodness! I cooked too much food, and I was just worrying about what to do with it all. It's always like this with sweet-and-sour pork and chop suey. I just know it's because the wok is so big. Right, you're okay with pineapple in the sweet-and-sour pork, aren't you, Haru? It's not Chii's favorite these days, but I'm the cook, so she doesn't get a say."

"I'm glad to be home...Mom, you keepin' an eye on the stove?"

Chiyuri asked the question quietly, and a hand flew to her mother's mouth. She ducked back into the kitchen with an "Oh, shoot!"

Letting out a sigh, Chiyuri stepped up from the entryway, grabbed some slippers with a blue bear appliqué, and set them before Haruyuki. She slipped pink rabbit slippers on her own feet and took a step forward to make space for him.

"...Eat the pineapples in mine, okay, Haru?"

"......Okay." He put on the slightly too-small slippers and followed Chiyuri to the room at the end of the hall.

The furnishings were simple, and the room was basically unchanged from the last time he'd visited—there were several large cushions of various colors on the floor and bed.

After setting her bag down next to her desk, Chiyuri undid the ribbon at her throat and sighed again. "Aaah. It's so humid. I get tired of being so damp every day."

"Well, it's the rainy season, after all. If you think about a Primeval Forest stage..." Haruyuki said, settling himself down on a starfish cushion on the floor.

"I hate that stage," Chiyuri said curtly, and then she peeled back the thin terry-cloth blanket on her bed as if having thought of something. She abruptly tossed this over Haruyuki's head and announced, "If you move an inch, I'll feed you to a giant snail in the Primeval Forest stage."

"Huh? Wh-what're you doing?"

"Come on! Don't move!"

His field of view closed off by the creamy white fabric, Haruyuki had no choice but to freeze. Soon, he heard the soft sound of fabric rubbing against fabric. This went on for about five seconds before he realized finally that Chiyuri was changing out of her uniform.

Wh-what are you thinking?!

And then:

Just you? No fair! I want to change, too!

While he was struggling to decide which of these he should shout, the blanket covering his head, through some deviation in weight, began to slip forward bit by bit. If it had been sliding backward, he could have grabbed onto the fabric in front of him to stop it, but given that it was sliding forward, his task was hard to accomplish with only small movements at his disposal. On the other hand, if he made any significant movements, it would fall completely and he would be dinner for an enormous snail.

Sounds like *snap, snap* continued to come from the outside world, and he had no idea what exactly was going on. The edge of the blanket finally reached the back of his head; it was only a matter of time before it passed the top of his head.

It's not my fault. It's Chiyu's for not balancing it properly when she threw it on me! Crying out in his heart, Haruyuki waited for the final moment. After about five seconds, the fabric flopped to the ground with a loud *fwup*, and waiting on the other side of it was Chiyuri in white shorts, with a green T-shirt pulled down to just above her stomach.

His childhood friend's arms snapped to a stop, and she looked at his exposed face with cold eyes. "I'm looking forward to the next Primeval Forest stage," she announced, yanking down her shirt.

"...So to get back to what we were talking about," Chiyuri said, sitting on the edge of her bed. "You think you can get the ability?"

Haruyuki, sitting on the starfish cushion formally for some reason, started to offer up the same ambiguous answer as he had in the elevator. But he stopped himself and cocked his head

slightly instead. "I-it's like...I'm surprised you're asking about this. You're that interested in the Metatron mission?"

"What? I *am* a member of Nega Nebulus, you know."

"I know, but, like, it's not Dusk Taker and the Armor of Catastrophe. This isn't just about Negabu, you know? From your usual thinking, I thought you'd actually get mad at the Six Kings for pushing this on us..."

For a moment, Chiyuri seemed to be deciding whether or not to get angry at this, but then, for some reason, her cheeks turned red. "Qu-quit it. I mean, talking like you've seen right through me...But, well, you're right."

"Huh?"

"When I heard about the meeting of the Seven Kings, I was actually a little annoyed. You worked so hard and had just finished purifying the Armor, and here they were pushing you to take on this serious role in the vanguard of a mission to take down a Legend-class Enemy! But, like, I...I saw *it* with you, and Taku too, and all."

Rather unusually, Haruyuki immediately understood what the pronoun "it" meant: the main body of the ISS kits they had seen in the Brain Burst central server, also known as the main visualizer. The jet-black brain eating into a corner of a beautiful galaxy. Even if he tried, he could never forget the way it reached out with countless blood vessel–like circuits to connect with all the kit users, including Takumu, to carry out its abominable parallel processing.

"It hasn't even been three months since I became a Burst Linker," Chiyuri said. "And there've been all kinds of hard things, but I like the Accelerated World. The duels are fun, and I've made lots of friends. So...I hate that something evil is eating away at that world. If you want to get rid of the ISS kits of your own will, then I'm rooting for you. And I'm sure there'll be something I can do. Although I can't use light techniques."

"...Chiyu..." Something abruptly pushed up in his heart, and Haruyuki desperately swallowed it back. Blinking both eyes rapidly, he took a deep breath before bowing his head. "…Thanks. I…I love the Accelerated World, too. And yeah, I'm scared of Metatron, but I figure if I've got a chance at defending against that laser, then I've got to give it a try." He lifted his head and grinned.

"I mentioned this before, but I've got kind of a hint at least. I learned some stuff from Izeki and Shinomiya. And even in the duel with Cerberus, I feel like I realized something important. It's probably no good to think only about repelling the laser. The ultimate mirror can't just be a slab with a high reflectance."

Speaking as though in a dream, Haruyuki didn't notice Chiyuri's gaze cooling sharply halfway through.

"Hey, Haru?"

"Rather than a physical presence, it's actually a passage— Huh? What?"

"Ui's one thing. But why is Izeki coming up here? You're just in the Animal Care Club together, right?"

"Huh? Oh, well, um. Sh-she showed me a mirror. She's got this hand mirror that seems super expensive, you know? It's so different from the ones they sell at the canteen, I was actually surprised. Ha-ha-ha!"

"If you're looking for a proper mirror, *I* have one, you know!"

"I—I guess you would." Haruyuki twisted his index fingers together, and Chiyuri suddenly stood up from the bed, stomped past him, and left the room. *She's not actually going to get a mirror from somewhere, is she? But there's a huge full-length mirror in the room already,* he mused, before she returned less than a mere minute later.

In her hands was not a mirror, but glasses of barley tea set on a tray. She placed one in front of Haruyuki. "Mom says it's another fifteen minutes until supper. That should be plenty of time."

"S-sorry? Plenty of time for what?"

"I was thinking about stuff yesterday, like maybe there was some other way to practice repelling a laser. I mean, you can't just get Niko to hit you with her guns every time, right? And I thought up something good."

I've got a bad feeling somehow! Although the thought filled his head, he didn't let it out of his mouth. Clutching the cold barley tea in both hands, Haruyuki swallowed hard and waited for what she would say next.

"It's not just Burst Linkers who use light techniques, right? I mean, you've got the problem itself to disprove that: Metatron. So then, if there was a reasonable Enemy who attacked with lasers, you could practice as much as you like with it, and then *bang*! Right?"

"G-giga wait!" he hurriedly interjected. "You can call it 'reasonable,' but even the small Enemies are seriously strong!"

Chiyuri shrugged lightly. "But the Wild-class one we hunted on the way back from special training the day before yesterday was a pretty easy victory?"

"Th-there were eight people hunting, and two of them were kings! And to start with, we're not going to be able to find a small Enemy that attacks with lasers that easily."

"And yet, wouldn't you know, there was one livin' real close." A catlike smile spread across Chiyuri's lips, and she snapped the fingers of her right hand. "Setagaya Area Number Two. With your wings, we can just zoom over."

"Huh. Y-you already found one? How…Did someone tell you about it?" Haruyuki asked in reply, baffled.

"I told you." Chiyuri's smile took on a bashful note. "If there was something I could do, I wanted to do it. I figured I should try finding it myself before turning to other people, so last night, I did some wandering in the Unlimited Neutral Field. And luckily, I found a teeny Enemy that shoots lasers."

"Bu— You…" After holding his breath for a second, Haruyuki shouted, at a volume that would just barely not leak outside the room, "A-are you crazy?! Diving *alone*, and on top of that messing with Enemies?! I mean, you could've run into some dangerous Burst Linkers or been targeted by a Beast class and ended up in unlimited EK!"

"It's fine. I made sure to set an automatic disconnect timer, and you know how hard Lime Bell is, right? On top of that, I have healing abilities, so I'm not going to end up in unlimited EK that easy."

"So you say—," he began, intending to argue even more vehemently, but then pinched his mouth closed.

Chiyuri—the Chiyuri Kurashima he'd known since he was born—was exactly this person. Moody, quick to anger, and more hardworking than anyone. She made incredible efforts when no one was looking, and no matter how hard it was for her, she never let it show on the surface; she always smiled sunnily.

She said she did special training to improve her reaction speed in a full-dive environment in order to succeed in installing the Brain Burst program. Back then, she couldn't accelerate, of course, so she must have sacrificed her life in the real and devoted herself to serious special training, the kind that makes you bleed, over tens—no, hundreds—of hours.

"Chiyu, how long did it take you to find that Enemy?" Haruyuki asked.

After looking a little undecided, Chiyuri clucked her tongue. "Um. A little over three days of inside time."

Honest-to-goodness absurdity. But Haruyuki couldn't reproach her at this stage. Instead, he sat formally on the cushion and bowed his head deeply. "…Thank you, Chiyu."

"Hey! Wh-what are you getting all serious for?! Ah! Yikes! We only have ten minutes until Mom calls us. Come on! Hurry up and dive!" Chiyuri shouted, her face red, and took a sip of her barley tea before pulling a small hub and three XSB cables out from her desk drawer. She connected the home server connector on the wall and the hub with the longest cable and then sat down again on the bed, gesturing to Haruyuki to join her. "Come on! Hurry up!"

"Huh?! Um, what—?"

"I don't have a sofa or anything in here, so our only choice is to lie back here! Hurry up!"

"O-o-okay!" Haruyuki stood up as he was told and sat down

next to Chiyuri. Instantly, the palm of her hand was pressing down on his forehead, and he fell back onto the bed. He stiffened up as one end of a cable stretching out from the hub was plunged into his own Neurolinker, and then Chiyuri immediately connected her own before lying down next to him.

A sweet smell wafted up from his childhood friend, who had only just changed clothes—but leaving him no time to even be conscious of this, a sharp voice flew at him:

"We dive on the count of three! Here we go. Three, two, one..."

""Unlimited Burst!""

Lucky I didn't get the command wrong, Haruyuki thought as he fell toward the rainbow-colored ring.

3

"I've always wanted to say that. The whole 'on the count of three' thing," Lime Bell said, touching down on the virtual ground with her trademark vivid lime-green armor, pointed hat, and the handbell Enhanced Armament that made up her left hand.

Landing in the field a moment later, Haruyuki grinned wryly beneath his mirrored visor. "You said that so suddenly, I almost shouted the usual direct-link command, you know."

"B-be careful! If you do that, you'll dive into my private space."

"That cushion hel— I mean, heaven. Heaven. I kinda want to see it again...almost..."

"Then once this special training is over—no, after supper—I'll let you in." Chiyuri nodded back at him. "Anyway, let's go outside."

Haruyuki looked around at their surroundings, but because they had dived inside a building, all his eyes took in were white walls. He couldn't identify the stage attributes from this.

The balcony window was gone, but a narrow passageway stretched out from where the door had been. It should've come out into the shared hallway of the condo, but to save time, Haruyuki turned back toward the wall that normally had a mirror in it. He clenched his right hand into a fist and then looked to Chiyuri, behind him, for permission. "Um. You mind if I smash this wall?"

"Seems overly complicated, but sure, whatever. We do have to build up your special-attack gauge and all."

"Okay. Excuse me, then." He turned to the wall once more, sank down slowly, and twisted his body sharply while at the same time launching a right straight without really pulling his arm back. He was basically unaware of it, but this was close to the way Wolfram Cerberus moved—focusing on avatar mass and rotation speed rather than the swing of the arm. Haruyuki had unintentionally absorbed the fact that the heavy metal colors were more suited to this type of movement than the normal colors from their second meeting and now used a similar technique.

The punch—which was more like his whole body slamming forward—landed smack dab in the center of the wall, and the shriek of the impact sounded like the bullet from a large rifle hitting its target. But not a single crack appeared in the smooth white surface.

"H-hey, Haru. Are you okay? Did you take damage?" Chiyuri asked, concerned, since players could only see their own health gauges in the Unlimited Neutral Field. Haruyuki said nothing; he simply continued to fire punch after punch at the wall. He knew without looking that his gauge was not decreasing—and that every bit of the force of his blows was penetrating the wall.

Crrrrack! Soon, this incredibly loud sound filled their ears, and the southern wall turned to dust. The field beyond it had no sooner sprung into view than Chiyuri shouted again. This time, her voice was bright and welcoming.

"Whoa! Incredible! It's so pretty!"

The sky was a milky white, lustrous like melted pearls. The buildings on the ground were also all pure white, looking very much like temples and sacred spaces, and large, regular octahedron crystals floated above roads and empty lots all over the stage. The transparent gems spun slowly, turning the light from the sky into rainbow spectra dancing on the terrain.

"A Sacred Ground stage," Haruyuki murmured as he looked

out over the rare, upper-level holy stage. "Been a while since I've seen this."

"I've only seen it once in a normal duel." Next to him, Chiyuri bobbed her head up and down. "Um, I'm pretty sure you can charge your special-attack gauge by smashing those crystals, right?"

"Yeah. And because you're smashing them in the Unlimited Neutral Field, sometiiiiimes, you get item cards. Apparently."

"What? Really?" Lime Bell swung her head to turn her eye lenses—some of the cat-slant of Chiyuri's own eyes in their shape—on Haruyuki, but she quickly shook her head back and forth. "Nope. No way! We can't! We're not here to play today; we've got special training. This is no time to go looking for items!"

"I—I didn't say anything!"

"We're wasting time. Let's get going! Carrying or piggyback-ing, which is better?"

"Uh, um. I'm usually the one who asks tha—"

"Then ask. Okay. Let's see. Carrying, then." The words had barely left her mouth when Chiyuri turned toward the right side of his avatar.

Fully aware that Chiyuri had managed to completely take the reins here, Haruyuki had no choice but to reach his arms out and fasten them around Lime Bell's back and legs before lifting her up.

The green-type avatar excelled in defensive abilities, but she was a little heavy; the resistance he felt in his arms was greater than with Black Lotus or Sky Raker, whom he had similarly car-ried in his arms like this. But his sense of self-preservation was developed enough that he knew to keep that thought to himself, so he simply remarked, "Okay, here we go," and his body danced up into the air.

The Kurashima home was on the twenty-first floor of the condo, so the ground was correspondingly far away, but Chiyuri had once jumped down from the top floor of the Shinjuku Government Building with him, so it was no surprise when she didn't cry out at the beginning of their free fall. Once they had dropped about twenty meters, he spread the wings on his back and shifted to gliding. Fixing his aim on one of the crystals floating on Kannana Street directly below, he kicked it as he flew past.

There was an ephemeral *clink*, and the rainbow crystal shattered. No item card appeared, but his special-attack gauge leapt up to being nearly half-charged. This was enough power in his gauge to be able to fly nonstop to Setagaya. He ascended again and then hovered for a moment at an altitude that allowed them to look out over the city.

"So where in Setagaya does this laser Enemy pop up?" Haruyuki asked the girl in his arms.

As she took in the beautiful sight of the Sacred Ground stage, Chiyuri's eye lenses flashed. "Oh, a little past Sakurajosui Station."

"So, this way?" He turned toward the southwest, but rethought this and started to fly due south above Kannana.

Aratama Suido Road stretched out ten kilometers from the Koenjirikkyo intersection, where Kannana Street crossed Oume Highway, to the Kinuta Purification Plant along the Tama River in the distance. This road was so perfectly straight, it was hard to believe that it lay within the twenty-three wards, and Sakurajosui Station was along it.

Getting onto Suido Road a little west of the intersection, Haruyuki dropped altitude and flew at full speed a single meter above the pavement. Naturally, his special-attack gauge started to drop precipitously, but there were crystals floating on this road, too, so he head-butted and shattered one he happened to come across.

Far from being frightened by any of this, Chiyuri cried out "Go-o-o!" like he was a thrill ride at an amusement park. In the blink of an eye, the raised bridge of the Keio Line came into view, running along the border between Suginami and Setagaya

Wards. He slipped under this, decelerated, and came to a stop, his legs digging out ruts in the smooth surface of the ground.

"Phew." Still tucked neatly in Haruyuki's arms, Chiyuri let out a small sigh and then lifted her head. "Ahhh, that was fun! We should've just kept flying all the way to the end of the road."

"Y-you were the one who said we're not here to play!"

"Don't stress about the detaaaails!" Here, she finally jumped out of his arms. She looked around for a minute and then pointed to the east side of the road. "I found the Enemy near that big building there."

"Big building?" Haruyuki cocked his head and called up a map of the neighborhood in his mind. If this were the real world, he could have just tapped the map icon on his virtual desktop, but there were no such convenient apps in the Accelerated World. Probably. "I'm pretty sure there's a university here, maybe? What school was it...?"

"All the universities are the same on this side!" Chiyuri pointed out in an exasperated tone. "It's not like you came to take their entrance exam. And there aren't any Burst Linkers in college."

"I—I guess." What he was actually concerned about was the possibility of a neighboring junior high or high school affiliated with the university.

In the Unlimited Neutral Field, the places you were most likely to have an unexpected encounter with other Burst Linkers were first, near a portal; second, near a shop; and third, at any point where a large, huntable Enemy popped up—but a junior high or high school was basically next in line. In cases where multiple Burst Linkers attended the same school, they sometimes would use the school grounds as a meeting place in the Unlimited Neutral Field. Haruyuki himself had chosen the Umesato courtyard as the place for his final battle with Dusk Taker two months earlier.

That said, the flow of time in the Unlimited Neutral Field was accelerated to be a thousand times faster than it was the real world. Haruyuki and Chiyuri could stay on this side for a full day, while only eighty-some seconds would pass in the real world. The odds of crossing paths with other Burst Linkers in the same time and place were basically less than one in ten thousand.

And for all that, I feel like I still run into people on this side, Haruyuki said to himself before concluding that Setagaya was an empty area and that they were probably okay for now. Automatically, he wrapped an arm around Lime Bell's waist in a tight hold and took off gently before he realized that his partner was staring intently at Crow's face.

"What?"

"Nothiiiing. I was just thinking you're getting pretty comfortable with grabbing me."

"I—I am not! A-and you were the one who told me to carry you!"

"Yeah, yeah. Anyway, get a little higher up."

"...Yes, ma'am..." Haruyuki would probably never win a discussion with his childhood friend. Fully aware of this, he ascended around twenty meters straight up. When he did, there was indeed a vast space on the east side of Suido Road. The large temples dotting the area were probably the university campus buildings in the real world. But...

"I can't see any Enemies or anything."

"Hold on a sec," Chiyuri said and, with some purpose in mind, brandished the large bell of her left arm: the Enhanced Armament Choir Chime.

As far as Haruyuki knew, the bell had two uses. First was a direct, striking attack. The bell was terrifically sturdy and heavy, and a blow to the head would cause a ferocious *bong* to assault a player's auditory system, temporarily stunning them, so it was a fairly useful weapon.

And the second was, of course, the special attack Citron Call. This had the extremely rare effect of turning back time for the target. When used on an ally, it recovered their health, while when used on an enemy, it returned their hard-won special-attack gauge to zero or forced their armament to unequip; it was appropriately showy for her tiny witch-like appearance.

But there should have been no need to rewind time in this situation. *Wait. That can't mean application number one. Is she going to hit me on the head?!* Haruyuki cringed into himself.

The bell started to wave back and forth in a slow movement, almost as if in invitation. After a slight lag, a sound more reminiscent of a bell than a chime spread out in waves—*riiiing, riiiing.* After about ten seconds, Chiyuri lowered her arm, but the sound didn't stop. Echoing off the surrounding terrain, it propagated endlessly, gradually weakening before fading out.

What on earth was that?

Before Haruyuki could ask the question, Chiyuri stretched out her right hand and said, hushed, "Look! There!"

To his surprise, his eyes followed where her finger was pointing and found something crawling out of one of the temples.

"Huh? An Enemy?! No way! Chiyu, did you call it?!"

"Calling it, it's kinda like— So, like, Enemies react to sound, right? When I was walking around looking for a laser-using Enemy last night, I had the idea that maybe I could call together Enemies from a wide range if I used my bell just right. So I tried a bunch of different things."

"A-a wide range? What would you have done if a whole lot of them had shown up?"

"It was a little iffy this one time, true." She stuck her tongue out playfully as she informed him of this rather serious fact, then moved her right hand to call up her Instruct menu for some purpose.

You could set all kinds of different conditions for the visibility or invisibility of this system window, but as a rule, tag-team partners and Legion members could see it, so Haruyuki could also see the window as it opened with a *kashak* sound effect. Chiyuri's finger moved once more, and the display changed to a list of abilities and special attacks.

Lime Bell's only special attack should have been Citron Call.

With this in mind, Haruyuki stared at the screen and then quietly cried out. Because, in the ability column, there was a row of text shining radiantly.

"Acoustic Summon…Call with sound? When did you—? This ability…"

"I told you, last night. After I managed to call an Enemy the first time, I opened Instruct, and surprise! There was this ability suddenly shining there."

"Th-there was? That's great…" Before the desire to applaud Chiyuri's hard work and creativity, Haruyuki honestly felt defeat. He had been assigned a mission with a high level of difficulty: Obtain the Theoretical Mirror ability. Even after he was evaporated ten times by the Red King's main armament, he hadn't been able to come up with anything; he couldn't help comparing his own dumb self with Chiyuri.

But having no doubt seen precisely what was going on in his head, Chiyuri bopped Crow on the head. "Okay, look," she said, in an exasperated voice. "Acoustic Summon and the Theoretical Mirror that you're trying for are on totally different levels! All I can use mine for is to call Enemies. Although if I could pull out hidden Burst Linkers, too, that would be super handy."

"W-well, you might be right…"

"And if you get Theoretical Mirror, it won't just be Enemies; you'll have a hundred-percent resistance to the light attacks of other Burst Linkers, too, right? There are kind of a lot of red types with lasers. You'll be able to use it all the time in the Territories. Don't get depressed. Let's get right to your training. I mean, I went to all the trouble of finding you an Enemy."

"Y-yeah, you're right. If I manage to get it today, Kuroyukihime and Master will both be surprised—I just know it. Okay! I'm gonna do it!" Haruyuki clenched his left hand into a fist—his right was holding Chiyuri. He felt like he heard a sigh near his ear, but he ignored it and started moving forward.

At first, the Enemy was nothing but a tiny silhouette, but as they got closer, its shape became apparent: an armadillo with a huge head. Covered in hard armor, the body was round, and the four legs were short. The forehead of its tapered head was excessively large, with an elliptical red gem, or maybe a lens, embedded in it. It moved its pointed snout from side to side, apparently looking for the source of the sound that had beckoned it to this place.

"You can see the red jewel in its forehead, right? It shoots lasers from there. I was far away, so I didn't take a direct hit, but it pierced the buildings of the Ancient Castle stage, so don't let your guard down, okay?"

"...The Ancient Castle buildings are pretty hard..."

"It's fine. You'll be fine. As long as you don't die instantly, I can heal you with Citron Call. Its aggro range is about thirty meters, so descend right before that."

"...R-roger." Haruyuki nodded and started to swoop so that he would land with room to spare, fifty meters in front of the armadillo Enemy. Since the Enemy was standing still in the middle of a large space that seemed to have originally been the university sports grounds, approaching it was easy.

The floor of the Sacred Ground stage was covered in tiles with a lovely arabesque pattern. Its opposite, the Deadly Sin stage, was also laid with white tiles, but blood-like fluid oozed from the joints of the lattice pattern in that stage, while these tiles were the very definition of purity. The friction coefficient was also just right; there was no fear of your feet slipping.

Thus, Haruyuki and Chiyuri landed fifty meters away, their eyes fixed on the Enemy ahead. However, the bottoms of their feet did not communicate the sharp hardness of tile, but rather something wet and mucusy.

"Whoa!"

"Aah!"

Crying out, the pair tumbled backward at the same time. Half-immersed in the sticky fluid, they stiffened up in tandem, too. In the Accelerated World, liquid on the ground generally caused serious issues, and so any liquid a Burst Linker encountered had to be dealt with immediately. Haruyuki first looked at the health gauge in the upper left of his field of view, but fortunately, it didn't appear to have dropped by even a pixel. Which meant that rather than being poison or a corrosive fluid, this was some adhesive liquid.

With that thought, he threw his upper body upward, again at the same time as Chiyuri. But their backs easily peeled away from the ground.

So then what was this sticky stuff? He dropped his gaze and saw that they were sitting in a brown pool about four meters in diameter. Ever so tentatively, he raised his left hand, but the liquid dripped off, seeming to leave his metallic armor unchanged.

"...What is this...?" Haruyuki cocked his head.

Chiyuri raised her right hand to bring the viscous brown liquid to her face. "Huh. No way. Is this maybe..." Muttering, she lifted her face and turned to Haruyuki. "Haru—I mean, Crow, open your mouth," she commanded.

"Huh?"

"Hurry! Aaah!"

He did as he was told and ran a finger from the bottom of his helmet to the top. His mirrored visor slid up a quarter of the way, revealing the hidden mouth of his avatar's exposed body. He had no sooner popped this open than Lime Bell's index and middle fingers—dripping with plenty of the brown sticky stuff—were thrust into his mouth.

"*M-mnghaamph!*" Naturally, he cried out at this sudden assault, but she didn't take her fingers out. Fluid was forced into his mouth, and the taste of it spread unbidden across Haruyuki's palate. Slightly bitter, with body. And sweet. More than sweet; it was terribly delicious.

When he grew still, Chiyuri yanked her fingers out. "What's it taste like?"

"...Chocolate..."

"I knew it."

So then taste it yourself! he wanted to shout, but the urge was circumvented by a massive question mark popping up in his brain.

Why? Why would there be a pool of chocolate on the ground—and sweet milk chocolate to boot, Haruyuki's favorite kind? This wasn't an attribute of the Sacred Ground stage. Or had they mistakenly assumed this was Sacred Ground when it was actually a Sweet stage or something?

Sitting there dumbfounded, he wrestled with whether or not to try having another taste when—

"Puppet Make!!"

The adorable voice of a girl rang out through the field. There was no doubt this was a special technique call—the voice command a Burst Linker shouted to activate a special attack. And if he was hearing one of those, then the basic idea was that something, at any rate, was about to happen.

Haruyuki quickly grabbed ahold of Chiyuri's torso again and fiercely flapped the wings on his back. As they rose up, he dashed backward about three meters and once again checked their surroundings—or he was going to check their surroundings, until what happened next stole his attention. From the pool of chocolate before them, *splrp!*—two human-shaped figures rose up.

"No way! It's totally not deep enough for an avatar to dive in there!"

Chiyuri was exactly right.

But the fact was that two 150-centimeter silhouettes stood before their eyes. Their forms were very simple: heads smooth and round, with arms, legs, and body all clearly visible. They had no eyes or mouths; instead, each of their faces bore only a single flowerlike mark. They were a semiglossy dark brown—the same chocolate color as the pond they'd leapt out of.

The avatars had no particular characteristics to speak of, but one feature they shared was unique to them: The pair, standing side by side, had the same external appearance. But in the Accelerated World, it was fundamentally not possible for multiple avatars to have exactly the same design. Even the senior members of the Blue Legion, Cobalt Blade and Manganese Blade—rumored to be twins—had slightly different colors and part shapes.

"Wh-what on earth—?!" Haruyuki shouted at the same time as the two avatars charged silently forward.

Without even the time to notice that the chocolate pool spreading out at the feet of the avatars had disappeared, Haruyuki and Chiyuri reflexively leapt into counterattack formation. Silver Crow launched a sharp left strike, and Lime Bell cast her Choir Chime, at the chests of their respective opponents.

Instead of the impact of his sharp fingers shooting through hard armor, Haruyuki felt something wet and soft, like he had plunged his hand into a lump of modeling clay. His strike dug deeply into the chest of the faceless avatar and continued out through their back. With the one blow, the torso was split in half, and he wouldn't have been surprised if their health gauge dropped over 50 percent. After taking an injury on this level in the Unlimited Neutral Field, they wouldn't be able to move for a while because of the pain dancing through their nervous system—twice the pain experienced in a normal duel field.

They shouldn't have been able to, anyway.

"Wha—?" His left hand still following through on the blow, Haruyuki opened his eyes wide.

The faceless avatar only staggered very briefly and then, without a single cry, countered with a right straight. The punch hit Haruyuki hard on the left side of his helmet, whisking away 5 percent of Crow's health gauge in one shot.

Throwing himself back to avoid a follow-up attack, Haruyuki glanced over to check on Chiyuri. She, too, had knocked the faceless body flying with a strike from her handbell. But that didn't stop her enemy, either. With a large hole in its body, the avatar shot off a right roundhouse kick. Chiyuri blocked it with her left arm. At the same time, she jumped and bounced over to Haru-yuki's side.

"What the—?! These guys are weird!" Chiyuri shouted, and Haruyuki bobbed his head in agreement.

And then they witnessed something abnormal that went far beyond weird.

Although both of the faceless avatars had taken serious damage to their bodies, the areas around their wounds suddenly melted, becoming a dark-brown liquid to fill in the holes. In just a few seconds, the bodies of the no-faces were completely restored, taking on their original smooth, dark-brown surface.

"So striking and hitting have no effect," Haruyuki groaned.

"To begin with"—Chiyuri cocked her head slightly—"are they really Burst Linkers? Their armor seems sort of made, like—to be honest, like chocolate, I mean…"

"Oh, yeah. And the chocolate pool from before is gone. If these two are dolls made from that chocolate…Maybe we could find out if we took a bite?"

"You *just* had chocolate ice cream!" Chiyuri retorted, and in that instant the faceless avatars who had been steadily closing the distance between them stiffened awkwardly. Or so Haruyuki felt. They actually started to retreat, and he gradually stepped forward after them.

Unfortunately, however, he didn't get the chance to taste the chocolate-color avatars. Before he caught up with them, the girl from before spoke again.

"Figuring out the weak point of my Chocopets so quickly! You're not so bad at this, hmm!"

The source of the very slightly nasal, sweet voice was not the no-faces before their eyes. Haruyuki and Chiyuri quickly looked over to their left and saw a tiny silhouette standing on the roof of a small temple about twenty meters away.

She was smaller than the faceless avatars. Her armor was a similar semiglossy chocolate color, but her shape was different.

From the long hair coming out on both sides from beneath a hat with a large brim and the large skirt-type armor covering her lower half, she was clearly a female-type avatar. Her eye lenses shone a clear pink.

The instant he saw her, Haruyuki was certain of two things. First, that this F-type was, this time, for sure a real Burst Linker. Second, that the two faceless avatars were combat dolls created with her power. The "puppet make" command they'd heard at the start of the offensive was probably a special attack that created dolls.

He had all kinds of other questions—for instance, what was a Chocopet?—but he put them aside for now and asked the one he had to ask before all others. "Why are you attacking us?! You... Are you a member of the Acceleration Research Society?!"

The chocolate F-type avatar blinked with surprise and then stamped a high-heeled foot down on the roof of the temple. "I belong to the Dessert Lovers' Society! And you! Playing dumb despite the fact that you came here to hunt Coolu! As long as my eyes are the color of strawberry cream, I absolutely will not allow you to do that!"

And there's another weird word. He searched the index in his brain, but he found nothing about a person called "Coolu," so he tried to confirm.

"Um. Who's Coolu?"

"It's pointless to feign innocence! I was witness to your attempted attack on little Coolu over there!" Her slender left hand snapped up and pointed to the center of the plaza.

Shifting his gaze, he saw the small armadillo-like Enemy sniffing just like it had been before. "Huh? The Enemy? That's 'little Coolu'?"

"She is! The species name is Lava Carbuncle—Coolu for short. She's my friend! I'll stand and lose all my points right here and now before I'd allow you to go ahead and hunt my poor baby!" Turning her left hand on Haruyuki and Chiyuri, the chocolate avatar continued boldly. "Now you'd better hurry up and use them! Those filthy...*ISS kits*!"

4

"Cocoa Fountain."

The small, chocolate-colored avatar uttered the technique name in almost a murmur, and a glittering pink light shot from the tips of her fingers.

The light carved out a parabola and fell to the ground. There, with a burbling sound, the same dark-brown liquid Haruyuki and Chiyuri had slipped in before—milk chocolate—came gushing up. Instantly, the lesser-class Enemy Lava Carbuncle, aka Little Coolu, started moving toward them at a trot and sniffed at the chocolate pond before plunging its tapered snout in and lapping it up.

"She's in the Enemy's aggro range, isn't she?" Chiyuri said quietly, and Haruyuki nodded.

The chocolate avatar was standing a mere three meters away from the Enemy now. No matter how slow and sluggish the Enemy, it would definitely attack at this close range. Haruyuki and Chiyuri had given themselves a margin of error and kept a distance of forty meters between themselves and it, but even so, they couldn't say for sure that they were at a safe range.

"So maybe it's been tamed?" Haruyuki wondered.

"But, I mean, don't you need a special item for that? Reins or something, like Kuroyukihime used to tame that flying horse?"

"I thought so, too. But, well, I guess there are a fair number of exceptions to the rule in the Accelerated World."

While they stood next to each other discussing the issue, the chocolate avatar turned her back to the Enemy, who was lapping up its treat in a trance, and marched toward them. The two chocolate puppets—Chocopets for short—that she had generated from the first chocolate pond had already disappeared, the technique having expired its effective time.

The avatar that stopped in front of Haruyuki and Chiyuri, wordlessly turning her eyes on them, was relatively small for an F-type. She wasn't much different in size from Utai Shinomiya's Ardor Maiden.

"I'll introduce myself first. Chocolat Puppeteer...I do not currently belong to any Legion."

"Oh!" At the abrupt self-introduction, Haruyuki hurriedly bowed his head. "Um, I'm Silver Crow. My Legion's Nega Nebulus."

"I'm also a member of Nega Nebulus—Lime Bell."

Once they had given their names, the small female avatar, who apparently went by Chocolat Puppeteer, traced her cheek with a slim finger and nodded sharply. "I see. So you're the famed Corvus of the Black Legion. And the Watch Witch."

"Is that your nickname?" Haruyuki asked in a quiet voice.

"I—I don't know!" Chiyuri's cheeks reddened slightly as she shook her head. "Anyway, focus on the conversation!"

"R-right."

Fortunately, Chocolat Puppeteer had fallen into a brief moment of thought. When she lifted her head, she nodded once more. "I understand that you are not ISS kit users. And that you did not come to hunt Coolu."

"Th-thanks." Haruyuki let out a sigh of relief before continuing in a more composed tone. "So is it maybe okay if we ask you a question, too?"

"Go ahead. Please."

"When did you dive here?"

It was clear that Chocolat was lying in ambush for Burst Linkers who came to hunt Coolu, aka Lava Carbuncle. But an ambush in the Unlimited Neutral Field was no simple thing. Or rather, an ambush was basically impossible without knowing the dive time of your target up to the very second.

Chocolat shrugged lightly. "I'm pretty sure it was ten—no, eleven days ago. Although it was a mere sixteen minutes ago in real time."

"E-eleven days?!" Haruyuki and Chiyuri cried out together.

The small chocolate avatar's mouth cracked into a slight smile. "It hasn't been boring in the slightest. I've been with Coolu the whole time. And...I don't care if ten days turns into ten months. I mentioned this to you before, but I'm prepared to give up all my points on this dive."

"..."

Haruyuki and Chiyuri unconsciously looked at each other. Losing all your Burst Points was the same as a forced uninstall of the Brain Burst program—that is, death as a Burst Linker. Too heavy a thing to say with a smile on your lips.

"Um. So what you're saying then is that you won't step back from protecting this Enemy—I mean, Coolu—even if it means losing all your points. Is that maybe it?" Haruyuki asked timidly.

"That is what I'm saying." Chocolat nodded, moving her bonnet-type hat calmly up and down.

"But— That— Maybe this is the wrong way to say this, but no matter how many times an Enemy's hunted, they're restored once the Change comes, right?"

"That is indeed true. But the Enemy that is restored is at best one of the same species; it's not as though the exact same individual is regenerated. The next Lava Carbuncle to pop up in this place will probably attack me the second I approach it." Her voice shook a little at the end, and Chocolat hid her face under the brim of her hat.

Lime Bell—with a totally different armor color, but a similar hat and an overall form that resembled the other avatar somehow—took a step forward. "How long did it take for you to get so close to this baby?" she asked, gently.

"...In real time, a little over two years."

"It did? So then you're really friends now, huh? I get how you feel. I mean, if I made such a cute friend, I'd definitely want to protect them."

"..."

Chocolat Puppeteer lifted her head slightly and looked at Lime Bell. "Do you really feel that way?" she asked quietly.

"Of course!"

"M-me too." While Chiyuri was emphatic, Haruyuki was timid in his assent.

"So, then..." Chocolat smiled once more, somehow sadly. "What if the one trying to hunt that friend was also a friend? And a Burst Linker who had been a comrade in the same Legion only three days before? What would you do?"

Legion: Petit Paquet; members: three.

The members had discussed and decided on the Legion name, which means "small package" in French, Chocolat Puppeteer told Haruyuki and Chiyuri in a subdued voice.

They had moved from the large sports ground to the inside of a compact temple. The three sat in a circle on the white floor, elegant cups before them, faint steam rising up. The cups held hot cocoa, but this chocolate was not pulled from the ground with Chocolat's special attack. Instead, it came from a porcelain pot that had appeared together with the cups, made into objects from her storage.

As a general rule, your only option was to buy items at the shop if you wanted food or drink in the Unlimited Neutral Field. The currency was, naturally, burst points, but players who had only just set foot in this world didn't really have the points to spare for that. Which meant Chocolat was somewhat of a veteran, but her level was four, one below Haruyuki's.

"Our Legion wasn't especially passionate about normal duels, much less so the Territories. We'd go to the Shibuya or Meguro areas next door on the weekends and fight a few tag-team matches, and that's about it. Which is why it took me nearly two years to reach level four, and the fact that I cleared the Legion Master quest was honestly miraculous."

"Huh? Don't you need a minimum of four people for the LMQ?" Haruyuki blurted.

The dark-chocolate avatar smiled ever so faintly. "The reason they say you need four people is because there are several puzzle gimmicks that require operation in four different places at the same time, but I have my Chocopets, so."

"Oh. Ohhh. I get it."

"That was also a part of my miraculous luck," the tiny avatar said, then brought her cup of cocoa to her mouth.

Haruyuki watched her for a while, pushed into silence. The members of Nega Nebulus almost never went on expeditions to Shibuya or Meguro, so perhaps it was only natural that he didn't know Chocolat's name, given that she'd made those areas her main battleground. But an apologetic feeling still rose up in his chest.

Up to that point, he'd always treated Setagaya like an empty area. He'd never turned his feet in that direction—even though it bordered his home of Suginami—but there were indeed Burst Linkers in that region, too. Chiyuri apparently felt the same way, as she took on a formal position and bowed her head.

"I'm so sorry. I thought there was no one in this area. So I came here looking for Enemies."

"It's fine. In fact, even if you combined Setagaya Areas One through Five, you'd still only get a couple dozen or so Burst Linkers. If you had dived an hour later, you...wouldn't have come across me or anyone else," Chocolat murmured. "They'll have taken care of everything by then."

Haruyuki lifted his hanging head. "Um. You told us a little about this before, but you're on standby in this place to fight the people coming to hunt Coolu, right?" he asked timidly. "And you said they're your friends—members of the Legion Petit Paquet. You all came this far together?"

"That's exactly right— No, our relationship goes beyond that. One of them is my parent, and the other my child."

"…!!"

Haruyuki and Chiyuri both gasped. But when he really thought about it, this wasn't strange at all. In fact, it was only natural that there would be parent and child among the members of a small-scale Legion. In the six-member army of Nega Nebulus, after all, there were four with parent-child relationships: Haruyuki and Kuroyukihime, and Takumu and Chiyuri.

But in that case, it was all the more curious—why would Chocolat's parent and child try to hunt the Lava Carbuncle she'd spent two years building a friendship with? From its size, that Enemy was no doubt a lesser class; they definitely wouldn't get that many points for defeating it.

Perhaps seeing the question in Haruyuki and Chiyuri's minds, Chocolat Puppeteer lowered her cherry-pink eye lenses sadly. "Three days ago, on Sunday evening, everything changed—no, everything was lost. My parent, Mint Mitten, and my child, Plum Flipper, were forcibly parasitized by ISS kits. In that instant—"

"What?!"

"Th-that's—!"

Simultaneous cries of surprise burst out of Haruyuki and Chiyuri.

"Ah!" Haruyuki leaned forward and squeezed his question out. "The ISS kits, they can only parasitize Burst Linkers who want that themselves, can't they?!"

"That's what I heard, too! I mean, if it was possible to force the parasite, then they wouldn't have needed to do that whole thing during the Hermes' Cord race, would they?!"

Chiyuri's observation was correct.

In the final stage of the Hermes' Cord race held on June 9, after secretly slipping in among the participating teams, the Acceleration Research Society's Rust Jigsaw had activated Rust Order, a fourth-quadrant Incarnate—negative will targeting a broad range—going so far as to slaughter not only the race participants but the many spectators in the Gallery.

The Acceleration Research Society's intention was assumed to have been to make widely known across the Accelerated World the overwhelming power of dark Incarnate and make Burst Linkers more likely to reach out to the ISS kit, an Enhanced Armament that could easily be attached to the body.

In fact, Ash Roller's junior avatar, Bush Utan, had turned to Haruyuki and said, "IS mode has that kind of incredible power. The ultimate power, skipping over all the rules of Brain Burst, even." And: "But this ISS kit makes even losers strong. Like the more of a loser you are, the stronger you can get."

The reason Utan had been overtaken by the ISS kit was because he had first had this awareness of that power. Put another way, if forced parasitization were possible, then just as Chiyuri noted, there would have been no need to carry out a demonstration like that during the race. If they simply challenged Burst Linkers on the matching list one after another, they could have easily succeeded in the Society's objective of spreading the ISS kits throughout the Accelerated World—although Haruyuki still didn't know what they were hoping to achieve with that.

Chocolat took this in and let out a long, deep sigh. "I, along with my two comrades, also understood this to be the case. We never sought out any suspicious power. It was enough for us to simply protect our small box in a corner of the Accelerated World. The truth is, I had no intention of going up any further levels. Our desire was to dive all together once or twice a week into the Unlimited Neutral Field, chat, feed Coolu, sit alongside one another and wait for the Change, simply spending the time like that..."

Chocolat hugged her knees tight, perhaps reliving sad, painful memories, and continued.

"That is why when *she* appeared before us to invite us to accept the ISS kit, we flatly refused. Because we had heard that you wouldn't be parasitized by that black eyeball if you sincerely refused it. However—when we did so, she said, 'Then you'll need surgery, hmm?' and attacked us. There were three of us and two of them, but we were basically no match for IS mode. They caught Plum first. They cut her chest open with large scissors and put the kit seed in."

"S-scissors?!" Haruyuki felt a pinch in his memory.

But before he could actually dig into that memory, Chocolat said, even more sorrowfully, "Seeing this, Mitten told me to escape through a portal and pull out their direct cables on the real side. I ran desperately for the leave point at Sakurajosui Station, returned to the real world, and pulled out the cables of the two who had dived with me. However, by that point, Mitten had also already fallen into their hands...but neither of them appeared much different immediately after bursting out. They laughed and said they hadn't been parasitized by ISS kits. But..."

"...It was too late...?" Chiyuri asked in a quiet voice.

Chocolat hung her head deeply. "In the space of one night...the next day...they were no longer the Mitten and Plum that I knew. They urged me to accept an ISS kit as well. When I refused, they said they were leaving the Legion. Since that day, they've been *her* comrades, hunting small- and midsize Enemies in the Unlimited Neutral Field in Setagawa."

"This 'her,' is it maybe"—Haruyuki timidly gave voice to the name that had finally come back to him—"is it maybe a Burst Linker called Magenta Scissor?"

Chocolat jerked her face up, only to drop her shoulders once more before nodding. "Yes, it is. She was likely the first ISS kit user in the Setagaya area. Now everyone other than me is already on her side."

Magenta Scissor.

Haruyuki had heard this name from the mouth of his best friend and Legion comrade, Takumu Mayuzumi. Eight days earlier—on the night of Tuesday, June 18—Takumu had visited the Setagaya area alone to get information on the ISS kits, and he had been given the very item by Magenta Scissor. At that time, the kit was in sealed card form, and Takumu had saved this in his storage. But the next day, June 19, he had been attacked by the most fearsome PK group, Supernova Remnant, and to fight back, he had activated the kit. That night, Haruyuki and Chiyuri went to sleep while connected with Takumu, and by attacking the ISS kit main body in the Brain Burst central server, they had just barely managed to remove the kit terminal parasitizing Takumu.

However, that said, naturally, it wasn't as though the kit's disappearance had destroyed the source of reproduction, Magenta Scissor's kit. Scissor continued to distribute the kits in the Setagaya area until finally—he supposed—three days earlier, she had attacked Chocolat and her Petit Paquet near the border of Suginami, where they had been living quietly.

"Then there aren't any more Burst Linkers in Setagaya for Magenta Scissor and them to target, so they're hunting Enemies instead?" Haruyuki asked.

"That appears to be the case." Chocolat assented once more. "And it seems that even with the power of IS mode, opponents of the Beast class and up are too much for them, so they're only hunting Wild and lesser classes. I...I begged and pleaded with the changed Mitten and Plum to at least let Coolu live, but..."

Here, abruptly, a single transparent droplet spilled out of Chocolat Puppeteer's cherry eye lens.

"With every passing day, the two of them grew colder. And finally today, they said this to me: That if Coolu died, then I would give up and also join Magenta Scissor. They said they and their friends would come to hunt Coolu after school...which is why...which is why I..."

Another tear spilled onto her chocolate cheek. Before it had a chance to fall to the floor, Chiyuri reached out and gently embraced Chocolat.

"That's why you've been waiting here all this time. To protect Coolu...I'm sorry we scared you."

There was no way he could also do something like hug Chocolat, so instead, Haruyuki bowed his head. "I-I'm sorry too. To make up for it, we'll help you. Let's protect Coolu together."

Even hearing this, Chocolat Puppeteer didn't react right away. Her shoulders continued to shake in Chiyuri's arms for longer than ten full seconds before she finally uttered, "I didn't think I could really protect Coolu. On the color wheel, I'm between yellow and red, more long-distance and indirect engagement—more of a support type. But I…I do have a means of an absolute direct attack that I can use against only Mint Mitten and Plum Flipper, my former friends."

Haruyuki wasn't immediately able to grasp the meaning of this, but from Chocolat's tense air, he caught her true intention. Chiyuri seemed to realize it at the same time. "Judgment Blow?" they murmured together.

Chocolat nodded very slightly and continued feebly, "In the Legion Master quest, we all worked together and took on the challenge, but the one who obtained the clear item…was me. Mitten and Plum have already left the Legion, but for one month, I have the right to judge them. I think that's my only choice now. Not to protect Coolu, but to save them. They're parasitized by the ISS kits, and it is having an effect on their real personalities, too."

"…"

An attack on Carbuncle by three or four people was something that could be fended off with the help of Haruyuki and Chiyuri. But it was impossible to get rid of the ISS kits parasitizing Chocolat's friends with an attack inside the Accelerated World. Last Thursday, Haruyuki had witnessed ISS kit users attacking Ash Roller and Bush Utan, members of the Green Legion, in this very Unlimited Neutral Field. Spurred on by a dizzying rage, he had summoned the Armor of Catastrophe that lay sleeping in his avatar and fought the six kit users. In the middle of that battle, Haruyuki had ripped out the kit parasitizing one of his enemies and crushed it.

A strange light had escaped from the destroyed "red eyeball," and he had chased after it to its destination, Tokyo Midtown Tower, guarded by the Archangel Metatron—but the light that had fled was itself most likely the core of the ISS kits. Even though the eyeball was crushed, the kit hadn't disappeared. If they were going to resolve the situation with offensive power in the Accelerated World, their only option was to hit what was thought to be the kit main body that existed on the top floor of Midtown Tower.

And if that was the case, then maybe the only option was to use the Judgment Blow to liberate Mint Mitten and Plum Flipper from their

ISS kits, just like Chocolat said. But—that was a final solution and at the same time a tragic conclusion. Because Burst Linkers who lost Brain Burst also lost all memories related to the Accelerated World.

Unable to find anything to say, Haruyuki simply and intently clenched his hands together. In his heart, one thought alone spun round and round: *If only I'd mastered the Theoretical Mirror ability already. Then maybe, right about now, the seven Legions would be cooperatively carrying out the Metatron mission and trying to destroy the ISS kit main body. And then, if they succeeded, Chocolat Puppeteer wouldn't have to be suffering like this...*

Wait. The thing I should really be yelled at for is my lack of imagination. Even though I found out however many days ago that the ISS kits were spreading through Arakawa, Koto, and then Setagawa, I acted like it was someone else's problem. I figured they were empty areas, so it was still okay. The thought never crossed my mind that there were Burst Linkers suffering there, too. I just selfishly kept thinking we'd figure something out before it got to Suginami and Nerima.

"Sorry. I'm sorry, Chocolat...I...If only I'd—," he squeezed out, unthinkingly.

"Crow." Chiyuri snapped her right hand up to cut him off. "This is a bad habit of yours. Making everything your own fault, and on top of that, thinking that it's already too late," she asserted curtly.

"B-but"—he raised his eyes a little—"if I hadn't been dragging my feet..."

"You've been doing everything you can! And there's still work you can do. Chocolat, you too; it's too soon to give up. I've got an idea."

Just as Haruyuki had guessed, the university that sat in this place in the real world had a neighboring affiliated high school and junior high. Chocolat Puppeteer and the two former members of her Legion were students at the middle school. The temples of varying sizes that stood in this part of the Sacred Ground stage were school facilities—in other words, Chocolat knew the terrain of this area very well. But so did their attackers, Mint Mitten and Plum Flipper. It would be hard to hide in a temple for an ambush.

There was also the risk of being on the receiving end of a surprise attack and having to fight in a free-for-all in close quarters.

Naturally, their attackers wouldn't know that Haruyuki and Chiyuri had joined forces with Chocolat. It might have been effective to use Chocolat as bait and then have Haruyuki and Chiyuri launch a surprise attack. But they couldn't use that method now. Because the strategy that Chiyuri had come up with required them to fight openly, head-on.

"I'm telling you, we don't have to wait for the enemy in the middle of the grounds," grumbled Haruyuki, a big lover of surprise attacks.

"Don't keep complaining after you've already agreed!" Chiyuri jabbed him lightly in the side. "Your job is to defend against any long-distance attacks from their side, Crow, so make sure you actually keep watch!"

"R-right." He nodded, but...

Waiting for other Burst Linkers in the Unlimited Neutral Field was a matter of intense patience. Even if, for instance, you managed to narrow down your opponent's dive time to within five minutes, that could end up being as much as five thousand minutes on this side: over three days.

And the preliminary attack warning Chocolat's former comrades had given her was "today after school." From a general perspective, that could have been a span of several hours, but having known the two Burst Linkers for many years, Chocolat had apparently narrowed it down somewhat to the thirty minutes between six o'clock and six thirty. Approximately twenty days inside. She had been planning to wait, earnestly and intently, that entire overly long time. In fact, eleven days had already passed by the time she ran into Haruyuki and Chiyuri. She had absolutely no idea at what point in time the attackers might appear during the remaining nine days.

Put in this position, Haruyuki keenly felt the tremendousness of the deceleration ability of the jet-black layered avatar who called himself the vice president of the Acceleration Research Society. If you could drop the speed of perception to a 1:1 ratio with the real world while diving in the Unlimited Neutral Field, it would be a fairly simple thing to lie in wait for other Burst Linkers and attack. But, of course, he couldn't be envious of a power that relied on the illegal BIC—brain implant chip.

In the Accelerated World, if you tried to acquire something, compensation of equal value to that thing was required. A very long standby time was one of those—and the Burst Linkers who obtained incredible power via the ISS kits were definitely losing something precious inside themselves.

Haruyuki had come now to Sakurajosui in the Setagaya area here with the aim of acquiring the Theoretical Mirror ability. He had come to have the rare laser-attack Enemy Lava Carbuncle be his partner in special training, but Chiyuri had spent three days here already to find this partner. No matter how many days they ended up waiting, this was not the time for Haruyuki to throw in the towel. This was even more true now that they'd met the Burst Linker who called Carbuncle a friend, heard her sad story, and been treated to hot cocoa.

"It's okay. I'll make sure to keep watch, so you two just rest now, while you can," Haruyuki said.

Chiyuri and Chocolat next to her blinked their eye lenses in surprise and then, for some reason, giggled at the same time.

"Wh-what are you laughing for?"

"It's just, like—you're saying stuff that just doesn't suit you."

"You are putting on airs a little."

"Tch..." Unconsciously, he hung his head and then hurriedly brought his gaze back up.

They were standing by in the middle of the university grounds where Haruyuki and Chiyuri had first encountered Lava Carbuncle. Coolu, the Enemy in question, had withdrawn to a midsize temple it used as a nest. In the real world, the building was apparently the university co-op store, where they sold all kinds of sweets. (Although Haruyuki didn't think this had any connection with that.)

A large school building rose up on the northern side of the grounds, while Coolu's nest was on the east side, so it was the south and west sides that were open. If the ISS kit users were going to come at them, it would be from one of those directions. Haruyuki glared that way, but he also had one more important clue as to the direction of their approach: the energy crystals floating all over the Sacred Ground stage. To come across one of these and pass by without smashing it required almost inhuman restraint. Just like Haruyuki had, players would simply punch them on their way past, even if their special-attack gauge was full. And the crystals made a particular sound when they were broken.

Thus, Haruyuki split his concentration between his vision and his hearing. Would a human form cutting blackly through the milky white sky be first? Or would he hear the bell-like sound of destruction first?

Still on guard, he glanced to his side and saw that at some point, Lime Bell and Chocolat Puppeteer had sat down on the ground, back-to-back. Both of their heads were hanging, and given that neither of them was moving an inch, they appeared to have somehow fallen asleep.

He was the one who had told them to rest, but even so, he grinned wryly at how easily they had dropped off. But he soon wiped the smile from his face. Chiyuri had spent three days looking for an Enemy with a laser for him, and Chocolat had already been on a continuous dive in this field for eleven days. It was no wonder they were both tired.

Have a good sleep, you two, he mouthed silently, and once again he took up his stance on guard.

About four hours after they had started on standby, the enemy still hadn't appeared, and Haruyuki was enduring a de-buff that came from within—hunger. It was true that his actual body in the real world was starving, but those signals shouldn't be able to transmit to the Accelerated World. So the hunger was a fake that his brain—no, his spirit was selfishly creating. He knew it was a fake, but that didn't make the sensation of his avatar's stomach tightening up go away.

If he had known this was what would happen, he would have eaten a double order of the chocolate gelato at Enjiya. And he would have added miniwaffles to the top.

Thoughts like this rolling through his mind, he pressed his hands against his stomach, and then he saw something flash in the corner of his vision: a shiny, burned brown. His eyes moved that way as if sucked in to see the armor skirt of Chocolat Puppeteer, asleep with her legs out to one side. The more he looked, the more it seemed like the wonderful color of chocolate.

The color of normal duel avatars came in a wide range and variety, but the material was basically the same. Not plastic, not glass, and of course, not metal—a hard crystal. Chocolat would have been no exception to this rule; the armor of her entire body was an inorganic substance that was only the *color* of chocolate. Haruyuki understood this in his head.

But as someone who had been eating chocolate ice cream at Enjiya's for many years, his instincts were telling him this kind of texture was not possible with a fake. Of course, he couldn't exactly bite into it to make sure, but if he cautiously tried touching it a little with a finger...

"What are you doing?"

Suddenly, he heard a murmured voice near his ear, and with a jump, Haruyuki yanked back the left hand he'd started to extend. Timidly shifting his gaze, he saw that the light-pink eye lenses of Chocolat, who he had assumed was asleep, were shining with a reproachful light. He almost shouted immediately, "Nothing at all!" but if he woke Chiyuri—who was sleeping against the girl's back—things would get dire.

"Uh, um. I just couldn't help wondering whether that chocolate color was real," Haruyuki replied in a quiet voice, still off balance.

Chocolat let out a sigh. "Nearly every Burst Linker who meets me says the same thing. Even my parent, Mint, and my child, Plum—that was the first thing either of them said to me in the Accelerated World."

"I-it was...I'm sorry. I didn't mean to make you remember."

"There's really no need for you to apologize," Chocolat said curtly, and then, for some reason, she raised her left hand and thrust it in Haruyuki's face.

"Huh…?"

"Go ahead. Please confirm it for yourself."

"Wh-what?!"

"I'd simply prefer it if you understood in advance, rather than getting curious about my armor during the battle and losing your focus."

"R-right." Given the go-ahead, Haruyuki couldn't hold back anymore. "Okay then, I'll accept your kind offer." He brought his face closer to Chocolat's left hand. The lower part of his visor slid up automatically, and his exposed bare mouth clamped down around the slender index and middle fingers.

Instantly, Chocolat shuddered with an "Eep!"

But Haruyuki's mind was basically taken over by the "flavor" spreading out in his mouth, and so he was unconscious to Chocolat's reaction. Moderately sweet, slightly bitter, highly fragrant: the perfect chocolate flavor, and far more delicious than the liquid of the Chocolate Fountain he had tasted a little while before. This flavor, right, it was the finest Belgian *couverture* chocolate…

"Excuse— I…I meant that you could taste the back of my hand." Stammering, Chocolat tried to pull her fingers out, but this did not work with Haruyuki at the peak of his hunger. He licked at the avatar's fingers again, dreaming of biscuit sticks covered in chocolate, and it felt as though his dreadfully painful pangs of hunger were gradually eased.

"Nngh…! Y-you must have understood by now." A faint voice slipping out of her, Chocolat twisted her body, and the motion knocked Lime Bell, sleeping up against her back.

"Nyah…" Chiyuri lifted her face and looked back to witness Haruyuki's act—and just as she was on the verge of doing so…

Kashak! The faint, distant sound touched Haruyuki's hearing.

"……!!"

His mind instantly switched gears, and he took his mouth off Chocolat's fingers and stood up. His visor had no sooner closed again than he was calling out sharply in a quiet voice, "Chocolat, Bell, they're here!"

Immediately, the faces of both Chocolat Puppeteer, holding

her left hand and panting, and Lime Bell, watching this curiously with sleepy eyes, stiffened.

"Where?" Quickly getting to her feet, Chiyuri surveyed their surroundings. "I can't see them."

"I heard a crystal breaking. Southwest. Probably about a hundred meters away."

"There's a passage there that goes between the university and the high school. If they come in through the gate and not over the wall, they'll be approaching here from the west. And, Silver Crow?"

Haruyuki reflexively shrank back. Naturally, he assumed he would be censured for his previous act, but Chocolat settled with simply glaring at him and then quickly saying, "My name does take quite some time, so when you call me, you can simply shorten *Chocolat* to *Choco*."

"Oh, then you should call me Bell."

"J-just call me Crow."

Chocolat nodded lightly at their responses and turned her face away. "All right, understood. They're coming."

Haruyuki shifted his gaze to the west once more at basically the same time as several figures assembled on the roof of a single-story temple. Four.

"Four, huh?"

"And one of them is excessively large, hmm?"

They were still some distance away, so Haruyuki and his defenders couldn't make out color or shape, but even still, they could clearly see that the one on the far right was a very large avatar.

Bigger than Cyan Pile—no, Frost Horn, even, Haruyuki thought.

"The two on the left are Mint Mitten and Plum Flipper," Chocolat murmured in a strained voice. Even from this distance, she could identify her longtime friends. So then the two on the right, including the large avatar, must be Burst Linkers given ISS kits by Magenta Scissor, or—

"Both of you, get down!" Haruyuki made Chiyuri and Chocolat step back while he himself took a step forward. He saw the large one on the right and the two on the left all raise a hand at the same time. He had seen this motion before.

Dark Shot.

He didn't know if their voices actually reached him, but Haruyuki distinctly heard the technique name in his ears.

Against the backdrop of the pure, pearl-white sky, their three hands were enveloped in a dark, sinister aura. This concentrated in the centers of their palms and built up for a moment before becoming ink-black beams and gushing out.

By that time, Haruyuki was already shouting, arms crossed in front of him: "Laser Sword!!"

Shkeeenk! The crisp sound rang out, and swords of silver light expanded in an X shape.

The dark beams, now fused into one, reached him, slamming into the intersection of the blades stretching out from his arms.

The pressure pushed him back about twenty centimeters over the arabesque patterns of the ground. But Crow stopped there and roared, "Unh…aaaaaah!"

He yanked his arms down sharply to the sides. The dark beam scattered and dispersed, melting into the atmosphere of the stage before disappearing.

Dark Shot was one of the two techniques possible when an ISS kit user activated IS mode. "IS mode" was short for "Incarnate System mode." Just as the name suggested, this was not a normal special attack but rather an Incarnate attack.

A trained imagination flowed into the Image Control circuit of the Brain Burst program, normally a supporting system, and caused an overwrite. This was the logic of an Incarnate attack. Although it was called an *overwrite*, the power of it basically rendered the normal defensive abilities of a duel avatar ineffective. The reasoning was that you could only handle an Incarnate attack with another Incarnate attack. Of course, this sort of attack was extremely difficult to obtain. To master just one of the four basic techniques—power expansion, range expansion, defense expansion, movement expansion—required many long hours of training in the Unlimited Neutral Field.

But simply by equipping it, a kit user gained the range-expansion technique Dark Shot and the power-expansion technique Dark Blow. Both were basic techniques, but with the two together, the user had all-purpose attack power. If the user launched the punch and laser, both impossible to defend against—and both of which had no connection with the special-attack gauge—in succession, there was no way for a midlevel Burst Linker without an Incarnate attack to resist.

Haruyuki had mastered the Incarnate attack Laser Sword under the guidance of his master, Sky Raker, but the category was range expansion, and the power was basically a normal thrusting attack plus a little extra. It wasn't suited to defensive use, and on top of that, the Dark Shot launched by the enemy group contained the power of three people. But even so, Haruyuki believed he would absolutely not be pushed back by this technique. As *if* they could beat him.

"Shoot as many times as you want—it's no use!!" Haruyuki shouted toward the attackers lined up fifty meters away, the overlay of his Incarnate still lodged in both arms. "I'll watch this technique any number of times, repel it any number of times! As if I'm scared of a technique that never evolves!"

The "any number of times" was a bit of an exaggeration, but this was a fact, at any rate. However, Haruyuki had repelled Dark Shot when he was transformed into the sixth Chrome Disaster, and now that he had sealed away the armor, his defensive power had dropped significantly.

Nevertheless, in a battle using the Incarnate System, simply taking a thought to the extreme had serious meaning. When it came down to a conflict between overwrites, in the end, it was a fight pitting the strength of different imaginations against one another. The Dark Shots he had knocked back left and right when he was Disasterfied had strengthened the image in Haruyuki's mind.

In contrast, the techniques of the kit users were not thus strengthened, because the sources of their techniques were not in their hearts but rather in the foreign objects parasitizing their avatars. Haruyuki was proclaiming that truth, but it seemed that this was not understood by their attackers; three of them raised their right hands once more.

"I'm telling you, it's pointless!!" Now, Haruyuki took on an attack posture. He readied his left arm in front of his body and drew his right arm back at shoulder height, a motion that strongly resembled the Black King Incarnate attack, Vorpal Strike.

"Dark Shot." This time, the lifeless sound of the technique name being called faintly reached him.

He howled his battle cry to overwrite that voice: "Laser Lance!!"

Wrapped up to the shoulder in silver light, he thrust his right arm forward with all his might, and the dazzling, shining Incarnate lance was launched with a metallic roar. It collided violently with the three black beams pressing in on him, and a spray of light and dark danced and fought each other.

Too far...?! No, it'll reach!! Haruyuki clenched his teeth and mustered up every bit of image power inside him.

If the Laser Sword he had used before had been a combat technique that expanded and contracted at high speed, a sword of light from either hand, then this Laser Lance was a mid-range attack that took time to launch compressed light from his right hand as a lance. The range in which it maintained 100 percent of its power was at present limited to twenty meters, and the power weakened dramatically after that.

The lance was already stretched out twenty-five meters, so it was fair to say that it was at its limit for practical distance. But ever since Kuroyukihime had informed him of the existence of a second stage for the Incarnate attack—the practical technique—he had been working independently on different kinds of tricks.

There were two types of practical techniques. A "composite attack," with two or more of the four basic attributes, and a "special attack," which did not fit in with any attribute. In order to cover the long-distance fighting that Silver Crow was so poor at, Haruyuki had explored ways to further expand the range of his

Laser Lance. The answer he had reached after countless failures was to cut the Lance with his Sword.

"Nngh…aaah!" A low cry slipping out, he pulled his fully extended right arm back bit by bit. The image of the lance trying to charge forward stretched like rubber. Once his right hand returned to his shoulder, the elasticity of the lance reached its limit. In that instant, a short sword of light was lodged in his left hand, readied in front of his chest.

"Go!" With a brief shout, he severed the lance of his right hand at the base with the sword of his left hand.

Zwwank! The air shook, and the now-freed lance of light shot forward with incredible speed. It sent the aggressive jet-black beam scattering in all directions, just like in the previous skirmish, and then closed in on the aggressors, as if following the beam's trajectory backward.

However, the technique—which Haruyuki had secretly named Laser Javelin—had a weak point: its hit precision would worsen from logic overpowering it. The lance carved out a faint arc in the air and plunged into the roof of the low temple the four enemies were standing on. After a pause, a flash whiter than the temple itself erupted and ripped a giant hole in the building.

Here, finally, two of the attackers—Mint Mitten on the right, and Plum Flipper standing to the left—looked shaken, albeit slightly. They'd probably never had their IS mode technique repelled and counterattacked to this extent before. Their silhouettes, small like Chocolat's, crept backward.

Yet, the tall avatar with her arms crossed threw her right hand up into the air, essentially ignoring Haruyuki's counterattack. Perhaps she had a sword-shaped weapon; the long, sharp tip checked the movement of the two starting to retreat. Here, likely having been given some instruction, the four enemy avatars jumped down from the temple that was starting to crumble to the ground and began to slowly walk toward Haruyuki and his comrades.

"Crow, that was really something."

"I'd like to say I expected nothing less."

Chiyuri and then Chocolat murmured from behind him.

"This is just starting, guys," Haruyuki replied in a quiet voice. "Or rather, now it's you two—Bell, Chocolat…er, Choco—taking the lead now. I'm counting on you."

"Yup! Leave it to us!"

"Indeed."

Even during this quick exchange, the four attackers continued walking directly toward them. The two on the left still moved rather awkwardly, but the tall avatar next to them—the apparent leader—and the super-large avatar on the far right held their heads high as they strode toward Haruyuki and his friends.

Once they had gotten about five meters away, the leader raised her right hand again. Everyone stopped.

At this distance, he could pick out the details of their duel avatars. Standing on the far left was an F-type with big gloves on both hands, large boots on both feet. The armor of her body, including a head part reminiscent of a knit hat, was a bright mint green. She was probably Mint Mitten.

The F-type next to her had shoulders, waist, and elbows enveloped by popping spherical armor. She wore a round hat on her head, and her coloring was a muted reddish-purple. This had to be Plum Flipper.

Both of them were small, cute avatars with the same air as Chocolat Puppeteer. However, their cuteness was significantly damaged by the crimson eyeball attached to their chests—the ISS kit. While the eyeball emitted a powerful light like it was starving, the glittering in their own eye lenses was empty. They seemed to recognize Chocolat standing behind Haruyuki—their friend until a few days ago—as nothing more than a target for destruction.

The interference of the kit is getting stronger, Haruyuki thought to himself. He remembered that when Bush Utan was parasitized, he had basically kept his original personality even three days in. In contrast, despite the fact that Mint and Plum had been parasitized a similar three days, their appearances were already those of automatons.

Since the ISS kit terminals were synchronized through the main body enshrined at Midtown Tower every night, the more of them there were, the greater their influence over those who equipped them. Without exaggeration, this was a race against time. Digesting this, Haruyuki turned his eyes on the tall avatar, who was apparently the leader, standing to the right of Mint and Plum.

She was tall, but her torso and limbs were as slender as Silver Crow's. Her entire body was covered with a film-type armor so that she looked like she was wrapped in bandages. Other than her mouth, her face was completely hidden, so it was hard to discern her gender. But from the lines of her body and the air about her, she was probably an F-type. In each hand, she held a strangely shaped weapon. They were probably in the sword category, but the single blades were extremely tapered, and the space between the blade and the grip was excessively long. The grip was incorporated into an enormous knuckle guard, making a distorted circular shape. The color of her armor was a bright reddish-purple.

And then the last avatar—a figure that could only be said to be bizarre. It was very large and much taller than even the reddish-purple leader; probably two and a half meters tall. It was also at least a meter wide. And its round, dark-green body had nothing in the way of a neck or a waist, but simply tapered slightly at the top. In other words, it was essentially a perfect egg shape. If it hadn't been for the short arms and legs sticking out from the sides and bottom, alongside the eye lenses shining yellow, it wouldn't have looked like a duel avatar at all. Even the ISS kit attached to the center of the oblong body looked ridiculously small.

During the time when Haruyuki and his comrades were quickly inspecting the enemy group, their adversaries were doing the same thing to them. The reddish-purple leader pulled the corners of her mouth—the only part of her face not covered by the film-type armor—into a grin. "That silver and the shiny head—so you'd be the Corvus of Nega Nebulus, hmm? Then the yellowish-green one behind you's the Witch. These are some unexpected guests, but we are glad to have you. Welcome to Setagaya area."

From her husky voice and tone, he instinctively knew his opponent to be a slightly older girl. This was the type of duel opponent he was worst with, but he couldn't shrink now. Haruyuki focused his strength within his abdomen.

"And you must be Magenta Scissor," he declared, certain from her color and attitude. But then his confidence disappeared abruptly, and he muttered, "Wait, no, was it Magenta Scissors..."

Although he felt Chiyuri sighing behind him, this wasn't the time to turn around and get her to tell him. He was pretty sure this should have been Scissor, but if that meant the office supply for cutting paper, he had a memory of learning in English class that it absolutely had to be in the plural, "Scissors."

If it had been a regular duel field, her name would have shown up under her health gauge, Haruyuki agonized.

The magenta avatar smiled bewitchingly once more. "Scissor is right for me. I'll tell you why, so don't add that *s* ever again. I totally hate those English words that are two things when they're one thing."

"Like shoes and pants?" he said, inadvertently drawn in, and Magenta Scissor nodded sharply.

"Right, exactly. Like chopsticks and stuff." She chuckled as she continued. "I mean, it's acting like these things have no value on their own. A single shoe, a lone chopstick. Don't you think that's terrible? The second they're not a pair anymore, no matter how beautiful they are, how untouched, they end up in the garbage."

Not comprehending what she was trying to say, Haruyuki fell silent.

"Does this have anything to do with the fact that you're going around handing out—no, forcibly infecting Burst Linkers in the Setagaya area with ISS kits?" Chiyuri snapped on his behalf from behind him.

The reddish-purple avatar moved her head, wrapped with winding ribbon armor, and laughed again. "If I had to say, it does...maybe? Once I give this to every Burst Linker, one concept of a pair that I hate so much will disappear from the Accelerated World. Because if everyone's using the same techniques, then tag-team compatibility becomes meaningless, after all."

"D-duels without any personality like that won't be fun at all!" Chiyuri shouted.

Magenta spread out her hands, clutching the strange swords, and shook her head in exasperation. "They're fun because they have personality? So then what about the Burst Linkers who were born with the kind of individuality that everybody sneers at, the kind they hate? What are they supposed to do? Like Avocado Avoider here?" She passed her left wrist through the ring-shaped grip of her sword and gently stroked the dark-green egg avatar with her now-free hand. When she did, the body—so large they had to look up at it—shuddered slightly, and a low purring voice came from somewhere unknown in that body.

The avatars generated automatically by the Brain Burst program came in all shapes and sizes, to the point where they had essentially nothing in common other than a roughly human shape. Inevitably, the great majority of Burst Linkers ended up with avatars with a cool or cute design, or with avatars that were the exact opposite. And unfortunately, in the Accelerated World as in the real world, the tendency for the former to be more popular and the latter to be the opposite was seriously pronounced.

"It can't be everyone doing that," Haruyuki said, before Chiyuri had the chance to reply.

"You're right there, too, aren't you, Magenta? From the way you're talking, you guys were comrades before the ISS kits came out, right?"

"Unfortunately, you're wrong. I met Avocado very recently. Only just having become a Burst Linker, he was the target of a group attack by several people and was on the verge of total point loss. One of the people attacking him was his own parent. He was cackling, saying how he didn't want a creepy child like this."

When Haruyuki and his comrades were at a loss for words, a rumbling groan slipped out of the massive green body. Whether he liked it or not, Haruyuki was forced to understand that this was not a voice of anger, but of sadness.

"I challenged Avocado when he was in a place where it'd all be over if he lost one more time and gave him an ISS kit. You should've seen him turn the tables after that. Those guys really were out of luck that they canceled the limit on the number of times they could be challenged with their Legion member privilege. Half of them were at total point loss. Including Avocado's parent. So? Can you still say a Burst Linker needs personality? Can you actually believe it's natural that there are Linkers anyone would pair up with and Linkers no one will join?" Hand still on Avocado's side, Magenta shrugged lightly.

The entirely unexpected question thrust at him, Haruyuki could only fall silent once more. He thought that Magenta Scissor was wrong, bringing the idea of winning and losing teams into the Accelerated World. But at the same time, it was a fact that when he first saw Avocado Avoider, his impression was "different, weird." At that moment, Haruyuki hadn't thought of Avocado as a fellow Burst Linker, but only as a monster to be defeated.

Breaking the silence was Chocolat Puppeteer, who'd been silent up to then. "Pushing his parent to total point loss...I wonder if that was really Avocado's will?"

"What do you mean, Cocoa, hon?"

Faced with Magenta, broad grin still on her face, the small chocolate-colored avatar took a resolute step forward. "The ISS kit doesn't just take away a Burst Linker's individuality. It also steals the user's kindness and empathy and gives them hate in their place. Even if, hypothetically, everything went according to your plan and all the Burst Linkers were kit users, unfairness and alienation wouldn't disappear from the Accelerated World! Absolutely not!"

"How can you say that, hmm? Your friends understand, you know, Cocoa? They get that instead of locking themselves up in a little box, it's way more fun to get stronger, get fighting power, and change the world."

"That's a lie!! That's your—that's what *you* want! You're simply forcibly infecting other Burst Linkers with this desire! And one more thing: The only people allowed to call me Cocoa are Min-Min and Pliko!!"

The end of this was a tear-filled shriek.

It seemed like Mint Mitten and Plum Flipper, who were standing lifelessly behind Magenta, shook slightly upon hearing this. But immediately after that, the eyeballs pasted to their chests flared with a red light, and the eye lenses of the two girls became empty once more.

"It's too bad, Chocolat Puppeteer. In the end, I guess I have no choice but to operate on you, too," Magenta Scissor said in an increasingly cold voice, removing her hand from Avocado. She twirled the sword hanging from her wrist and grabbed it once more. The sharp, tapered end glittered coldly. "Silver Crow, Lime Bell. If you sit and watch quietly, I won't do anything to you. I only came with one kit seed, anyway. But if you get in my way, we'll kill you over and over and over until we get bored of it, you know?"

Haruyuki reflexively called the surrounding terrain to mind. From the university here to the portal at Sakurajosui Station wedged along Aratama Suido Road was about eight hundred meters as the crow flies. He could make it there with his wings in a single bound, but if the fighting power of Magenta Scissor and her gang far exceeded his expectations, it was a little far for all three of them to retreat together. However, Chocolat Puppeteer probably wouldn't try to run. She was prepared to free her friends from the control of the ISS kits with the Judgment Blow, even if it meant being killed over and over and losing all her points.

Their one hope to avoid this tragic end was the Mint and Plum Recovery Mission drafted by Chiyuri. And the possibility of this mission succeeding rested on whether or not they could defeat Magenta Scissor and Avocado Avoider while leaving the other two alive.

It was a fact that Avocado's past as recounted by Magenta did move his heart. But faced with him in this situation, there was no road other than fighting, not due to hatred, but in order to talk to each other through the duel—the very meaning of a Burst Linker's existence.

"Sorry, but we can't just stand by and watch," Haruyuki declared. "We have our own reason we have to fight you."

"Oh?" Smile still on her face, Magenta cocked her head slightly to one side. "And what's that?"

"Don't tell me you forgot you parasitized our precious comrade with an ISS kit last week."

"Oh, Cyan Pile, right? And I had high hopes for him, too. I mean, a change of heart in the middle of syncing and then attacking the main body—that was disappointing. You're barking up the wrong tree complaining about that to me. After all, Cyan was the one who came all the way to Setagaya wanting the kit, you know? All I did was give it to him as a present in card form, just like he wanted."

"Even if you did, you had to have known. That even if it was sealed in card form, the kit would whisper to the owner's mind and tempt them into equipping it. You've probably experienced that yourself, haven't you?"

"…"

At this from Haruyuki, the smile vanished from Magenta's lips. She raised the bizarre swords dangling from each of her hands and lightly brought the points together with a *clink*. "I'm a bit offended by that. I accepted this of my own free will. In order to remake the Accelerated World into what it should be."

When Magenta slowly opened the swords crossed in front of her to both sides, almost as if that was a signal, part of the ribbon armor wrapped around her chest peeled away. The crimson-red eye snapping open on the surface of her exposed avatar body was, of course, the same ISS kit that Mint and the others had attached to their chests. But for this one, the coloring, so reminiscent of blood, was darker, and the eyeball was also a size bigger. Because Magenta's face was hidden under the layers of ribbon wrapped around it, it almost looked like the kit was her own eye. After this eye, inorganic and yet clearly hate-filled, glanced at Haruyuki and his comrades, Magenta declared coldly, "I guess we're going to have to make you disappear, after all, hmm? And if you two are gone from the Accelerated World, Cyan'll probably come back to me, too."

It had to have been more than ten days since the ISS kit had taken up residence in her body, and yet it appeared that she had almost completely retained her self; did that mean the power of her will was incredibly strong?

Banishing the fear that threatened to rise up in him, Haruyuki shouted, "A-as if that's going to happen! No matter what, he'll never come back to you again!"

"Well then, let's test that theory. I'm getting pretty tired of chatting already. Just as you wished, I'll be your opponent. Mint, Plum, the two of you take Lime Bell. Avocado, you can *eat* Chocolat."

Haruyuki and his comrades were startled by this last order, and in that moment of stunned surprise, Magenta Scissor brandished the sword of her right hand high—and then dropped it sharply. The two former members of Petit Paquet to her left and Avocado Avoider on her right started to move.

"Bell! Choco! Just like we planned!"

"Leave it to us!"

"Absolutely!"

Haruyuki and his team exchanged quick words and then started to act. First, Chocolat thrust both hands out in front of her.

"Cocoa Fountain!!"

Together with the call of the technique name, pink light poured down in a broad range from her ten fingers. With a burbling sound, large amounts of chocolate gushed out of the ground. This spread out and covered a diameter of thirty meters of the field, and Mint, Plum, and Avocado got their feet caught and staggered.

"Tch!" Clicking her tongue, Magenta Scissor leapt back and then stepped even farther back, avoiding the pool of chocolate—more like a chocolate lake, actually.

Naturally, Haruyuki too was within the effective range of Chocolat's technique, but he had used his wings as she activated it and so was hovering ten or so centimeters above the ground.

Behind him, Bell and Chocolat also retreated to get some

distance and immediately got to work on the next part of the plan. Bell brandished the Choir Chime of her left hand and whirled it in large circles. "Citron Call!"

She swung it down. Accompanied by the tinkling of a bell, the Chime's light zeroed in on Chocolat, standing beside Bell. The brown avatar had broken an energy crystal before the arrival of their enemies to charge her special-attack gauge and had then used up that charge for the full-power Cocoa Fountain, but now, thanks to the effect of Citron Call Mode I, which rewound the status of the target in units of seconds, her special-attack gauge was replenished once more.

No sooner was it fully charged than Chocolat was calling out her second technique. "Puppet Make!!"

Snap! She turned four fingers toward the chocolate lake. The smooth milk chocolate surface bulged up in four places, and the now-familiar chocolate puppets—Chocopets—jumped up from within. Two of them flew at Mint and Plum, while the other two headed toward Avocado to surround the enemy avatars. With their feet caught up in the chocolate on the ground, the enemy was unable to move freely.

Long/midrange duel avatar Chocolat Puppeteer had the ability first to make chocolate bubble up in the field with the prerequisite technique of Cocoa Fountain, which also hindered enemy movement. And then with her special attack Puppet Make, she could create automatic combat dolls from that chocolate pond and make them attack specific targets.

The scale of the chocolate pond and the number of Chocopets were determined by the number of fingers she held up when activating the techniques. With ten fingers, she could create a chocolate pond thirty meters in diameter, but that completely exhausted her fully charged special-attack gauge. Which meant, essentially, that if she created the biggest pond possible, she couldn't call any Chocopets until she charged her gauge once more. But when working in combination with Citron Call, she could smash through that limit.

Although the chocolate pond was 40 percent smaller after the creation of four Chocopets, it was still more than large enough to hold the feet of Mint Mitten and the others.

Haruyuki first confirmed that step one of their strategy had succeed and then shouted, "You guys take Avocado! I'm going after Magenta!"

He spread his wings and flew at top speed, skimming the surface of the sticky-sweet pond. He slipped between Avocado and Plum and closed in on Magenta Scissor beyond them.

"This is some seriously cheeky action!" The reddish-purple avatar readied her swords to meet Haruyuki. The thick blades glittered and glinted, but he charged forward regardless. Of the metal colors, Silver Crow's antiphysical defenses were on the low side, but even so, his resistance to severing attacks was higher than the average regular color. He caught the swords that sliced down from both sides at the same time with the armor on his upper body.

Skreeek! A high-pitched metallic screech sawed into his ears, and bright sparks shot out, lighting up the armor of both fighters. Of course, he couldn't escape from this unscathed; the health gauge in the top left of his field of view dropped the tiniest bit, a few pixels, but he ignored it and flapped his wings as hard as he could.

"Aaaaah!!"

As if pushed back by Haruyuki's roar, Magenta Scissor's feet floated up. Not letting this chance get away, he started in on another charge, still at close range. Cutting directly across the grounds, he shoved her back to the temple where she and her team had first appeared. Magenta crashed thunderously into the wall right beside the hole Haruyuki had opened up with his Laser Javelin. Her body half-embedded in the white wall, a groan escaped her lips.

Using the reactive force to get a little distance from her, Haruyuki began another rush on his opponent to settle this match before she managed to pull herself back together.

"Hngaaah!"

Barely touching the ground, his Aerial Combo—which used the instantaneous thrust of both wings to launch both hands and feet at her over and over—ripped into Magenta, and she was steadily hammered deeper into the wall. Her two swords took about half his strikes, but Haruyuki had four limbs. Punches and kicks slipped past her guard to smash into her reddish-purple ribbon armor one after another.

He had suspected from the start that her defensive abilities were not that great. Reddish-purple was a little closer to long-distance than close-range on the color wheel. She shouldn't have been able to really take a hit in close combat.

But hold on a sec. In that case, why is her weapon a sword? If she's a sword user, then her color ought to be way closer to blue...

Haruyuki continued his onslaught, but just as this question popped up in the back of his mind, Magenta crossed the swords in both hands in front of her body. *Ka-ching!* It was the sound of the two metal elements fitting together. What had been two swords were in that moment transformed into something else: two blades opening like a jaw with a single rivet as the fulcrum and large ring-shaped grips.

Those aren't swords anymore! Those are scissors! Haruyuki realized.

"You're in danger! Dodge!!" Chocolat's voice reached him from behind.

"Nngh!" He forcibly stopped the right roundhouse kick his leg was in the middle of and forced some backward thrust with his wings.

Magenta started to move her arms, but Haruyuki was already more than three meters away. It seemed to him that the range for the swords and the scissors was the same—or maybe the range for the scissors was smaller, since she had to operate them with both hands?

But a faint smile played on Magenta's lips. In a movement filled with certainty, her arms slowly closed the scissors. The blades, opened to their maximum of nearly a meter, closed in on seventy centimeters, and then fifty.

Snip! He heard the jarring sound through his avatar body. He felt cool, chilled metal touching him on either side of his waist. He hurriedly turned his eyes in that direction, but there was nothing there. But the hard pressure increased with each instant, and the chill turned into pain.

"Wha—?!" he cried out in surprise, and just as he was on the verge of flying even farther back, the sound of metal ripping through metal echoed across the stage.

A crimson damage effect cut across Silver Crow's stomach. A dizzyingly fierce pain raced through his nervous system, and he very nearly screamed, but managed to grit his teeth and endure it.

Glancing up to check his health gauge, he saw that it had dropped nearly 20 percent in just this single hit. If his dash backward had been half a second later, his avatar would no doubt have been cut right in half. But more importantly, why had the attack reached him? There were nearly four meters between the scissors and Crow now.

"Ability: Remote Cut. And now that you've made me use this technique, you won't die quickly," Magenta Scissor said in a whisper, then opened the two blades all the way once more. When they had been separated, they were smallish swords, but now that they were fused, they were enormous, sinister scissors. The weapon, its sense of presence orders of magnitude greater now, closed again with a cold *snap*.

Haruyuki instantly folded his wings up as he jumped to the right, but even still, she managed to inflict a shallow cut on his left arm, and then a burning pain assaulted him. His health gauge decreased another 5 percent.

Snip! Snip! Snipsnipsnip! Still embedded in the wall of the temple, Magenta opened and closed her scissors over and over. Haruyuki moved intently to avoid the line extending from the tip of them, but in the blink of an eye, his body was peppered with countless cuts.

He badly wanted to escape into the air with his flying ability, but his instincts told him that was not a good move. After all, he didn't know how far the cutting power of the scissors reached. If he deployed his wings, the projected area of Silver Crow would nearly double—her target would get bigger, in other words. And if she took aim to cut even one of his wings, that was basically the end of the plan he and his allies had put together.

Intently slipping through snip after snip of invisible blades on the ground, Haruyuki groaned. *This is definitely a red long-distance attack—and a fairly powerful one at that.*

The power to cut a target at the end of a line extending from the scissors was, if looked at in a different way, perhaps the same as a rapid-fire slicer gun. The problem, however, was that he couldn't see the attack. All he could do was guess at the line of sight from the direction of the scissors, and Magenta Scissor could freely adjust the timing for generating the cutting force. She could throw in all the feints and the random shots she wanted.

But if she had this kind of powerful technique, then why hadn't she used it right from the start? Why had she actually had the scissors split into two pieces? These doubts in his mind, Haruyuki continue to do his best to dodge the double blades.

And then, suddenly, a human shape leapt in from the side in front of him. Simple body, a face with no eyes or mouth, entirely a dark brown. One of the Chocopets, the combat puppets created by Chocolat Puppeteer. The puppet, with nothing other than its fists as weapons, faced Magenta resolutely, as if to hide Haruyuki behind it. Ahead of it, the blades of the scissors closed cruelly.

Snap! Simultaneous with the metallic sound, a red line raced across the Chocopet's neck. Whether Haruyuki wanted to or not, he was forced to visualize the puppet's head tumbling to the ground. But naturally, it didn't.

The head did separate momentarily from the torso, but the cross-section melted and fused the two back together in the blink of an eye. When he thought about it, the Chocopets had apparently taken absolutely zero damage from Haruyuki's striking hand or Chiyuri's bell attack when they were first fighting them. Most likely because their entire bodies were made of chocolate, cutting and piercing attacks were normally ineffective.

Seemingly annoyed at the Chocopet recklessly charging in, the scissors snapped together even more violently. Instantly, the puppet's body was cut into five, six parts, but they were indeed soon all stuck together again.

Mouth twisting, Magenta switched from holding the scissors in both hands to carrying them in her right as she clenched her other into a fist.

The ISS kit attached to her chest emitted a crimson light. Her entire body was covered in a faint, dark aura, and this quickly concentrated in her left hand. Even seeing that inky black pulsation that warned of overwhelming force, the Chocopet showed no sign of fear. Wordlessly, it kicked at the ground and brandished an empty fist as it flew forward.

A cool smile spreading across her lips once more, Magenta murmured the technique name: "Dark Blow."

Her left fist, enveloped in a viscous darkness, shot out, making the air and the earth shudder. It met the Chocopet's descending right fist in midair. Rather than melting, the chocolate arm—immune to striking attacks—crumbled as if sucked into the surface of contact. The affinity of the Incarnate technique generated by the ISS kit was a nihilistic energy type. Even a chocolate puppet had no way of resisting it.

The right chocolate arm was instantly blown off from the elbow to the shoulder. However, not stopping there, the Dark Blow began to swallow the puppet in darkness from its torso to its head. *Whmm!* A heavy vibration sound shook the air, and when Magenta yanked her fist out, the remaining lower half of the Chocopet turned back into liquid chocolate and scattered into the air.

Through the brown mist, he could see Magenta Scissor's mouth open wide.

Charging forward as if chasing after the puppet, Haruyuki finally noticed it. Perhaps to shoot off another Dark Blow or unsure about whether to pick up the scissors again, her left hand scratched at the air. But before it could choose either one—

Your sacrifice won't be in vain! Haruyuki vowed to the Chocopet as he brought his right hand down in a sharp chop.

"Laser Sword!!" The silver sword of light that extended from his fingertips cut through Magenta's left arm above the elbow. After the faintest time lag, her arm slipped apart, top and bottom. Without a sound, the bottom fell, bounced once on the arabesque patterns of the ground, and scattered into tiny fragments before disappearing.

"*Nngh!*" Magenta Scissor groaned deeply and bent in half. She was likely withstanding the pain of losing a limb.

Haruyuki turned to her. "Now you can't use your scissors anymore. You can't open and close them with just one hand."

"And that's why I hate them, the two things that are one. I despise them. Scissors, shoes, the bilateral symmetry of the human body." This was Magenta's response.

He had the feeling that her words also contained the reason why she hadn't moved to use the scissors right from the start, and also why she was trying to eliminate the concept of the tag-team pair from the Accelerated World. But before he had the chance to think very deeply about it, her lips moved once more.

"I'll admit that was some fine work realizing you can render me nearly useless if you take one of my arms, boy. But, you see, you've seriously gotten the wrong idea about one thing."

"Th-the wrong idea? About what?"

"Well, that…That's the fact that you judged me to be the main power of the enemy."

"But I mean, no matter how you look at it, you're the leader, aren't you? You were giving all kinds of instructions and all."

"It's not necessarily the case that the leader is the strongest, you know? Me luring you all the way over here means we win," Magenta said, grinning. "Go on, take a look behind you."

"C-Crow!!" Chiyuri's scream reached Haruyuki's ears. "What should we do?! I keep hitting him and hitting him, but it's not doing anything at all! If we don't hurry, Choco's—!"

Haruyuki whirled around to find the enormous avatar Avocado Avoider standing imposingly over Lime Bell, who was slamming the Choir Chime against his egg-shaped body over and over.

And then, swallowed up to her chest in Avocado's massive mouth clamped shut around her, Chocolat Puppeteer screamed in agony.

5

"Nngh…unh…aaaaah!"

Chocolat's thin screams reached Haruyuki's ears.

"Avocado doesn't have any teeth in his mouth. Instead, he licks at the armor of a Burst Linker to dissolve it, although the time it takes depends on the Burst Linker," Magenta said, leaning against the wall of the temple, the look on her face indicating that she was suffering real pain from the missing-part damage. "But Cocoa's chocolate armor seems like it'd melt pretty quick? You better hurry over there?"

Haruyuki glanced at the reddish-purple scissors user and hesitated, unsure whether he should strike the killing blow or not. But given that she was unable to operate her scissors with just one arm, it was impossible for her to activate her most powerful weapon, Remote Cut. There was the possibility she'd come at him with Dark Shot, the long-distance Incarnate attack, with her right hand, but in order to do that, she would have to throw aside her scissors. He had no evidence to back it up, but he was certain she wouldn't do that.

"I don't need you telling me that!" he shouted, then spun on his heel. Running with all his might, he accelerated spectacularly with the added thrust from his wings, and in the blink of an eye, he was closing in on Avocado Avoider's massive form.

"Let go of…Chocoooooooooo!!" Roaring, he kicked at the ground and shot the sharp tips of his left toes straight forward, adjusting his rudder angle with thrust from his wings so that his entire body spun at top speed. Spiral Kick: a technique effective against large avatars because it doubled his power and penetrative force, although accuracy was slightly sacrificed.

His left leg, spinning like a drill, touched Avocado's dark-green armor, which didn't appear to have any thickness to it, and ripped through it easily. *Splrt!* There was the thunder of a heavy, wet impact, and Crow's foot plunged deep into the right side of Avocado's back.

But that was all. The massive egg-shaped avatar continued to move his mouth in a chewing motion as though he felt nothing, even with Crow's foot sunk more than half a meter into his body. And yet he shouldn't have been able to stay on his feet after taking that kind of damage because of the pain—especially given that one's pain sensors in the Unlimited Neutral Field operated at twice the normal amount.

Dumbfounded, Haruyuki nevertheless applied reverse thrust with his wings and pulled his left foot free. Normally, the light of a damage effect would gush out like blood, but not a single spark spilled from the large hole in Avocado's back. Just the opposite: A green buffer material thinner than the surface immediately filled it, actually going so far as to regenerate the thin armor.

"E-even with that blow just now, there's no damage?!" Haruyuki groaned.

"Exactly!" Chiyuri ran over, staggering in the chocolate pond to answer him in a panic. "You can kick him and punch him, but he just regenerates right away! He probably absorbs all physical attacks!"

"That's—he's not a Chocopet or anything," he said reflexively, before suddenly realizing something and looking around quickly.

In a spot about ten or so meters away, Mint Mitten and Plum Flipper were trying to eliminate the two Chocopets circling them nimbly, but their feet were caught in the chocolate covering the ground, and they couldn't move freely. There should also have been two Chocopets getting in Avocado's way, but they were nowhere to be seen. One of them had probably come to Haruyuki's aid, but the other one—

"He ate it!" Chiyuri shouted quickly, reading Haruyuki's thoughts.

"A-ate it?!"

"She said that at the beginning, remember? That was the weak point of the Chocopets. Avocado sucked the Chocopet in right along with the air and chomped it up. And then, when Choco got closer to make another Chocopet, she got..."

Here, the two of them looked up at Avocado's massive body. From a mouth nearly two meters above them, Chocolat's upper body hung out, an expression of agony on her face.

"Nngh!" Gritting his teeth, Haruyuki took off from the chocolate pond, and hovering in front of Avocado's mouth, he grabbed onto Chocolat's arms. He pushed his wings with everything he had and tried to pull her free, but she didn't move so much as a centimeter. On the contrary—red sparks of damage flew from her shoulder joints.

"Unnh!"

Hearing the weak scream, Haruyuki hurriedly stopped his propulsive power. But Chocolat's face still looked like she was suffering serious pain. Most likely, her armor skirt, reminiscent of flower petals, was being dissolved inside Avocado Avoider's mouth.

Above the meter-wide mouth, relatively small—although they were still five centimeters in diameter—eye lenses blinked at short intervals. In time with the fluctuating light, a low, heavy voice rumbled from deep in the egg-shaped body, "Like... Chocolat...like..."

Haruyuki was momentarily speechless, and then, still holding Chocolat's arms, shouted, "Just 'cos you like her doesn't mean you have to eat her! If you want to be friends, then just say—"

Here, he was at a loss for words. Because when he thought

about whether he himself could do that, he realized it would certainly be impossible. Just inviting Rin Kusakabe to the school festival had nearly brought him to dehydration; there was no way he could take action beyond that.

And Avocado Avoider was at present parasitized by an ISS kit, which amplified negative feelings. He was in no state of mind to be persuaded by words.

So if physical attacks were absorbed, Haruyuki would also fail to pull Chocolat free. Could he and Chiyuri eat this massive body like Avocado had the Chocopet? Impossible! As he racked his brain, he heard a halting voice.

"Heat...or ice plus attack is. The key...That's the real weak point of the Chocopets...I'm sure Avocado also..." The owner of the voice was Chocolat, swallowed up entirely to the point just below her chest. The chocolate-flavored armor, which didn't seem strong at the best of times, was most likely dissolved inside Avocado's mouth. Chocolat dying was equivalent to their mission to free Mint and Plum failing. Her health gauge was already down to less than half.

"G-got it! Hang on a little longer!" Haruyuki shouted as he let go of her arms. Once he had gotten a little distance, he thought hard about the problem.

Neither Silver Crow nor Lime Bell had anything in the way of fire or ice techniques. If the Shrine Maiden of the Conflagration had been in the battlefield, she could have roasted Avocado's massive body to a crisp in the blink of an eye, but naturally, they didn't have the time to escape through a portal and contact Utai in the real world.

"Haru! Is your laser sword no good?!" Chiyuri shouted from the ground, likely having heard what Chocolat said.

Haruyuki shook his head quickly from side to side. "It's not hot!"

His Incarnate technique Laser Sword did have the word "laser" in the name, but its affiliation was basically a pure severing. It didn't produce a drop of heat. And naturally, his piercing-type

Lance and Javelin were the same. Even if he attacked Avocado with them, the soft armor would regenerate in an instant.

But maybe if he threw out physical attacks faster than the regeneration, he would at some point reach the body beneath the armor (assuming it existed). The problem with that, though, was that in the process, Avocado's special-attack gauge would be infinitely charged, the power melting Chocolat's armor would be enhanced, and Haruyuki would run the risk of some other new technique being activated.

If this were a Century End stage, there'd be tons of burning oil drums. There's no fire or anything in the Sacred Ground— The instant his thoughts reached this point, his eyes flew open wide. He sent his gaze racing around their surroundings until his eyes landed on a small temple in the east of the grounds.

"Choco, your friend." He quickly turned back to Chocolat and instructed her tightly, "You have to call Coolu! Coolu can shoot a real laser!"

Chocolat opened her peach eye lenses wide, as if momentarily forgetting her agony. But she soon shook her head. "I—I…cannot. Coolu would attack…you two…"

"It's okay!" Haruyuki took a deep breath, put his strength in his stomach, and shouted the rest. "I'll reflect the laser!"

"…!"

Chocolat was speechless once more, but after she shifted her gaze to glance up to the left and check her own health gauge, she nodded slowly, but firmly. "I…understand. I trust you, Silver Crow." Then she mustered up the little life remaining to her and clenched both hands before closing her eyes and shouting, "…Help me, Coolu…!!"

The reaction was instantaneous.

From the temple in the east: *Krrrrrr!* Haruyuki had no sooner heard the shrill voice growling than the armadillo-like figure was racing out onto the grounds. Although it was a lesser Enemy, it was easily over two meters long from its head to the tip of its tail. Its bulky mass—much larger than that of the majority of Burst Linkers—shook the ground and began to dash across the white earth.

"Choco, hold on twenty more seconds!" Haruyuki spread his wings and moved away from Avocado, charging full speed toward Lava Carbuncle.

"Leave the healing to me!" Chiyuri's voice chased after him.

"Thanks!" he responded briefly. After just seconds of flight, he landed a scant twenty meters ahead of the Enemy, its eyes glittering red and burning with rage.

"*Krrrrrrr!!*" Howling sharply, Carbuncle had clearly recognized Haruyuki as its master's enemy. It stopped, bracing its four limbs against the ground and dropping its head low. The interior of the elliptical ruby embedded in its forehead flickered with a crimson light, almost exactly like the effect when the Red King's main armament was preparing to fire.

Apart from the Four Gods, the Super-class Enemies that guarded the Castle, the monsters that lived in the Unlimited Neutral Field—"Enemies"—were categorized into four classes.

The strongest was the Legend class, which made the deepest level of major dungeons in each region or famous landmarks their territory. A few dozen experienced Burst Linkers could meticulously prepare and strategize to challenge one of these Enemies and might still be totally annihilated by the slightest misstep. The Blue King, Blue Knight, was said to be the only one who had ever succeeded in defeating a Legend class solo, and for that, he had been presented with the nickname "Legend Slayer."

Next were the large Enemies known as Beast class. If you got a party of twenty or so people together, it wasn't impossible to safely hunt these creatures, but naturally, it required closely coordinated movement. And since Beast-class Enemies often moved along bullet-train tracks, occasionally, an unlucky few would stumble upon them and meet the sad fate of targeting and instant death. Very few people knew that the Green King, Green Grandé, had continuously defeated these Beast-class Enemies solo and turned the vast points he earned from this endeavor into card items to replenish other Burst Linkers.

Third was the Wild class. Their average size was about five meters, and when someone talked about "hunting," they meant this class. However, even veteran Burst Linkers were said to have difficulty defeating these Enemies solo—and even then, the Enemies occasionally formed herds. So while a single avatar was focused intently on fighting one of them, other Enemies of the same type would link together and stampede; these sorts of tales were often told in the Accelerated World.

And the fourth class of lesser Enemies was used as a trial for recognition as a senior Linker in many Legions. The idea was that if you could defeat one solo, you had attained full Burst Linkerhood. The majority who took on this challenge were strong players who had reached level seven. Or put another way, a single lesser-class Enemy possessed fighting power equivalent to a level-seven Burst Linker.

Naturally, Haruyuki, still at level five, had never challenged a lesser class on his own. More than a few times, he had been careless and ended up targeted, but in each of these instances, he had run for his life and yelped each time his health gauge dropped dramatically at taking just a single blow from a seemingly subdued long-distance attack.

However, right now, he could not run away. For Chiyuri, who spent three days going around the dangerous Unlimited Neutral Field looking for Enemies. For Chocolat, who stood up all by herself against the encroachment of the ISS kit in Setagaya area. For Mint and Plum, who'd been forcefully parasitized and had had long years of friendship ripped away from them. And he couldn't put the reason into words, but for Magenta Scissor and Avocado Avoider as well, he could not lose this fight.

"Come!!" Haruyuki shouted, and he crossed his arms firmly in front of his body.

Immediately, the jewel in Carbuncle's forehead flashed crosswise, and a ruby-red laser beam shot out.

Compared with the main armament of the Red King—which had vaporized Crow ten times in a row—the torrent of energy pushing on him felt more concentrated, proportional with the narrower diameter of the beam. The instant it collided with the metal armor of his chest, the area was red-hot.

The majority of the energy was reflected into their surroundings, due to the 95 percent reflectance that was silver's special characteristic. But the remaining 5 percent would penetrate his armor and sap his endurance. If his metal shell—his armor and greatest weapon as a metal color—were destroyed, the naked body of his avatar inside would be instantly vaporized. If he simply guarded the way he was now, it was obvious the end result would be the same as in the training with Niko.

It's not enough to bounce back the light. Enduring a burning heat like every nerve in his body was aflame, Haruyuki began to talk himself up. *A mirror isn't just a panel that reflects light. Reflection is, in other words, rejection. Something that rejects light couldn't be so beautiful, so unwavering.*

In the back of his mind, he saw the massive three-sided mirror he had been shown in the mirror room of the Suginami Noh Theater that was Utai Shinomiya's family home. Before a Noh performer put on a mask and stepped onto the stage, they focused their mind in front of the mirror. Utai described the mirror as the boundary between this world and the other world.

Boundary. A border, but also a path. In other words, rather than a simple flat panel, a mirror was an entrance and an exit. It accepted light, guided it, and released it once more.

As of the previous evening—when he had been shown the three-sided mirror at Utai's house and been told the sad story of her older brother, Kyoya Shinomiya (aka Mirror Masker)—Haruyuki had sensed that mental state, albeit only vaguely. The trigger for this vague instinct to sublimate up to understanding had been the fierce battle with the mysterious metal color, Wolfram Cerberus. At the beginning of the contest, Haruyuki had suffered so thorough a loss that he didn't even know what to say as an excuse.

But then there was the second fight with him, in which he was the challenger after special training during that day's lunch hour. With the Way of the Flexible that he had learned directly from its master, Kuroyukihime, Haruyuki secured his victory with the strategy of warding off Cerberus's fierce blows, turning them into power for throwing techniques, and slamming his opponent into the ground.

If, in the midst of this current offensive, he'd even once tried to resist his opponent's power with power, in that moment he would no doubt have had his armor smashed, just like the previous day. It was precisely because Haruyuki had accepted Cerberus's punches and been able to merge them with his own movements that he'd succeeded in his Guard Reversal.

In which case, maybe the same thing was possible against a laser attack? A true mirror accepted light and changed its direction only to send it out: the Way of the Flexible *against light*.

Don't be afraid!

The guards on his arms were still in one piece somehow, but even so, his health gauge was steadily decreasing. Haruyuki ripped his mind away from the fact and told himself firmly, *I am Silver Crow. I am the duel avatar currently most like a mirror in the Accelerated World. I'm probably far short of Shinomiya's older brother—"mirror" was part of his name, after all—but even still, for one moment, just one moment, I know I can fuse with the light. I can be a boundary to guide the light.*

Okay, then. Abandon your fear and your power. Accept it! Haruyuki still had his arms crossed, but he relaxed his tense, forward-pitched body slightly and lifted his face.

On the other side of his field of view, dyed red, his eyes met those of the small Enemy shooting the intense laser from the jewel in its forehead—or so he felt. In that instant, the decrease in his health gauge and the scattering of the light stopped simultaneously. It wasn't that the laser had been interrupted. Rather, it had become a crimson sphere condensing in the center of his intersecting arms.

"That's...iiiiiiiiiiit!!" Haruyuki thrust his right arm out straight ahead as he spun his body to the left. Toward the massive bulk of Avocado Avoider ten meters away, who was still licking at a dissolving Chocolat.

Shppksh! The air shuddered, and Carbuncle's laser shot forward once more, bent at an angle of 120 degrees or so. The laser made a direct hit on Avocado's armor and was almost sucked into the lower part of his body, and in short order, it was digging into his armor.

But the laser wasn't piercing that armor. The thick, soft cushioning was absorbing the energy like it had the physical attacks.

If this attack had been successive firing of actual bullets or a collision wave, Avocado's soft armor might have been able to completely withstand it. But just as Chocolat had suspected, heat seemed to be his Achilles' heel. In the blink of an eye, the dark-green surface armor was bright red, the color radiating outward from the point of entry. Haruyuki had to admire the determination of the other avatar when he still did not spit Chocolat out, but a Linker couldn't endure the attack of an Enemy—even a lesser one—with determination alone.

In a mere three seconds, the entirety of the egg-shaped body was incandescent, and cracks started to appear here and there in the armor. Haruyuki barely had time to register this before he heard a heavy, viscous sound.

Splrt! Avocado Avoider's massive body was melting, the thick liquid evaporating and disappearing before it even hit the ground. Naturally, the large mouth also vanished, and Chocolat was thrust out into midair. Just as she was on the verge of falling helplessly to the ground, Chiyuri raced over to catch the chocolate avatar in her arms. Almost as if the creature were aware that

Chocolat had been released, the laser emitted from Carbuncle's forehead also weakened, until it finally stopped.

"Haah." Heaving a long sigh, Haruyuki relaxed his shoulders. When he looked down at his arms, the armor that had been burning red hot was a silver far more clear than usual—or rather, he realized, it had changed into a "mirror color." He stared hard as the mirror in his arms disappeared and his limbs returned to their original silver sheen.

Was that the Theoretical Mirror ability? Did I actually manage to get it? he asked himself, but of course, no one answered. If he opened his Instruct menu then and there and looked at the status column, he would have been able to check whether or not he had more abilities, but he didn't have time for that now.

Because they were coming up on the final stage of the battle.

He checked that Lava Carbuncle's aggro had stopped, and then Haruyuki turned toward Chiyuri and Chocolat, and he opened his eyes wide in surprise.

There was a strange object on the ground not far from the two girls: a brown sphere about thirty centimeters in diameter. He thought it was maybe some kind of Chocopet, but the material was different. As he stared, dumbfounded, short arms and legs popped out of the sphere, and once it stood upright, it ran as fast as the little legs could carry it toward the west side of the grounds. To where Magenta Scissor was watching the battle, still embedded in the temple wall.

Haruyuki went up to Chiyuri. "What...is that?" he asked, in a low voice.

"D-don't ask me..."

"Probably...Avocado's main body," Chocolat answered, still in Lime Bell's arms. "Or a pit, I suppose. I don't think there's any harm in leaving him."

"P-pit...He really is a nonstandard duel avatar in all kinds of ways, huh?" Shaking his head shortly, Haruyuki switched tracks and checked Chocolat's injuries. Her large armor skirt was almost completely gone, and the chocolate color of both legs was half peeled away. But it didn't look like it had gone so far as her losing any parts.

As if to affirm Haruyuki's judgment, Chocolat said weakly, "Thanks, Bell. Please put me down. I'm all right."

"...Right." Chiyuri stooped forward slowly, and Chocolat stepped onto the ground and stood up, albeit staggering slightly. She turned her bonnet-covered head and stared resolutely toward the south side of the grounds.

Almost as though it had been waiting for her eyes to turn in that direction, a heavy vibration, one Haruyuki was already intimately familiar with, shook the air—the sound of a dark Incarnate attack being activated by the ISS kit. Mint Mitten and Plum Flipper had pulverized the two Chocopets hindering their movement with Dark Blow.

The Cocoa Fountain covering the ground had also reached its time limit and was disappearing. On the original white tiles of the Sacred Ground stage, the two small F-type avatars walked lifelessly toward them. The eyes attached to each of their chests blinked with a red light reminiscent of blood.

Haruyuki and Chiyuri started to get into battle-ready positions, but Chocolat shook her head lightly and stopped them. Injured, battered, she took a step forward, and a few seconds later, her former best friends stopped a mere two meters away from her.

"Why won't you come with us, Cocoa?" Mint Mitten spoke first, her head like a knit hat and her hands large and swollen.

"Come on, let's be stronger," Plum Flipper murmured, a perfectly round beret on her head. "Let's get strong and change the world, Cocoa."

The voices sounded intimate, but they were hollow somehow. Their eye lenses were also dim, so that it seemed almost as though it were the eyes on their chests speaking rather than themselves.

Though perhaps that was exactly what it was.

The most significant feature of the ISS kit was that night after night, synchronized processing of the seeds was carried out

while the user slept. The kit took in the negative thoughts culti-
vated by surrounding users and spread the user's own negative
thoughts out around them. Mint and Plum were synchronized
now with the dark will of Magenta Scissor, the parent of all the
kits plaguing Setagaya.

"Min-Min. Pliko. You don't need that kind of strength to
change the world," Chocolat replied earnestly, her injured avatar
just barely managing to stay upright. "If you just believe...*that*
will change the world. The two of you taught me that."

She glanced back at Haruyuki and Chiyuri and then quickly
turned her gaze forward again.

"In the real world, and in the Accelerated World, we have
feared the outside. We closed ourselves off in a gentle, comfortable box...we never turned our eyes toward the past or the future.
But that was a mistake. The reason we became Burst Linkers
was...to accelerate. To shake off painful memories and move
forward. With every step forward we take, the walls of our box
expand that much, and the world changes. The gifted power you
have now...we don't need to rely on that, Min-Min, Pliko!" Voice
tearful, Chocolat made her injured body take a step forward, just
like she'd said. Then another. And another.

Now she was standing in front of Mint and Plum. Their eye
lenses grew even darker, and in exchange, the shining of the ISS
kits increased. On their right hands, different in both size and
shape, was the exact same black aura. Haruyuki started to step
forward reflexively, but beside him, Chiyuri lightly shook her
head.

In a stiff movement, as though their joints had rusted, the two
raised their right arms. Unflinchingly exposed before this, Chocolat spread her slender arms and wrapped them around both of
her friends at the same time.

The two ISS kits flickered intensely. The inorganic sense emitted by the eyeballs could be taken as hatred but also as fear. In
sync with the disturbance in the kits, a change came over the
actual eyes of Mint and Plum. Eye lenses that had been essen-

tially grayed out continually increased in brightness, and fists that had been raised and held in midair trembled and shook. The dark, swirling aura shuddered unstably, even as it increased in concentration.

If they launched Dark Blow at the same time from that distance, Chocolat would disappear without a trace. If she was going to achieve the result she had first thought of—force Mint and Plum into total point loss with the Judgment Blow—this was her first and last chance.

However, Chocolat didn't move. Head hanging, she kept hugging her friends tight. From Mint and Plum's irregularly blinking eye lenses, droplets of white light spilled out and fell into the air.

In that instant, it wasn't the three members of the Legion Petit Paquet who moved, nor was it Haruyuki or Magenta Scissor off in the distance watching the scene unfold; it was Chiyuri—Lime Bell.

She brandished the Enhanced Armament of her left arm, Choir Chime, up high, and spun it in quick, broad, counterclockwise circles.

Bong! The echo, reminiscent somehow of school bells, came once, twice, then three times, and then four times. A pure citrus-green light gushed out of Lime Bell like a liquid and came pouring down directly ahead of her. At the same time, she called out the technique name: "Citron...Caaaaaaaaall!!"

The light surging out from inside the chime flowed forward in a straight line, making countless sparkling, glittering crosses, and enveloped Mint and Plum at the same time. In the center of the pillar of light that rose up from below, their two bodies were lifted ever so slightly off the ground.

Dropping her hips and supporting the bell of her left hand with her right hand, Chiyuri continued to emit the light with an intent expression on her face. Haruyuki approached her by habit and supported her back with a hand. Her body, as slender as those of Chocolat and the members of Petit Paquet, trembled all over, demonstrating her desperate mental focus.

In addition to Mode I, which restored Chocolat's special-attack gauge in the opening stages of the fight, Lime Bell's special attack Citron Call had a Mode II, which used up her entire gauge. Its effect was to cancel out up to four levels in the status of the target avatar. Specifically, it made it as though things like an avatar losing its limb—or being parasitized by an object, or equipping or obtaining of Enhanced Armament—had never happened.

Since the ISS kit was, in fact, a parasitic object and was also the obtaining of an Enhanced Armament, the group assumed cancellation with Mode II would be effective. However, a week earlier, Takumu, parasitized with a kit himself, had asserted that this method would not make his own kit disappear. Because the kit activated a sort of pseudo-Incarnate system with the desire for power in the heart of the user as its energy source, it could overwrite Citron Call.

In which case, it would seem that theoretically, they shouldn't be about to get rid of Mint and Plum's kits now, either, but there was just one decisive difference here than from Takumu's case. And that was the fact that Mint and Plum had had their bodies cut open by Magenta Scissor and been forcefully parasitized with their kits. They had said words earlier to the effect that they wanted power, but that was not a feeling generated by their own hearts; it was something poured into them by other kit users through the nightly parallel processing. In which case, if they had inside them a resistance to the kit—no, a love for Chocolat—then there was a possibility that Citron Call could cancel the parasitization.

"P-please!!" Chiyuri shouted in a thin voice, as she continued the technique.

"Go away!!" Haruyuki also prayed intently, squeezing the words out as he held Chiyuri's shoulders. If their plan failed, then either Chocolat would be killed or she would use the Judgment Blow on her friends before that happened.

But he didn't want to see that outcome again. Absolutely not.

In the pale-green light, the ISS kits attached to the chests of

Mint and Plum shot out a flash the color of blood in its resistance. The eyeballs swelled up enormously, the blood vessels entwining them throbbing fiercely.

And then the right arms of the two girls, still up in the air, slowly started to come back down. The dark, miasma-like aura had basically disappeared. Their fists were released, and thin fingers reached out to Chocolat, trembling.

"Min-Min! Pliko!" Chocolat shouted, taking up both their hands to clutch.

A moment later, the black blood vessels extending from the ISS kits dried up, and the eyeball weakly closed its lids. The parasite turned into black mist and evaporated in verdurous light. When Citron Call was finished, there were no objects on the chests of Mint Mitten or Plum Flipper.

Chiyuri crumpled, and Haruyuki held her up, his eyes open intently wide. When he'd crushed the ISS kit that had parasitized the Burst Linker Olive Grab, a ball of red light had flown off into the sky. But this time, there was no mistake; nothing had escaped. That could mean only one thing: Their strategy worked—the existence of the kits had been rewound, and they had disappeared completely.

"You did it. You did it, Bell!" Haruyuki clenched his left hand, and Chiyuri, in his right arm, lifted her face and grinned through her exhaustion.

Mint Mitten and Plum Flipper had lost consciousness temporarily, and Chocolat was also leaning against them, eyes closed.

As Haruyuki and Chiyuri started walking toward them, the chocolate-colored avatar lifted her hanging head. There were streaks of white light on her smooth cheeks.

"In the end, when I held their hands...I could heard their voices. 'Cocoa, we're sorry,' they said...," she murmured hoarsely.

"Yeah, they're okay now." Haruyuki nodded deeply, together with Chiyuri. "They should be back to their old selves."

"You really fought hard, huh?" Chiyuri said. "It's because

your feelings reached them, Choco, that I could make the kits disappear."

The girl nodded sharply and paused a second before speaking again. "You can both call me 'Cocoa,' too."

Unwittingly, Haruyuki smiled wryly at this sign that Chocolat was quickly getting back up to full speed. But this was soon followed by "However, I will not let you taste me again."

He stiffened immediately.

"What?" Chiyuri cocked her head, and Chocolat started to open her mouth to expose Haruyuki's deed.

Before she could, they heard a sharp cry of *krrrrrr* from a slight ways off. At this warning, Haruyuki reflexively whirled his eyes around.

A slender silhouette jumped into his view, approaching slowly from the west. He braced himself, but soon relaxed. Magenta Scissor had her greatest weapon, the enormous scissors, split into two once more, and those pieces were dangling from her sides. Naturally, she was still equipped with an ISS kit, so a long-distance attack with Dark Shot was a possibility. But she didn't look like she had it in her now. Her left arm was missing, having been severed by Haruyuki's light sword, and her right arm held a brown ball about thirty centimeters in diameter—the seed of Avocado Avoider.

"Cho— I mean, Cocoa, don't let Coolu attack. She's probably not here to fight," Haruyuki said, quietly.

Chocolat nodded, albeit with a worried look on her face. She raised her right hand toward Carbuncle on the east side of the grounds, and with just that, the Enemy obediently lay down.

"Wow. Well trained," Chiyuri murmured admiringly. She also seemed to feel that the battle was over, but even still, she joined Haruyuki in stepping out in front of Chocolat and her friends to wait for the reddish-purple avatar.

Magenta Scissor came fairly close before stopping. Silver Crow was covered in injuries, cut with scissors and burned by Coolu's laser, but their fuchsia enemy was much the same. Her ribbon armor was smashed all over, leaving a fair amount of her actual body exposed. Above all, she should still have been hurting from having her arm cut off. However, not only did none of that show on her face, but the tall F-type avatar smiled faintly.

"I was plenty surprised just at you bending the Enemy's laser and melting Avocado's armor, but then you go even further and get rid of the ISS kits, huh? Just like that girl's subordinates, I suppose."

"Do you know the Black King?" Haruyuki asked.

Her sharp shoulders bobbed up and down. "At the very least, I don't want to have any more to do with you lot lest she herself appear...is about the extent of my knowing her."

"If you're saying that, then you're not going to come at Cocoa and her friends anymore, right?" Chiyuri pressed.

Magenta smiled again. "It's annoying, but I don't really have a choice. If I do parasitize them again, you'll just make it disappear, after all. I'm giving up on the north and moving east."

These words were a declaration that, even if she did temporarily abandon the idea of recruiting Chocolat and her friends, she had not given up on her larger, true objective—spreading the ISS kits to the whole of the Accelerated World. Haruyuki was about to ask why she would go that far and then gave up on the idea. He had already heard her motives—that she was going to remove inequalities caused by differences in abilities and appearances from the Accelerated World.

Tightly gritting his teeth beneath his mirrored goggles, Haruyuki turned his gaze to the brown, ball-shaped avatar in Magenta Scissor's arm. He had a hard time believing that the small sphere was the true form of Avocado Avoider, that massive avatar, two and a half or more meters tall. But the short arms and legs and the beady eye lenses shared the same design as his original appearance. And a shrunken ISS kit was attached to him in a place that corresponded to the chest.

"So then it's on, huh?" Haruyuki said, swallowing back all kinds of feelings. "Are you going to achieve your goal first, or will we destroy the ISS kit main body first?"

"I didn't expect this kind of trash talk from you. It's weird." Magenta smiled more broadly than she had so far. "Okay, fine, let's say it's on. But first. You all won here today, so I have to give you your prize, hmm?"

She snapped out two fingers of the hand holding Avocado, and two rectangular shapes were suddenly embedded in between them, although Haruyuki had no idea where she'd pulled them from. He was more than familiar with card items, but these were a matte black. This was the first time he'd seen them in this color. It looked like the item name was inscribed on the front in a crimson-red font.

"These are the ISS kits cut out of Mint Mitten and Plum Flipper. They came back to my storage, but the data might be contaminated, you know...by considerateness or kindness. I have no use for them, so I'll leave it to you all to dispose of them," she said, her tone making it impossible for him to grasp her true intent. She flicked her fingers, and the two cards spun through the air to plunge to the tile at Haruyuki's feet.

"D-dispose...I mean..." He twisted his neck as he wondered to himself if they were burnable or nonburnable garbage.

"Do whatever you want with them." Magenta shrugged once more. "Boil them, fry them, analyze them...Hmm? Oh, right! And tell Cyan Pile. That when I said I was giving it to him in that form because I liked him when I gave him the kit card last week, I was serious."

"Hey!" the so-far-silent Chiyuri snapped to attention and shouted the instant she heard this. "Wh-why should we give him a message like that?! More importantly, why do you like Pile?!"

"Goodness! Well, he is wonderful, isn't he? That asymmetrical form...Oh my, now that I'm thinking of it, you're quite nice as well, hmm?" Magenta retorted coolly, and as an added bonus, flashed Lime Bell a bewitching smile.

This apparently was impossible for even Chiyuri to process immediately, and Magenta's smile deepened momentarily at the other girl's frozen form before she wordlessly turned on her heel. Resettling Avocado's seed in her arms, she walked toward Sakurajosui Station.

Staring after her, Haruyuki was taken by a brief conflict. Magenta Scissor would likely keep disseminating the ISS kits in the Accelerated World. If he was going to try to stop her, maybe he should attack her here, defeat her, and then defeat her again when she regenerated in an hour, continuing to kill her and force her into total point loss. With the difference in their current battle abilities, it was definitely possible.

However, Magenta also had to know that Haruyuki and his comrades had that option. If, at the point in time when Mint and Plum's ISS kits were purified, she had instantly withdrawn to a leave point, she probably could have removed the danger of successive kills.

But rather than doing that, she had walked over to exchange words with Haruyuki and Chiyuri. He found it hard to believe that she had intended to set some malicious trap, including the gifting of the two cards to them. Most likely, Magenta had dared to stay on the battleground as the loser for the sake of her own pride—pride she still had even after playing host to an ISS kit.

Haruyuki couldn't attack an opponent like that from behind. He took his eyes off the receding shadow and crouched down to pick up the black cards at his feet.

"I-is it okay to touch them?" Chiyuri asked, in a worried voice.

"I guess maybe it's okay as long as I don't press the 'use' button or shout the activation command or anything." Even as he said this, he was reluctant to hold them for a long period of time, so he quickly opened his Instruct menu, moved to his storage screen, and tucked the two cards away there. When he lifted his head, job finished, the figure of Magenta Scissor was already gone from the large grounds.

Clenching his teeth against the complex mix of emotions that he himself didn't really understand upwelling in his chest, Haruyuki turned around. In the arms of the kneeling Chocolat, the two girl avatars were just starting to wake from their slumber; their slender limbs trembled.

Haruyuki moved to approach them, but Chiyuri grabbed his arm.

"Let's just leave the three of them to themselves," she whispered, and he nodded in agreement.

He couldn't hear their exchange, but Chocolat Puppeteer, Mint Mitten, and Plum Flipper appeared to be talking slowly. After the passage of some time, brown and green and purple arms were stretched out, and the three girls hugged one another tightly. Captivated by this beautiful scene, Haruyuki snapped back to reality when a massive shadow entered the frame suddenly from the left. The shadow turned out to be an Enemy with short limbs extending from an armadillo-like body wrapped in armor, an elliptical ruby glittering on its forehead—Coolu.

Chocolat had ordered it to stand down, but it probably couldn't hold on any longer. It rubbed its streamlined head against the girls, a sweet voice slipping out of it. *Krrr, krrrr.*

At some point, Haruyuki had grabbed Chiyuri's hand beside him, and they watched over the three girls and one creature that made up the Legion Petit Paquet. They had originally come to the Setagaya area with the sole goal of special training with an Enemy opponent and had then gotten dragged into an unplanned, fierce battle that had started with an unexpected encounter. But from the bottom of his heart, Haruyuki was glad that they had visited that place at that time on that day.

Chiyuri appeared to feel the exact same way; her slightly teary voice reached his ears. "Thank goodness."

It felt like they had been accelerated for a fairly long time, but when they returned to the real world via a portal, only the seconds displayed on the clock in the lower left of his virtual desktop had changed.

From the faint crack under the door, the tantalizing scent of sweet-and-sour pork with pineapples wafted in, but it was still nearly ten minutes until the six-thirty suppertime. Even though he was starving from all that flying and waiting and fighting! But no matter what kind of Burst Linker you were, you still couldn't fast-forward time. Body still flat on the mattress that was a little softer than his own bed, Haruyuki let out a long sigh.

"C'mon, Haru. There's no need to be crying on this side."

He heard Chiyuri's voice from his immediate left and reflexively turned his face in that direction. When he did, a mysterious fluid that had indeed built up in both his eyes spilled out and cut across his cheek to make a light stain on the sheets.

"I-I'm not crying!" Trying out a protest like an elementary school kid, he rubbed his eyes with the back of his hand. But perhaps the tear-gland bubble was broken; the droplets welled up one after another and slid along his cheek. He gave up on interrupting them and tried to turn his back to Chiyuri. And then he noticed that Chiyuri's face, twisted through the film of fluid, was also shining with little drops of light.

"I mean, *you're* crying, aren't you?" he asked, pursing his lips.

"It's just"—Chiyuri didn't try to hide her tears, but rather smiled through them—"I mean, like, I'm just about the same amount of happy and sad. A double dose. I can't help it."

"Well, if it's a double dose, I guess you can't, huh..." Agreeing with this curious logic, Haruyuki thought, *Oh, that's it.*

After he had seen Magenta Scissor and Avocado Avoider off, a major ingredient in the mix of feelings that had risen up in his chest was "sadness."

Why was he sad? Because he thought they could also have a different future.

"Why—?" Turning his face to the ceiling once more, Haruyuki squeezed his voice out from his nearly blocked throat. "Why do we have to fight like that...?"

If the duels that took place in the Normal Duel Field were a fighting game in which opponents pitted their knowledge, technique, and willpower against each other, then the Incarnate battles in the Unlimited Neutral Field were life-and-death conflicts, with rage and hatred alone slamming up against each other.

It had only been eight months since he became a Burst Linker, and Haruyuki had just finally reached level five, but he had been put in that position several times already. None of those fights had given him a shred of the excitement and fun of the duel, though. The fierce battle with Magenta Scissor that day was the same. He had found the opening in the Dark Blow she relied on and launched his Laser Sword to win with difficulty, but all that was left in his chest was a deep despair.

"If we hadn't treated Setagaya like an empty area and had gone to hang out there more…If we had met just as Burst Linkers, all of us, and dueled normally, I'm sure that—"

We could've been friends with them, too. He swallowed this part back and moved to turn over onto his stomach on the bed, when Chiyuri grabbed his shoulder tightly.

"It's…It's not over yet, Haru. We're going to get rid of all the ISS kits in the Accelerated World, and then we'll go see Magenta and Avocado again. Next time, we'll invite Taku and Kuroyuki and our sister Fuko and little Ui, too, right? And then…And then…"

"Yeah. We will." Haruyuki nodded, wiping at his face with his right arm, and this time, he managed to stop the tears somehow.

Chiyuri sat up, pulled some tissue off the headboard, and dabbed at her eyes. Then she removed the cable from their Neurolinkers and wound it up. "Anyway, anyway, Haru!" she said, shifting gears rather remarkably. "I saw it! You seriously reflected Coolu's laser, didn't you! So that means you obtained the ability, right?!"

"Huh? Uh, um. I dunno." He sat up on the bed and scratched his head.

"Cooome on." Chiyuri turned a magnificent look of exasperation on him. "It's your own self. You should at least know whether you got it or not!"

"B-but, like—to confirm it, I'd have to get someone to shoot me with a laser again."

"O! Kay! Look! Here! You don't have to do all that. Just open your Brain Burst console right now and look at Silver Crow's status screen, and that's that!"

"......!!"

Haruyuki slapped his knee in a moment of understanding, and the look on Chiyuri's face advanced from exasperated to eyeball-rolling. But he paid her no mind and ran a finger across his virtual desktop. He tapped the flaming *B* logo and displayed the avatar status in the console screen that opened.

He nervously switched from the default normal attack tab to the abilities tab, and then turned his face away for a moment. But when he gritted his teeth and stared at the window out of the corner of his eye—there were two rows of alphabet text.

"O-oh! There's two!" Haruyuki shouted.

Chiyuri leaned forward, unable to stand it anymore. "Hey, show me, too!" She unwrapped the XSB cable she had been about to put away and with her left and right hands inserted the ends into their Neurolinkers. Normally, the Brain Burst program menu screen was invisible to other people, even while directing, and that restriction was canceled only when the other person was also a Burst Linker.

"Let's see. Where? Show me..." Chiyuri pressed her face in from the left, practically sticking her cheek up against his, and they read the text that had popped up in the window together.

The first line: AVIATION. It went without saying that this was his flight ability.

The second line: OPTICAL CONDUCTION.

"...Huh..." slipped out of Haruyuki.

"Whaaat...?" Chiyuri cocked her head hard to the right. "I'm pretty sure the English for the mirror ability was...Theoretical Mirror, wasn't it?"

"Y-yeah. I feel like that's what I heard..." Haruyuki nodded, sensing the bad feeling oozing into his chest in drips and drops grow enormous in the blink of an eye. *But I definitely reflected the laser, right. I became a mirror, right*, he told himself as he launched the English-Japanese dictionary app on the right side of his virtual desktop. He pressed the voice entry button.

"Opticull. Conducshun." He specified word lookup with the most Englishy pronunciation he could manage, and with a wait time of basically zero, the meaning was displayed.

Since Chiyuri was looking at the same screen, the two of them read it out loud together. "'...Light. Guidance...'?"

Even knowing the definition, he couldn't grasp the meaning of the ability at all. He cocked his head from the right to the left in sync with Chiyuri, and then they heard the long-awaited voice of Chiyuri's mother on the other side of the door.

"Chii! Haru, hon. Suppertime!"

He worried that the ability he had worked so hard to awaken was somehow apparently not the Theoretical Mirror that he had been asked to obtain at the meeting of the Seven Kings, but his anxiety could not cancel out the impetus of his empty stomach seeking sweet-and-sour pork with pineapple.

Haruyuki took a deep breath and looked at Chiyuri next to him. "Let's finish this after supper."

His friend of fourteen years shook her head lightly from side to side. "Very occasionally, there are times when I think you might be extremely strong mentally."

6

A bright June 27. That day, too, the sky had been sprinkling them with rain since morning, as though the seasonal rain front was stubbornly sitting in the sky above Tokyo.

Having finished getting ready for school ten minutes earlier than usual, Haruyuki left the house with the slightly too-large umbrella that his father used to use in one hand. He headed south on the sidewalk of Kannana Street, slipped under the Chuo Line Bridge, and set his sights on the usual Koenjirikkyo intersection. It was Thursday, the day of the routine Ash-Crow duel.

According to rules that had been set at some point, the winner of the previous duel had to use a Burst Point to accelerate and challenge his opponent. But in the duel two days before, on Tuesday, Silver Crow and Ash Roller had both been struck by the lightning of the Thunder stage and had their gauges sent flying simultaneously.

In the case of a draw, the rule was they changed the challenging side, and according to this, it was Crow's turn to be the challenger. However, even after he had climbed up the pedestrian walkway at the lights, Haruyuki did not connect to the global net, but rather kept going to descend on the inner-loop side of Kannana and come to a stop in front of a convenience store on the corner.

About two minutes later, a green EV bus stopped at the bus stop nearby. Only one passenger got off. After opening an off-white umbrella, she approached him at a trot, the pouch slung across her body, swinging from side to side.

"K-Kusakabe, don't run. It's—" The moment he hurriedly started speaking, a brown loafer slipped on the wet road. The girl lost her balance and listed first to the left, then the right—somehow, mysteriously, not falling down—until she managed to just barely bring herself to a stop right in front of Haruyuki.

He quickly pulled back arms he had started to stretch out to support her in case of the worst and said his greetings. "Morning, Kusakabe."

"Good. Morning, Arita." Bowing deeply along with her umbrella was, of course, Ash Roller in the real: Rin Kusakabe. Like Haruyuki, she was in eighth grade, but she attended a girls' school in Sasazuka in Shibuya Ward; she commuted from her home in Egota in Nakano.

Sasazuka was on the Keio line, and the station a mere four stops farther out was the very Sakurajosui which they had visited the previous night. As the crow flies, they weren't even four kilometers apart, but since the borders between Suginami, Shibuya, and Setagaya wards got complicated in that area, in the Accelerated World sense, the distance was greater than this small number. In fact, during the dive the previous day, Haruyuki had not once realized that Sasazuka station was fairly close by.

That said, there was no mistake that Shibuya Area No. 3, where Rin's school was, was immediately adjacent to Setagaya area on the east. This fact caught at his thoughts for some reason, but Rin's smile appearing from beneath the edge of her white umbrella instantly pushed the question away.

"Um. I'm sor-ry for being selfish." With this, Rin went to lower her head once more, so Haruyuki shook his free hand and his head back and forth at the same time.

"N-not at all! It's fine! The only difference is the duel coming first or after."

The selfishness Rin was referring to was the extremely modest request to talk at the intersection before their usual duel. Haruyuki had intended to talk with her after the duel, like they had two days before, but he couldn't believe there would be any issue in just changing that order.

However, in that case, why did Rin want to put the duel off on that day alone?

"Um." As if intuiting Haruyuki's question, Rin pulled her head back into herself with an embarrassed air. "If the duel's first, I thought my brother might. Say something unnecessary to you."

"Unnecessary? Like what kind of thing?"

"Um, like 'A million years too early to invite my baby sis to the school festival, you damned Crow' or something."

"…R-right. I get it. I totally get that." It was a realistic concern. Haruyuki involuntarily burst out into a sweat.

It was a fact that Rin Kusakabe was Ash Roller in the real, but the personality—or rather, the spirit that lived in the duel avatar that fought in the Accelerated World—was not hers. Rin's older brother, the former ICGP racer, Rinta Kusakabe, operated the fin de siècle rider—or that's how Haruyuki understood it, although the logic wasn't clear.

Ash Roller adored his little sister, and although he lost it whenever Haruyuki got near her, if Haruyuki didn't invite her to event-type things, he would get angry about that; he was truly an irrational figure. Haruyuki had invited Rin to the Umesato school festival after the duel the day before yesterday, so he assumed that Ash also shared that memory—in other words, there was a strong possibility he would be in Mega Heat mode in that day's duel.

Huh? Wait? But then does that mean that talking to Kusakabe now before the duel will make Ash's anger go beyond Giga and up into Tera Heat?

The thought crossed his mind, but he didn't have the time for indecision right then and there. According to the bus information transmitted from the sign pillar at the bus stop, the next bus for Rin to catch had already arrived at the third stop back.

Putting aside the question of the big brother for the moment, Haruyuki manipulated his virtual desktop. The document file he called up was an invitation to the school festival, coming up in three days. Each student was given three invitations, but since it was assumed that the invited guests would be close relatives, there was a restriction that did not allow them to be transmitted over the global net.

Haruyuki turned toward Rin and transmitted the invitation, which he had gotten his mother's stamp of approval on from her bed that morning through an ad hoc connection between their two Neurolinkers. The number of files remaining dropped to two, but he didn't have anywhere to use those anyway.

"If this is in your Neurolinker, you'll be able to pass through the gates of Umesato," Haruyuki said. "If you let me know a little before you arrive, I'll come meet you."

Rin rested her umbrella on her right shoulder and wrapped both hands carefully around the invitation file displayed in her virtual desktop. A huge smile popped up onto her face, a face with thin lines reminiscent of a boy's somehow. "Thank...Y-ou. I...M. Very happy. I'll definitely, definitely come."

"R-right. Although I'm basically not doing anything except helping with my class exhibit."

After a quick bit of research the other day, he had learned that the kendo team that Takumu belonged to was going to present in the dojo a "cosplay martial arts demonstration," the true nature of which was unknown, while Chiyuri's track team was going to do a crepe booth. When he additionally heard that the student council, on which Kuroyukihime served as vice president, was planning to open a secret program on the local net, his mouth inevitably turned down slightly at the corners.

Haruyuki had also been officially appointed to the impor- tant role of president of the Animal Care Club, but it had only been ten days since the launch of the club itself. Even so, he *had* thought about borrowing a classroom somewhere, decorating it like a jungle, and displaying the lone animal they were caring for, the northern white-faced owl, Hoo. But in addition to being a nervous type, Hoo had only just moved to Umesato from Matsunogi Academy, so Haruyuki had determined that the burden of having so many people traipse by him would be too much and had given up on the whole idea before getting to the stage of proposing it to the "super president," Utai.

The exhibit by the seven students in grade-eight class C, who were not participating with a team or club, was "Koenji Thirty Years Ago," a fairly cultural and inoffensive topic. When people entered the classroom, static images of the Koenji shopping street in the 2010s would be displayed in their field of view, and if visitors followed the path laid out, the images were set to scroll automatically. At first glance, it seemed elaborate, but they had actually adopted the basic program from something extant, so Haruyuki and the others working on it simply had to find and load pictures from the period from the Umesato archives and individual websites. They planned to finish this task in just one day, on Saturday, and regrettably, these were not details he was particularly proud to share with Rin.

But Rin's smile was not clouded in the least. She took a step toward Haruyuki and gripped her umbrella tightly with both hands again. "Um, I *am* looking forward to your class exhibit. But. I. I'm just so incredibly happy. That you invited me to your school festival. Arita. I mean." Here, she brought her face even closer and lowered her voice as much as possible. "Bringing Burst Linkers from other Legions. Into your school. Is like the most taboo of taboos. In the Accelerated World."

It could be said to be something of a miracle that Haruyuki, who had a tendency toward a direct link between his inner heart and the look on his face, managed to maintain his smile upon hearing this. Because he hadn't discussed inviting Rin to Umesato's school festival with anyone in the Legion, much less its master, Kuroyukihime. He had simply decided on his own that it wouldn't be a problem, since Rin and everyone in Nega Nebulus were already cracked in the real to each other. But what if it was actually a huge problem? And if it was, what kind?

"I-it's fine." Concealing the sudden apprehension, Haruyuki bobbed his head up and down. "Everyone in the Legion's looking forward to seeing you, Kusakabe. So. O-of course, I am too."

"...Thank. Y...ou," Rin murmured, her eyes tearing over, and closed the distance between them with another step. The fronts of their umbrellas overlapped, and the gray-and-white water-repellent fabrics created a modest shelter, cutting the two of them off from the outside world for a moment.

The sound of the rain and even the noise of the EV motors coming and going on the main road right next to them grew distant, and in the mysterious quiet that was born, Rin's voice came, faltering.

"I. Always. Always. Imagined it. If the Burst Points. System disappeared. From the Accelerated World. If the whole of the duel. Was just being happy when you win. And being frustrated when you lose. There'd be no need to worry. About being cracked in the real. Anymore. And all the Burst Linkers. All of us could just. Be friends in the real world, too." Her voice stopped momentarily here, and lovely, glittering droplets sprang up in her gray-flecked eyes. Her lashes caught them as they were on the verge of falling, and Haruyuki stared as he listened wordlessly to her murmured voice. "But. Even with the system now. I thought that day. Would probably come. That you. Would change. The world, Arita."

"Huh? Oh, I— That's—"

Totally impossible, his mouth wanted to say, but Rin's left hand pressed against it gently. His heart leapt and jumped at the sensation of her slender, smooth fingertip touching his lips.

"Right now. It's enough. That you fly in the sky. Of the Accelerated World. People who see you. They all, they all feel something. They should. A precious something. Like me."

She pressed the fingertip she pulled away from his mouth up against her own lightly, and then grinned. The expression on her face was so innocent and transparent that Haruyuki didn't realize that her finger had brought about an "indirect kiss."

Still smiling, she took a step back and their umbrellas separated, and the noise of the world returned at once. Mixed in with it was the heavy engine of the bus approaching from the north.

"The bus. Is here," Rin said, blinking rapidly, and gently stroked the metallic-gray Neurolinker equipped on her slender neck. The machine, with its lightning bolt crack on the exterior, was the one her brother, Rinta, had used during the fateful race. "I'm looking forward. To the festival. And I'm sure. My brother is, too."

With these last words, she bowed together with her umbrella and then turned around and ran—splashed—away. She slipped again on the wet pavement, but she didn't almost fall this time. She made it safely to the bus stop and got on the bus that arrived a few seconds later.

She waved slightly through the closed door, and finally coming back to himself, Haruyuki hurriedly returned the wave with his left hand. The bus departed with a low hum, passed through the Rikkyo intersection, and disappeared to the south.

Replaying her words over and over in his head, Haruyuki started to walk. He climbed the pedestrian bridge and stopped when he was somewhere in the middle to connect his Neurolinker globally. No sooner had the confirmation dialogue appeared than he was murmuring, "Burst Link."

Skreeeee! The sound of impact roared, and the world was frozen blue. Haruyuki appeared in the blue world of the initial acceleration space in his pink pig form and opened the Brain Burst matching list. From the dozen or so names listed there, he of course selected Ash Roller.

If the whole of the duel. Was just being happy when you win. And being frustrated when you lose. Murmuring this in the back of his mind, he pressed the DUEL button.

Instantly, the blue world began to transform. At the same time, his pig avatar also started to change into his silver duel form. After passing through a faint floating sensation, his metal feet came down on the thick trunk of a tree on its side. The scene around him had also changed completely; the road surface was now a valley covered by green grass, while the clusters of buildings had turned into enormous, mossy trees. A natural-type, wood-affiliated Primeval Forest stage.

As the timer dropped to 1,799, the throaty roar of a V-twin engine came to him from the south side of the valley. The bus Rin was on could have only gotten about two hundred meters away, and that distance was the blink of an eye for the American motorcycle Ash Roller rode.

Haruyuki spread the wings on his back and flew gently from the tree that had been the pedestrian bridge down into the middle of the valley and waited for the approaching motorcycle. The emotion he felt at Rin's words lingered in his heart, and he decided he wanted to have a few words with Big Brother Ash, too, before the duel.

Mere seconds later, the hooded headlight shone yellow from the other side of the plain. Time in the Primeval Forest stage did actually change, and it felt like it was currently a little before evening, but Haruyuki could still clearly make out the rider straddling the bike.

It was a familiar figure, clad in a leather jacket with metal armor, a skull-faced helmet on his head. But something was different than usual. Quickly taking a closer look, Haruyuki realized that red flames were burning in the eye sockets of the skull. And a tail of white steam appeared to be stretching out from the slit of a mouth.

"Uh, um, Ash—" Haruyuki had gotten that far when a leather boot kicked the shift pedal violently. At the same time as the accelerator roared to life, Ash crushed the clutch and yanked the tough front wheel up. The bike charged forward, ripping up the green grass.

"Yooouuuu goddaaaaaamned crooooooooooow!" A roar of anger shook the stage, loud enough to compete with the howling of the engine.

"Eee!" Haruyuki jumped a little. "Eeeee?!" Reflexively, he tried to fly, but his special-attack gauge was empty. He turned and started to dash away, but the glow of the headlight got closer with each breath he took.

"Yooooooouuuu! In-indirect—Indirect kiss with my siiiiiiiiis! Whaaaaat the helllllllll?! Yooooouuu! Shall! Craaaaaaash!!"

"N-no thank yooooouuu!!" Haruyuki sprinted desperately, and the front wheel of the bike—spinning with inertia—scraped his back lightly. His health gauge dropped the tiniest amount, while his special-attack gauge increased by a mere hint. Haruyuki immediately took this and poured it into thrust for his wings. He couldn't take off, but somehow he managed to avoid a crash with a long jump, waving his arms about in the air, as he fled to the north.

However, a few seconds later, a massive wall appeared ahead of him for an unknown reason, and Haruyuki opened his eyes wide. Since this valley had originally been Kannana Street, it should have continued all the way to the edge of the stage. Which meant the wall was not a real wall, but something big enough to look like a wall.

"Ah! Crap! Ash, you can't—!" Haruyuki shouted, flustered as he finally realized what the wall actually was.

But the big brother was burning with an unprecedented rage and showed no signs of letting up on the throttle. If Haruyuki slowed even slightly, he would definitely be pressed flat by the rear tire after being pulled down to the ground by the front tire, so he had no choice but to keep charging forward. Once they had broken the twenty-meter mark to the dark, wetly illuminated, reddish-brown wall-like thing, the small mountain shuddered and began to move.

The most significant feature of the Primeval Forest stage was that large creatures lived there, on scale with the Wild-class Enemies in the Unlimited Neutral Field. And without a doubt, lifting its thick head ahead of Haruyuki and Ash Roller at that moment, having been disturbed in its nap and in a foul mood, was the most powerful identified among these creatures: Tyrannosaurus rex.

"I've never seen anyone wake a sleeping Tyranno in this stage before!" one of the members of the Gallery following on the branches of the trees around them cried out, dumbfounded.

"Just like an Ash-Crow fight, giving us the goods!"

Immediately after someone offered this in response, Haruyuki and Ash and the motorcycle became a single lump that slammed into the side of the Tyrannosaurus.

"Ahhhh." Haruyuki leaned back on the bench and expelled a long sigh as he looked upward.

The rain that had been falling in the morning stopped during third period, and the gray coloring in the sky had increased considerably in brightness. Many students were seizing this chance to go out into the courtyard, and a slightly chilly breeze brought the tumult of the lunch break up to the roof.

"You think you'll make it in time for the class exhibit?" Takumu asked from beside him as he opened the package of his sandwich.

Haruyuki brought his head back up and nodded. "Yeah, we've basically got all the photos we need. All that's left is to put them into the display program on Saturday, and we're done. So, like, what kind of cosplay are you doing?" he asked in return, likewise ripping open the package containing his bun with *yakisoba* noodles.

"The boys' kendo team is in charge of the choreography for the performance." Takumu grinned wryly, almost shrugging his broad shoulders. "The girls' team is doing the costumes. They were super careful about measuring our sizes, so I kind of have a bad feeling about it."

"Ha-ha! Can't wait to see it. I'll definitely be there." After a brief laugh, Haruyuki took a big bite of his bun, and for a while, the pair simply moved their mouths, taking yogurt drink packs in hand at the same time and slurping them down.

"So? Didn't you have something you wanted to talk with me about, Haru?" Takumu asked as Haruyuki was on the verge of going for a second bite; his teeth clamped down on empty space. Haruyuki lowered his *yakisoba* bread, and an awkward smile spread across his face.

"Y-you saw through me, huh? Just like you, Professor Mayuzumi."

"Well, you know, when Professor Arita is kind enough to invite someone as humble as me to lunch, I figure something's up." His friend grinned before resuming a straight face. "So? What'd you do this time?"

I feel like I've heard that line really recently, Haruyuki thought, but he gave up on thinking too deeply about it. After quickly confirming there were no other students around, he put out a slightly circuitous question. "Uh, so, like, Taku. I was just thinking. Isn't the school festival pretty risky? In terms of Burst Linkers."

"Oh. Yeah, it's an event we need to be careful at. I mean, twice a year, students from other schools can legitimately connect with the in-school net, after all."

"T-twice a year? What's the other time?"

"The entrance ceremony, of course. But current students aren't at school on the day of the entrance ceremony, as a rule, so the risk is a little greater at the school festival."

Hearing this smooth explanation, Haruyuki nodded in understanding. "S-so then…it'd be pretty bad to give a student from another school an invitation when you know they're a Burst Linker…I guess?" Ever so timidly, he put forth this question, circling in on the heart of the matter, but fortunately, Taku appeared to be thinking of it in general terms. A broad, wry smile crossed his face.

"Actually, I think that would be safer. I mean, that means that you're both cracked in the real to each other, right? Like the Red King or Leopard. We could invite those two to the festival, and I expect there wouldn't be any security risk. But there would be other kinds of risks," he added in a quiet voice, though this did not reach Haruyuki's ears.

Instead, the boy secretly felt a rush of relief. If Niko or Pard was okay, then Rin Kusakabe—similarly mutually cracked in the real—would naturally be okay as well. In which case, he could assume that there was no need to obtain the understanding of his Legion members in advance.

Right. I still have those two other invites. Maybe I should ask Niko and Pard, too. No point in wasting the invitations. Okay! After school, I'll send them a quick message—

"What we should actually be careful about is the relatives and friends the other students invite. There's definitely a nonzero possibility that one of them is a Burst Linker, you know."

After a time lag, Takumu's increasingly serious voice reached Haruyuki's brain, and he blinked rapidly. He thought for a moment and then nodded; that was true. "If one of them checked the matching list just once during the festival, they'd know at a glance that Umesato here is the headquarters for Nega Nebulus, I guess."

"Yeah. But the invited guests all have their real info on the register, so they're carrying a certain amount of risk themselves. For a Burst Linker, a school festival is an event that requires caution, but that goes both ways. Students at the school hosting the festival, don't let your guard down. And don't just stop in on other schools' festivals. Right? I think Master'll probably talk to us about it soon."

"Right...I guess so..." As Haruyuki digested this information together with his *yakisoba* bread, Takumu grinned once more, pushing up the bridge of his glasses.

"So who're you inviting, Haru? Or did you already invite them?"

"Huh? O-oh, that's, I mean..."

"The number of Burst Linkers from other schools you know in the real is fairly limited. Master's probably inviting Raker and Maiden, so then there's the two in the Red Legion, and—"

"Uh, um, a-a-a-anyway, we should talk about what to do if there really is some strange Burst Linker mixed in with the invited guests—"

What saved Haruyuki, as he flapped his right hand clutching what little remained of his *yakisoba* bread, and his left hand, still holding the yogurt drink pack, was an icon informing him of the arrival of a text message. Takumu appeared to get one at the same time, and he turned his gaze away.

Together, they opened the message, which was a brief missive of two lines in a light-purple font against a black background: I APOLOGIZE FOR THE SUDDENNESS, BUT I'D LIKE TO HAVE A MEETING IN FIVE MINUTES. YOU'LL COME INTO THE STAGE THROUGH THE LOCAL NET AS AUTOMATIC SPECTATORS, SO PLEASE MAKE YOUR PREPARATIONS. IF THERE'S A PROBLEM, REPLY TO THIS MESSAGE. At the end of the message, there was a butterfly mark as a signature.

When the two boys closed their windows, having finished reading the message, the mail deleted itself, which erased the "mail arrival" mark as well. Haruyuki and Takumu exchanged a glance and cocked their heads to one side in sync.

"I know she's impatient, but even for her, this is sudden. And I mean, a meeting in a duel stage—you think something happened?"

"Hmm. If it was about how to respond as a Legion on the day of the school festival, she wouldn't have to be so urgent about it, right?"

Since there was no way Haruyuki was going to be able to understand something Takumu didn't, he stopped thinking about it. "At any rate, let's eat. Like they say, you can't accelerate on an empty stomach."

"They don't say that. But yes, let's."

They made what was left of their *yakisoba* bread and sandwich lunches disappear in one minute, and then for dessert, Haruyuki polished off a chocolate cornet and Takumu a package of milk pudding before they nodded at each other, finished. Chiyuri was having lunch with her girlfriends in the cafeteria, but if the meeting was through a normal duel, then at most, it would take 1.8 seconds. As long as she pretended she was on a full dive in the local net, she wouldn't have any problems.

By the time they had thrown their garbage down the chute in a corner of the roof, they had one minute left. Haruyuki and Takumu got ready to accelerate on the bench. Not even a second past the time they had been warned of, a cold thunder roared in their ears, and their consciousnesses were cut away from the real world.

7

His second battlefield of the day was a Wasteland stage with a dry wind howling through the gaps in strangely shaped, reddish-brown rocks. Of the natural-type, earth-attribute stages, it was one of the most peaceful; there were no troublesome terrain effects or fearsome moving objects.

Thinking how lucky they were that they had gotten a stage suitable for a meeting, Haruyuki checked the health gauges on the left and right. On the right side—in the place of the challenger—was Black Lotus. Which meant the challenged was Lime Bell. The thought had no sooner come into his head than he saw that the name on the left was Sky Raker.

"Huh?! Why is our sister connected to the Umesato local net?!"

The voice came from directly behind him, so he looked back and found the vivid yellow-green of Lime Bell. He sensed the same question from Cyan Pile beside him, so Haruyuki explained, having been made aware of this mechanism earlier.

"Kuroyukihime finally managed to set up a secret access gate from outside."

"O-oh." Chiyuri sounded strangely impressed. "That's just like our Black King. Nothing she can't cut through, huh?"

Takumu also nodded his head, wearing a face mask with its

horizontal slits, before looking around at their surroundings. "So then Maiden would have to be in the Gallery, too."

"Yes, I'm right here." The response came from a fissure in the rocky mountain that had originally been the first school building of Umesato, rising up immediately to the north of them—a place where the small shrine maiden avatar revealed herself.

They exchanged hellos with Utai Shinomiya, who would have been connecting from the elementary division of Matsunogi Academy to the south in Suginami Ward; then all four gazed into the northwest. Guide cursors indicating two more duelists pointed in that direction, but there was no sign of them yet.

Entry into buildings wasn't possible in a Wasteland stage, or rather there was no interior construction to the rocky mountains that the buildings turned into, but the massive rocks that had been the school and other large buildings in the real world were laced with narrow cracks like a labyrinth. If you accidentally ended up in one, it took a fair bit of effort to get out again.

"This is the direction of the student council office, right? Should we go look for them?" Haruyuki proposed, wondering if Kuroyukihime and Fuko were lost inside the mountain.

But before anyone could respond, a gray light flashed along the surface of the mountain. The enormous rock offered up a magnificent cross section before crumbling, and from within appeared Black Lotus, the jet-black duel avatar with long swords for limbs, and Sky Raker, her long hair reminiscent of fluid metal as it fluttered in the faint breeze, her slender body wrapped in a white dress. The two of them looked at Haruyuki and the others and then began to approach at a brisk pace.

"Sorry to keep you all waiting. We tried to leave the mountain, but all the paths were dead ends."

"Although, that said, cutting down the wall as a method of tackling giant labyrinths is a good bit of heresy."

"A-and who was it who suggested using Gale Thruster to fly out?"

"You're allowed to fly out of labyrinths with no roofs. That's always been allowed."

"L-liar. That is a lie."

Haruyuki was more than willing to listen to the back-and-forth of Kuroyukihime and Fuko, perfectly in sync as always, but unfortunately, the timer in the top of his field of view continued to steadily decrease, so he timidly interjected, "Uh, um, Kuroyukihime, Master, maybe we should start the meeting?"

"Mmm. R-right. This isn't the time to be talking about labyrinths." Kuroyukihime cleared her throat and straightened up while Fuko stepped back to one side in the same beat. "First, I apologize for interrupting your hard-won lunch hour. Sorry for calling you here so abruptly."

"I have to apologize as well. I was the one who asked Lotus to convene the Legion."

So it was Fuko who had such urgent information that she couldn't wait until after school for all the Legion members to come together. Haruyuki and the other three at his side turned their eyes on her, but she appeared to be leaving the telling to the Legion Master; she urged Kuroyukihime on with a gesture.

The Black King nodded lightly and took the conversation in an unexpected direction. "Do any of you know a boys' junior high/high school called Meihoku Academy in Shimokitazawa?"

This was the first Haruyuki had heard of it, but Takumu, who was standing on the left end, raised the Pile Driver equipped in his right arm slightly. "Yes, Master. It's a fairly high-ranking academic school in the city."

"Mmm. Their average scores on the national tests for the junior high division are about ten points higher than any year for us at Umesato."

Utterly unable to see where the conversation was going, Haruyuki cocked his head. Unmoved by the reactions of her Legion members, Kuroyukihime continued smoothly.

"This sort of earnest academic school often is not very passionate about in-school events. They have a simplified version of the school trip; they take care of gym tournaments and school festivals with minimal energy—things like that. Meihoku Academy in Shimokita is one of these, and they hold their school festival for half a day on a weekday. To be specific, this morning."

"Uh, uh-huh." As he made a noise of assent, thoughts wandered through his head: They wouldn't get very many people coming on a weekday, and finishing it before lunch meant there probably wouldn't be too many things on offer or anything.

"Master, you can't mean"—from this bit of information, Takumu had gleaned something Haruyuki hadn't, and he put it forward in a tense voice—"a raid on this school festival?"

"R-raid?!" Haruyuki cried out at the same time as Chiyuri, and then finally understood the meaning of this. Although Takumu used the word *raid*, no one had ever gone in and punched students from a rival school or occupied the building like armed terrorists. He was talking about the Accelerated World, naturally.

"It seems that three members of Great Wall are enrolled at Meihoku. They were challenged by a single Burst Linker via the local net, which had been opened up for invited guests for the festival. And they lost."

"…!"

Haruyuki and Chiyuri were not alone in gasping; even Takumu and Utai, who had likely figured out where this was going, took sharp breaths.

Since the duel fields in Brain Burst were based in reality, if you dueled in school, then the terrain was re-created with the placement of the school buildings and gym just as they were in the real world. In other words, the terrain advantage would have been with the three students at Meihoku Academy.

"Sacchi. Do you know the difference in level between the raider and the three who lost?" Utai asked.

"This is just hearsay," Fuko responded in Kuroyukihime's place, "so it's not certain, but the three were at level five and six. In contrast, the raider was apparently level six."

"Essentially the same level. And yet total victory on enemy territory. This is no small matter. What if the raider was using…?"

"That does appear to be the case. The three from Meihoku were apparently helplessly defeated by beams and punches with a black effect," Fuko noted.

"Ah!" Haruyuki shouted instantly, in perfect harmony with Chiyuri once more. "ISS kit!"

"There's no doubt about it. An ISS kit user has finally knocked on the front door and attacked a corner of the six great Legions." Kuroyukihime paused there before announcing the rest in a voice that was increasingly tense. "After handily beating the third one, she apparently left a message: 'If you want this power, come to Setagaya Area Number Five.'"

Haruyuki unconsciously clenched his hands into tight fists. At levels five and six, these were solid Linkers who had long since left their newbie days behind. And people who belonged to Great Wall wouldn't give in to such blatant temptation—or so he wanted to believe. But the power of the ISS kit was too overwhelming. Even Haruyuki, about to advance to the second stage of the Incarnate System, felt a deep terror toward that comprehensive long- and short-range power.

The desire to become stronger was a basic one shared by all Burst Linkers. Shown a power that was impossible to oppose and then told they could have it, too, how many people in the Accelerated World would not be moved at all? Haruyuki himself had given in to the temptation of the Armor of Catastrophe more than once and called its name.

"The key point here is that rather than a duel via the normal global net, she targeted the school festival and attacked on the local in-school net."

At Takumu's voice, Haruyuki's thoughts stopped, and he lifted his face. The indigo duel avatar, while being the most heavyweight, close-range type in Nega Nebulus, was also something of a staff officer.

"For the majority of Burst Linkers," he continued as he brought his left hand up to his face mask, "I think the school they go to is the 'final fortress,' equally or more important than their own homes. Even more so when there are several Linkers in the same school—when you have comrades there. To be attacked at that school and completely demolished on top of that has to be a fairly serious mental shock. Like what we ourselves experienced this April."

"Taku," Haruyuki said without realizing, but Takumu shook his head slightly as if to say he was okay. When the "marauder" Dusk Taker took everything two months earlier—or when they had believed he had—Haruyuki for sure and most likely Takumu as well had been more than shocked; he had been beaten down to the depths of despair.

In fact, hadn't Haruyuki at that time clung with all his might to the hope that Ash Roller had shown him? It was fortunate that Ash had introduced him to Sky Raker, but what if he had encountered an ISS kit user before Ash and been told that they would give him that power? He wasn't sure he would have refused.

"If the three Linkers at Meihoku Academy are thinking that the thing they should protect above all else is destroyed, the possibility that they will accept the raider's invitation is not zero...I think," Takumu said, almost murmured, and lifted his face to look at Kuroyukihime and ask her in a firm voice, "Master, what was the name of the Burst Linker who attacked the Meihoku festival?"

"Mmm. Yes. I didn't tell you yet, did I? Magenta Scissor."

The instant he heard this name, Takumu nodded as if his suspicions were confirmed, but Haruyuki and Chiyuri were unable to hear this without reacting violently.

"What?!"

"That's—"

Their simultaneous shouts drew the eyes of the other four members.

They looked at each other and nodded. They had been planning to tell everyone that day after school. This meeting could actually be said to be a windfall.

"Um. This report is a bit late, but last night, Chiyuri and I crossed swords with Magenta Scissor in the Setagaya area," he offered ever so timidly, and now it was Kuroyukihime and the others crying out in surprise.

"What?! So if you were with Chiyuri, a tag-team match then?! Who was Magenta's partner?!"

The questions came at a rapid-fire pace, and he brought his hand to the back of his helmet as he replied, "Uh, um, more than a tag match—it was like a group fight. It wasn't a normal duel. We ran into them in the Unlimited Neutral Field, so..."

The other four appeared speechless, so Haruyuki cleared his throat once before explaining in order the events of the previous evening.

The fact that Chiyuri discovered an Enemy that attacked with a laser near Sakurajosui Station in Setagaya Area No. 2. That they visited the Unlimited Neutral Field to do special training for the Theoretical Mirror ability with this Enemy as his opponent, and that an unexpected encounter was waiting for them there. And about the fierce battle with the shock troops led by Magenta Scissor and their hard-won victory.

"And the three members of Chocolat Puppeteer's Legion Petit Paquet want to come to Suginami soon and say hello. I didn't think that would be a particular problem, so I said sure. That's okay, right?" Haruyuki wrapped up his story with that question.

Kuroyukihime exchanged glances first with Fuko and then Utai before shaking her head back and forth, even as she assented. "Yes, well, that's not a problem. But I'm surprised you had the energy for such a grand adventure right after your revenge match with Wolfram Cerberus."

"I-if I had known all that would happen, I wouldn't have gone!" Haruyuki replied reflexively, but then quickly took it back. "N-no, if I had known, I probably would have actually invited you and Master and Mei and Taku so all of us could go."

"Exactly. We couldn't just leave Choco and them. I'm really glad we dived at that time yesterday. If we had been even five minutes later, it might have all been over."

Haruyuki nodded deeply at this from Chiyuri, and then

continued with a *but*. "But, Chiyu, if—no, probably, Magenta Scissor attacked Meihoku Academy *because* of the fight yesterday." He turned his face toward Kuroyukihime. "Kuroyukihime, after the fight yesterday was over, I told Magenta Scissor that it was a contest to see whether she reached her objective first or we destroyed the ISS kit main body first. And she said she would give up on the north and head east. Shimokitazawa's on the eastern edge of Setagaya area, right? So then, Magenta Scissor is acting on that declaration. In a sense, it's like I made her do this."

"You're wrong, Haruyuki."

At some point, Haruyuki had dropped his head, but at the sound of his master's voice, he jerked his face up again.

Because his face mask was almost completely covered by amethyst-colored, semi-mirrored goggles, the expression on the face of the Black King couldn't be seen, unlike with the face masks of Sky Raker and Lime Bell. Even so, Haruyuki sensed that Kuroyukihime was smiling sternly and gently.

"What you did was protect a Legion that might well have been wiped out last night and release two Burst Linkers from the control of the ISS kits. That's all. Given that she subdued Setagaya Areas Two through Five with force, it was only a matter of time before Magenta Scissor made her way into Setagaya Area Number One, which includes Shimokitazawa. How could you be responsible for that? ...Although I'm just a little displeased I was not invited to your special training."

"That's right, Haru, Chii. If you had just said something, I would've gone, too," Takumu interjected after Kuroyukihime, sounding a little hurt.

"N-no, that was just—" Haruyuki hurriedly waved both hands. "It was sort of like things just kind of went that way, like in the moment. Like I said before, if I had known we'd end up in that kind of fighting, I would have dragged you along whether you liked it or not."

"Ha-ha! I know. And...Chii was probably just watching out for me. I mean, you were in Setagaya and all."

Haruyuki was slightly surprised at this from Takumu, but Chiyuri shrugged and said, in a tone that wavered between rejecting and agreeing with this statement, "Um, more than watching out for you, it was more like it might make you remember something you didn't want to."

When Haruyuki thought very carefully about it, it had only been nine days ago, on Tuesday of the week before, when Takumu had headed out to Setagaya area on his own and been given the ISS kit by Magenta Scissor. The following day, he had been attacked in the real by the PK group Supernova Remnant and forced to activate the ISS kit; for a time, Takumu had squared himself with the idea that he might soon no longer be a Burst Linker. He would need a little more time to completely shake off those hard memories.

However, Takumu shook his head slightly after Chiyuri spoke. "Thanks, Chii," he said calmly. "But I'm okay. Right now, I feel like the fact that I lost to the temptation of the ISS kit, my fight with Haru, and you and Haru pulling me back are all part of my strength."

"We grow only stronger from the number of our mistakes." Utai nodded, her small face mask shifting as she spoke. "It is exactly as Mayuzumi says. We, too, have made many of our own mistakes." Fuko and Kuroyukihime—likely included in the "We, too"—cleared their throats, looking uncomfortable. Once the mood had relaxed, Utai announced in a clear, adorable voice that could only be heard in the Accelerated World, "But I do not think that Arita's behavior at this time was a mistake. Arita, and Kurashima as well, did whatever they could in a difficult situation. Just like they have in the many fights up till now."

"It'd be nice…if that was true…"

"It is true. It's important to reflect on the past, but more important is what we will do from now on. You told Magenta that this was a contest, yes, Arita? In that case, we must simply do exactly that."

"Um, 'exactly that'? So you mean…destroy the main ISS kit body?" Haruyuki put the question forward timidly.

"Yes, I do!" Utai replied sharply.

The only thing to do to eliminate the ISS kits plaguing the Accelerated World was to cut them out at the root. Haruyuki also understood that, but the kit main body was hidden away on the top floor of the Tokyo Midtown Tower rising up over distant Akasaka. And on top of that, it was guarded by the Legend-class Enemy, the Archangel Metatron, unbeatable outside of a Hell stage.

There was only one power that could resist the immediate death dispensed by Metatron's laser—a legendary ability possessed only by Ardor Maiden's parent and real-life older brother, Mirror Masker, the power to reflect all light techniques, Theoretical Mirror.

"Oh!" The cry slipped out of not just Haruyuki's mouth, but also Chiyuri's at the same time. They had finally remembered the unresolved question of the investigation interrupted by Chiyuri's mother's special sweet-and-sour pork with pineapple the previous evening.

"Right, right! Kuroyukihime, it's serious! I mean, Haru—"

"A-ah! I'll tell her!!" Haruyuki tugged on Chiyuri's cloak-type armor from behind to make her stop talking. After thinking for a minute about where to start, he first turned to Kuroyukihime and asked a roundabout question, "Um. Kuroyukihime, I just want to check something first. What kind of effect did the Theoretical Mirror ability actually have? Like, did it change the direction of a laser fired at the user…and let it flow off?"

"Mmm. Mmm. I've only seen it in action a few times. What about you, Fuko?"

"The same. You and I have nothing to do with light techniques, after all."

Kuroyukihime and Fuko glanced at Utai, seemingly concerned. The small shrine maiden avatar nodded as if to say she was okay, too, before speaking clearly: "I will answer that, Arita. Rather than let the laser flow off, it might be more accurate to say that Theoretical Mirror dispersed it. To be more specific, my brother would take an unmoving posture and break up the light-type attacks focused on himself into countless thin lines and erase them. Something like that."

"Break into countless lines and erase..." Repeating her words, Haruyuki instinctively replayed in the back of his mind the scene in which he dealt with Lava Carbuncle's red laser the previous evening. He had repelled the laser that hit his crossed arms back and to the left. Or rather, he had bent its trajectory and targeted Avocado. No matter how he looked at it, the expression "break apart and erase" just did not fit.

Wait. I've had this vague awareness of it ever since I was eating sweet-and-sour pork with extra pineapple in the Kurashima dining room last night. That I awakened some counterfeit ability to the Theoretical Mirror that I was supposed *to get. Because...*

"The name of the technique was different, right...," Chiyuri announced mercilessly.

Haruyuki dropped his head. His body kept moving until his knees were on the ground, and he shifted into a formal kneeling position.

"Wh-what is the matter, Arita?" Utai's scarlet eye lenses opened wide.

Haruyuki turned toward her and the similarly dumbfounded Kuroyukihime and Fuko and tragically confessed, "I-I'm sorry! I...learned the wrong ability!"

Three minutes later.

Having heard the rest of the story, Kuroyukihime and the others crossed their arms, put their hands to their mouths, and groaned together.

"Mm-hmm. This is indeed an unexpected development," mused Kuroyukihime.

"So rather than Theoretical Mirror, Optical Conduction?" said Fuko.

"We can't say anything until we see it in action, right?" asked Takumu.

Haruyuki took all this in with his head hanging deeply, and a small hand was placed gently on his shoulder. The slender white fingers were those of Ardor Maiden.

"Please lift your head up, Arita. You have nothing you need to apologize for."

"B-but I…After you took the trouble to tell me about mirrors and all kinds of stuff, Shinomiya…"

"Acquiring new abilities outside of level-up bonuses is essentially a very difficult thing. And yet a mere three days after the meeting of the Seven Kings, you were able to awaken a new power. You should instead be standing tall. Now please get to your feet."

Utai tugged on his arm, and Haruyuki stood up, shrinking into himself as he did. When he lifted his eyes, immediately before him were the forms of Kuroyukihime and Fuko. A black, sword-shaped hand and a slender, sky-blue hand reached out from either side to gently touch his arms.

"It's just as Utai says, Haruyuki. As far as I know, you are the only one who has twice succeeded in awakening your potential."

"And even if the name of the ability is different, it's still too soon to despair, Corvus. All it has to do is defend against Metatron's laser. From what we've heard of the phenomenon, I believe it has that possibility."

Hearing these warm words from his masters, Haruyuki was finally able to relax his shoulders. The truth was, he'd wanted to go for a while without telling Kuroyukihime and the others about the fact that he had gotten the wrong ability. He was afraid of being scolded or disappointing them, but when he thought about it, staying quiet was much more disloyal. There wasn't a single good thing about Legion members hiding things from each other. Haruyuki should have learned that much during the Armor of Catastrophe incident.

I'm going to just say the things that need to be said. Because Kuroyukihime and Master and Shinomiya and, of course, Taku and Chiyu are my precious comrades. Murmuring this to himself, Haruyuki thought about whether there was anything else he should tell them and remembered one other critical concern. They still had nearly half of the duel time remaining, and if he didn't take this chance to tell them, he'd probably drag it out again.

"Um, Kuroyukihime, there was one other thing besides the ability thing." As he spoke, he opened his storage and turned the two cards tucked away there into objects. He offered them to her, crimson font on their black surfaces.

"Mmm." Kuroyukihime brought her semi-mirrored goggles closer, suspiciously. "What's this?"

"Um, ISS kits."

The instant she heard this from Haruyuki, Kuroyukihime threw her head back and then retreated with a hovering movement. A moment later, everyone else—other than Chiyuri—also got some distance, almost flying back. Takumu's sliding step was particularly large.

"Huh? What...Wh-what's the matter, Kuroyukihime? And Taku, you too?" Haruyuki took a step toward them, cards still in hand.

"D-don't come near me, Haru!" Takumu shouted, leaping back again. "I made a decision not to come within two meters of those things!"

"But you just said you were okay now. It's fine; they're in a sealed card state."

"Th-they're still dangerous!"

Getting this violent of a reaction, Haruyuki was suddenly seized by a childish urge to gradually close in on Takumu, cards thrust out in front of him. *But you're almost in high school*, he told himself, and he gave up on the idea.

"C-Corvus, why do you have those things?" asked Fuko, who stood to his right.

"Um." Haruyuki turned to face her. "After the fight was over yesterday, Magenta Scissor gave them to me." The looks on everyone's faces grew more severe, so he quickly added, "But it wasn't like she was expecting me to use them or setting a trap that would just activate them on their own or anything."

"But I heard you can't replicate the ISS kits unless you fight and cultivate them. So then for Magenta, the ISS kits should be quite precious. Why would she hand them over to you, C?"

Utai's question was a natural one. Haruyuki had said it wasn't a trap, but he still couldn't even guess at Magenta's intention.

"She said something about how the ISS kits had been tainted by true feelings or kindness or something," Chiyuri murmured, and everyone turned their eyes on her. "But I don't think that's the real reason. I mean, she knows my power is to rewind. So like, she had to understand that the kits she got back after I rewound things were in the state they were before she parasitized Mint and Plum."

"I see. She could have used them to parasitize other Burst Linkers, and yet she gave them to Haruyuki, hmm? Excellent. Fuko and I shall take them." Kuroyukihime nodded once and then hovered over to him as she reached out the sword of her right hand.

Secretly relieved, Haruyuki moved one of the black cards to his other hand and offered them up simultaneously. With the tip of her sword, which had the function to adhere to small objects, Kuroyukihime took one, while Fuko took the other with a fairly wary look. Together, they held the cards up.

"Uh, um, they—" Haruyuki unconsciously called out a warning as he watched intently. "If you activate them with a voice command or use them in a pop-up menu, they'll parasitize you, so please be careful, okay?"

"Mmm. Understood. However, the idea that you could have two Incarnate techniques, short- and long-range, just by using one of these..." Kuroyukihime sighed, as if it were hard to believe.

"Honestly, you know?" Fuko nodded beside her. "How on earth did they make such an item? At this stage, we don't have the slightest—"

At that moment, a small gap opened up in the rows of cirrus

clouds filling the sky of the Wasteland stage, and the slightest red sunbeam reached the ground. The light hit the backside of the cards Kuroyukihime and Fuko held up, and the dense matte black grew a tiny bit lighter.

Instantly, stunned cries came from both girls.

"Wha—?"

"Th-this crest?!" Kuroyukihime appeared to be the more surprised of the two. The card moved away from the tip of her sword and fell spinning to the ground.

Haruyuki quickly reached out his right hand to catch it in midair and then held it up to the light himself. On the jet-black surface, "Incarnate System Study Kit" was inscribed in crimson roman letters. And then the red light that hit the back of the card brought out a small mark in the center of the row of text.

The design was of two revolver-type guns crossed. He had no recollection of ever seeing it before. If pressed to note some special characteristic of the mark, he would say the barrels of the guns were fairly long, but that was about it. He couldn't think of any Burst Linker who used weapons like this, either.

"Is this someone's crest?" he asked, pulling his gaze away from the card and turning toward Kuroyukihime, but he received no reply from her.

On behalf of their Legion Master, for whom the shock still hadn't worn off, Legion Submaster Fuko announced softly, "This crest…is that of the previous Red King, Red Rider."

Incarnate System Study Kit

8

After school.

Having finished taking care of his Animal Care Club duties, Haruyuki avoided the front yard, crowded with students busy preparing for the school festival, and returned to the first school building through the inner courtyard. When he stood in front of the sliding door of the student council office, deep inside on the first floor, an entry request window popped up in the center of his field of view. But before he could tap it, the door was unlocked from inside.

"Excuse me," he announced himself in a quiet voice and slid the door open. On the other side, the usual dignified atmosphere filled the room, so solemn it was hard to believe the room was in the same junior high. When he closed the door behind him, the hustle and bustle of the school at the end of the day receded at once, and only the faint sound of the student council office server machine could be heard.

Haruyuki took pains to walk softly—although the floor was covered in a thick carpet, so he wouldn't have made much of a sound even if he had walked normally—and took a few steps forward when the person hard at work at the large desk facing him lifted her head and said, coolly, "Oh, sorry for calling you in when you're busy."

"No, I'm pretty used to taking care of Hoo now, so."

"Mm-hmm. Sorry, just give me five more seconds...Okay, done."

The person who saved the file she had been working on and then stood up was, of course, the vice president of the Umesato student council, Kuroyukihime. None of the other council members were there, so he was alone in a closed room at school with Kuroyukihime, a situation that gave Haruyuki heart palpitations in a variety of ways.

He had actually invited Utai Shinomiya, aka the super president of the Animal Care Club and person with whom he had been working until a few minutes earlier, to come along with him, but for some reason, she had grinned and said, I'LL HOLD OFF TODAY. Takumu and Chiyuri were at practice, and Fuko went to a school in far-off Shibuya Ward.

Thus, Haruyuki was forced to stand at attention alone in the center of the room at the unexpected situation, while Kuroyukihime moved with a gallant step from the desk to the small kitchen built into the wall on the west side.

"Is tea all right with you, Haruyuki?" she asked.

"Oh! Y-yes!"

"With milk, lemon, or perhaps brandy?"

"M-milk, please," he replied, after judging that the last option was probably a joke.

"Mmm, understood." Kuroyukihime nodded casually and yet was surprisingly smooth in her tea preparations. Carrying a tray, she walked over to the sofa set in the southwest corner, and Haruyuki awkwardly followed.

"Please, have a seat."

"O-okay." He lowered himself onto the sofa—synthetic leather but with a soft touch—and she arranged cups and saucers for two on the low table before pouring tea from the pot. Her words and movements were extremely natural, but even so, Haruyuki sensed the faintest hint of pain in the expression of his beloved sword master.

That, too, was natural. The text message Kuroyukihime had

sent him between fifth and sixth periods had included the following: I NEED TO TALK TO YOU ABOUT THE FIRST RED KING, RED RIDER.

In January of that year, Kuroyukihime, at the request of the second Red King, Scarlet Rain, had gone on a mission to subjugate the fifth Chrome Disaster together with Haruyuki and Takumu. However, lying in wait for them in the Ikebukuro area of the Unlimited Neutral Field was a large attack force from Crypt Cosmic Circus, the Legion led by the Yellow King, Yellow Radio. Kuroyukihime had nonetheless turned resolutely to face them until Radio played a certain replay card.

Recorded on it was the ghastly scene of Black Lotus, the Black King, taking off the head of Red Rider, the first Red King, in a single blow at the first meeting of the Seven Kings, which had been approximately three years earlier at the time. Being shown this out of the blue had given Kuroyukihime an enormous shock, which went so far as to trigger the zero-fill phenomenon, and she had collapsed on the spot. It had been six months since then. As the leader of the new Nega Nebulus, Kuroyukihime had cut down numerous powerful enemies, but the wound carved in the depths of her heart could not have disappeared completely.

So with the surprise reveal of Red Rider's crest on the ISS kits, I guess Kuroyukihime's trying to face her own wounds, but is it really okay if it's just me here? Haruyuki couldn't help but have this thought—in fact, only recently, he would have gone so far as to drag another Legion member along with him there, or perhaps simply run away. Now, however, he said nothing, but rather quietly waited for her to speak.

Kuroyukihime was indeed Haruyuki's parent and Legion Master, as well as an absolutely invincible level niner. But at the same time, she was just a junior high school girl, a year older than he was, a girl who had the same struggles, pain, and fears as he did, as well as the desire to be rescued from time to time, like he did. He couldn't always be the one leaning on her and being protected.

Kuroyukihime. If I'm what you want, I'll always be right by your side. I'll never try to keep anything quiet from you again.

There was no way she could have heard these words he whispered to himself, but she touched her cup of chai to her lips and then abruptly began speaking as she lowered it again. But the details of what she said were, for Haruyuki, fairly unexpected. "Say, Haruyuki, what do you think the ultimate long-range attack power is?"

"Huh? The ultimate...long-range attack power?" After parroting her words back at her, he thought it over. "I guess it'd be an attack with serious range and firepower that could send a distant enemy flying in a single shot. Like Niko—I mean, Scarlet Rain's main armament."

"Mmm. I suppose. The Immobile Fortress's real armament is undisputedly the most powerful long-range attack currently in the Accelerated World. If it came down to a one-on-one shoot-out, even Crikin's robot couldn't beat her."

"Huh? C-Cri— Who's that?"

"Sorry, a tangent. I'll explain later. Let's continue with the main topic for now." The smile bleeding out around the corners of Kuroyukihime's mouth disappeared, and she leaned her slender body back against the sofa. "Just as you note, it goes without saying that Niko is the *most powerful* red type. But I wonder if that equals *ultimate*."

"So you mean there's a difference between *most powerful* and *ultimate*? What kind?" At some point, Haruyuki had been completely drawn into the conversation, and he leaned forward on the sofa.

Kuroyukihime moved her gaze around like she was thinking about something and then lifted a finger in a very teacherly gesture. "You said before: serious range and firepower, hmm? So then which do you think is the true nature of the red-type duel avatar's power?"

"I think..." He only had to contemplate for a second before replying almost immediately. "It's the range. The absolute firepower—the instantaneous force—is maybe higher with the blue types."

"Mmm. Exactly. If, hypothetically, the attack had something like a damage meter attached, the Blue King, Blue Knight, would likely get a higher reading than Niko. So then, the true nature of Niko's power is the long range. I suppose. Assuming a max of three thousand meters…"

What? Three kilometers is just too—, Haruyuki was about to say, but then he stopped himself. Because although that was the distance from one edge of a normal duel field to the other, he actually thought Niko could probably shoot that far. He wiped away the cold sweat that sprang up on his forehead with the back of his hand and bobbed his head.

"Which means even that girl couldn't hit an enemy farther away than that. This is the reason I say the most powerful is not the ultimate. Don't you think if the ultimate blue-type power is to cut through anything, then the ultimate red-type power is a shot that reaches anywhere?" Kuroyukihime grinned, and Haruyuki was at a loss for words for a moment.

Blinking his eyes rapidly, he shook his head quickly from side to side and objected, "B-but, Kuroyukihime, that means, then, unlimited range…doesn't it? Like, a bullet fired in the Unlimited Neutral Field in Tokyo would just keep going to Okinawa… sort of. That kind of power, I mean, serious firepower just doesn't exist. I don't think."

What if it does *exist, though?* Haruyuki broke out in a sweat once more, but fortunately, Kuroyukihime smiled again and laughed off the idea herself.

"Ha-ha! It's true—I don't know of any avatar *that* incredible. But…the idea that a bullet fired by one's own weapon could reach an enemy no matter how far away they are…In a certain sense, there was someone who expressed this ultimate ability in the Accelerated World."

Here, a moment of pain raced through Kuroyukihime's eyes again, but drawn into the conversation as he was, before he noticed it, Haruyuki was already asking, "Wh-what do you mean? Not unlimited range, but reaching however far? I feel like that's a contradiction."

"It's simple. It's like this. The weapon is yours, but someone else pulls the trigger. In that case, theoretically, you could shoot an enemy in Okinawa from Tokyo? You'd just have to entrust the weapon to someone in Tokyo and have them go to Okinawa."

"Th-that kind of cheat," Haruyuki retorted, flapping his hands. "I mean, the weapon's an Enhanced Armament, right? I don't think you can really just hand those over to someone else so easily as that."

As far as Haruyuki knew, there were only four ways to obtain an Enhanced Armament: (1) initial equipment, (2) level-up bonus, (3) shop purchase, and (4) driving another Burst Linker to total point loss and taking the Armament from them; that was it. Even if (4) was out of the question, the other three were also fairly difficult. Buying it in the shop seemed easy, but since a powerful Enhanced Armament actually cost enough points for a player to go up an entire level, in a certain sense, buying it wasn't all that different from sinking the points into a level-up bonus.

"It's just as you say, Haruyuki." At some point, a tranquil expression had come across Kuroyukihime's face, and she nodded gently. "However, there used to be a lone exception in the Accelerated World. *The power to produce one's own Enhanced Armament*: the ability Arms Creation. The person who possessed this ability...was the first Red King, also known as Master Gunsmith, Red Rider."

The Legion meeting over the lunch break approximately four hours earlier had ended in confusion: Immediately after Fuko gave voice to the name Red Rider, Kuroyukihime had told all of them, "Give me a little time," and brought the topic of the ISS kits to a close there. Then she and the others had discussed the main agenda item she'd called them together for: confirming their course of action for a Magenta Scissor raid at the school festival (though, that said, the plan was basically just to be on maximum alert at the Umesato festival on Sunday), and then the meeting had been abruptly called to a close.

When they were about to leave, Fuko had sidled over to him and murmured, "June's almost over, you know? ♥" but it was still clear the double-gun crest hidden on the ISS kits was seriously troubling her.

During his afternoon classes, 10 percent or so of Haruyuki's brain was occupied by the former Red King. He noted in his mind all the information he had ever heard about Red Rider, but the list was surprisingly short. His name, the fact that he had been the leader of Prominence before Niko, and the fact that three years earlier, he had been hit with Black Lotus's sudden death technique, lost all his points, and been forever banished from the Accelerated World. That was basically all he knew.

Even still, from the fact that his color name was crowned with red—the pure color itself—Haruyuki had vaguely assumed that he had boasted incredibly awesome long-range attack power: massive firepower exceeding even that of Niko in fortress mode. However, this ability of his that Kuroyukihime was now telling him about was far beyond anything Haruyuki had imagined.

The power to produce Enhanced Armaments...

"Arms Creation? Th-that means the power to make as many gun-type Enhanced Armaments as he wanted?" Haruyuki asked ever so timidly.

"It wasn't quite that impressive of an ability." Kuroyukihime shook her head, a faint smile crossing her lips. "I remember him telling me that to forge just one gun required serious payment on his side. Although, of course, he didn't tell me exactly what that payment was."

"Still, that's an amazing ability. He could gradually enhance his Legion members with his own power."

"Indeed. In fact, there were plenty of Burst Linkers in Prominence at the time equipped with handguns and rifles made by

Rider. Apparently, some even switched over from their own original Enhanced Armaments. For that alone, I suppose Rider would have been adored by his Legion members." Kuroyukihime cut herself off there and turned her gaze on the evening scene on the other side of the window before continuing, almost in a murmur, "The guns he forged were all extremely accurate, you see. They gave us quite a bit of trouble in the Territories. About the only one who could shake free of the barrage of bullets and break through to the enemy was Fuko, equipped with Gale Thruster. The ICBM strategy, where she would fly in carrying Uiui and airdrop her into the enemy firing squad, was something we came up with out of necessity."

"I—I get it." Nodding his agreement, he took another sip of milk tea before giving voice to the question that abruptly popped up in his mind. "But I mean, listening to this, it's like Red Rider was really generous. He trusted the Legion members unconditionally, huh? I mean, there was the possibility that the Burst Linkers he gave the guns he made to would take them and transfer to some other Legion, right?"

"Mmm. I suppose. It's true Rider didn't concern himself with the details; he was a thoroughly positive, passionate fellow. But it isn't as though even he would hand out his weapons without any kind of safety whatsoever."

"Safety? What do you mean?"

"Exactly what I said. All the guns Rider made were equipped with a safety modeled after the crossed guns crest you saw at lunch today. And he could lock that safety from a distance. Even after he handed the gun over to someone else, mmm? So supposing a Legion member were to switch Legions, gun and all, they would never be able to pull the trigger of that gun again."

"Whoa, this power just keeps getting more amazing," Haruyuki groaned admiringly. "He couldn't actually fire long distance, could he?"

"It does appear that he indeed could not, and we kings used to roll our eyes at it." Kuroyukihime smiled faintly. "If he's going to activate a safety, then the power to recover the gun itself would be better. Rider would always say in response, 'It's not like I designed the ability, you know.'"

Here, Kuroyukihime lifted her teacup and, without bringing it to her mouth, returned it to the saucer a few seconds later. She let out a thin sigh, head hanging, and murmured in an almost soundless voice, "Haruyuki...Is it all right if I come sit next to you?"

"Huh?! Oh, uh, um, um." His heart suddenly began to move at double speed, and he fell into a half-frozen state, unable to say yes or no.

But without waiting for a reply, the older student, clad in black, stood up smoothly from the sofa. She went around the coffee table and soon sat down immediately to his left. A refreshing scent tickled his sense of smell, and a faint warmth that would have been impossible to re-create with avatars in the virtual world stroked the skin of his left arm.

"There are social cameras in this room as well. But for this distance, no security's going to come charging in." As she whispered this, Kuroyukihime leaned her slender body against Haruyuki. Her arms, stretching out from her short-sleeved shirt, touched his own, and his mind raced. At this distance, he could hold in his feelings or he could leave zero distance between them—but he forced down the feelings quickly rising up within him.

He knew instinctively what Kuroyukihime wanted. She was about to confess something very difficult, and during that confession, she wanted him to support her. In which case, as her child, as a Legion member, and as a male student who adored the vice president, he had to do what he had to do.

"Kuroyukihime. I said this before, too, but...no matter what happens, I'll always be right by your side," Haruyuki said as if firming up his resolve.

"Before?" Kuroyukihime cocked her head curiously, still extremely close to him. "When are we talking about?"

"Huh? Uh, um." Panicked, he replayed the movie of his memories and paused on a certain scene. He had definitely said almost the exact same thing immediately after sitting down on this sofa—"Ah! I-I'm sorry! I didn't so much say it as just think it in my head."

It was one thing to get mixed up with a neurospeak voice-directing, but something was wrong with him mistaking speaking for a simple thought. Haruyuki was thoroughly embarrassed.

"Honestly." A slender finger reached out abruptly and poked his cheek. "You never change. It's basically all right if you stay like this, but next time, make sure to communicate these kinds of thoughts in words. Out loud."

"R-right. I will."

"Mmm. Please do." She nodded primly and pulled her finger away from Haruyuki's check, tucking it back into her hand before taking a deep breath and speaking somewhat abruptly. "Summer three years ago. I was in grade six. If we cut straight to the reason I sliced off Red Rider's head with an Incarnate-enhanced special attack, it's…it's directly connected with Rider's abilities Arms Creation and Distance Safety."

"Huh?!" Haruyuki was stunned. "It wasn't because of the non-aggression pact the Red King was advocating?!"

"There was indeed that." Next to him, Kuroyukihime pulled her chin back a centimeter or so. "But immediately before the first meeting of the Seven Kings was held and became the stage for tragedy, I received certain information from one of the kings. Red Rider wasn't just proposing a mutual nonaggression pact among the seven major Legions—he was also completing 'physical means' of essentially forcing it to be enacted."

"Physical…means…"

"Yes. You might well call it an absolute power. A gun that would be distributed to all of the seven major Legions on which the safety would only be released in the event of an attack by another Legion. In appearance, it was a very ordinary revolver-type handgun, but it was no mere Enhanced Armament. It shot immensely powerful Incarnate bullets, the accuracy rate was one hundred percent, and the number of bullets it held was infinite. So, for example, if a hundred people came at you in the Territories, as long as the defending side had this gun, they would have the power to easily wipe out the enemy."

Kuroyukihime's words at once brought Haruyuki's temperature—which had started to rise at being pressed up against her—back down at once. Aware of the gooseflesh standing up on his arms, he shook his head in a motion that resembled shivering. "Th-that's...I mean, he might have been a king, but there's no way he could make something like that, that kind of powerful Enhanced Armament from scratch. I mean, even the Seven Arcs don't have that kind of power."

"I...also thought that when I first heard this; I didn't believe it. But, well, the king who told me about it had an actual Incarnate gun. Said that it was a sample from Rider. She demonstrated it for me in a duel stage with just the two of us. It was a Demon City, with its solid terrain, but...I saw a third of the stage become level ground pocked with craters in mere seconds. And the side of the gun was indeed emblazoned with the crossed guns emblem and a safety."

Having gotten this far in her explanation, Kuroyuki slumped against Haruyuki's shoulder. Her face was turned far downward, and he couldn't see the look on it. After a brief silence, the voice that came was tinged once more with an echo of sorrow somehow.

"I was pushed into a state of serious confusion and anxiety. The fact that Rider hoped for the stagnation of the world so much that he would create this gun, so like the nuclear deterrence forces of old, was a shock to me. I believed his motivation for creating weapons was simply that he was seeking the excitement and delight of the duel."

She laced the fingers of both hands together and squeezed before continuing her monologue.

"Until I was shown that gun, I thought I would be able to persuade Rider with words—ask him what the meaning was of the existence of Burst Linkers that didn't fight, tell him we should continue to duel even if we were saddled with the level-nine sudden-death rule. I thought the other kings and Red Rider himself would accept my assertions. Because I believed—no, I was convinced that like me, everyone, from the bottoms of their hearts, more than anything else, was seeking the thing that lay beyond level ten."

The instant he heard this, a faint, distant voice came back to life in the depths of Haruyuki's mind.

I…I want to know. Whatever it takes, I have to know.

Accelerating your thinking, you can get money, grades, fame. Is this really the meaning behind our Duels? Is this the compensation we seek, the limit we can reach? Isn't…isn't there something beyond this? This…shell called a human being…outside…something more…"

Kuroyukihime had said this the previous fall at a coffee shop in Higashi Koenji, the day after Haruyuki had become a Burst Linker. He'd known basically nothing about the Accelerated World at that point, but her words had made their way deep, deep into his heart and lingered there. Even now, eight months later, he felt like he could hear the faint echoes of it if he listened hard.

"Something…more," he murmured, and then he raised his voice to continue. "I don't think it's just the kings. I'm sure all Burst Linkers are thinking like that from the bottoms of their hearts."

"…Yes, I suppose. But at the time, I thought I had been betrayed. I believed that Red Rider was so afraid of losing Brain Burst that he brought forward this nonaggression pact, and on top of that, he developed a gun incorporating the prohibited Incarnate System—the ultimate weapon. I believed he was trying to make the world stagnate. The respect I had for Rider, the solidarity I felt with him as a comrade in arms, vanished. I attended the meeting of the Seven Kings with one resolve—a murderous intent. To take Rider's head while the safeties for all seven of the

Incarnate guns that had supposedly been already completed were locked and make it so that those guns could never be fired."

Still leaning against Haruyuki, Kuroyukihime raised her right hand slightly and stared at it for a while. Almost as though she were searching for traces of blood somewhere on those pale fingers.

"Naturally, I was prepared for the fact that the other Kings—especially Rider's sworn ally, Blue Knight, and Purple Thorn, who was basically in a romantic relationship with him—would not understand my actions. In fact…I even suspected these two had already agreed to Rider's plan behind the scenes. Thus I was tormented with the thought that I would never get another chance outside of this meeting to take the heads of five level niners and reach level ten. I would first push Rider to total loss with a surprise attack, and then, in the massive confusion that was sure to follow, four others."

She paused for a moment and squeezed her right hand tightly shut.

"No, I'll be precise. I would defeat Blue Knight, Purple Thorn, Yellow Radio, and Green Grandé. I attended the meeting of the Seven Kings with this murderous intent. You already know what happened after that. In the end, I took only Rider's head and shamelessly lived on myself. Immediately after that, we took on the Four Gods of the Castle with the full mobilization of Nega Nebulus, and I destroyed the Legion itself."

"…Uh-huh…" Haruyuki could only offer a small voice as he nodded. He had been told about the brave and sad end of the initial Nega Nebulus ten days earlier, when he had met Utai Shinomiya. The Legion had succeeded in rescuing Ardor Maiden from the altar of the God Suzaku at that time, but the remaining two Elements of the Legion were still in a sealed state, and Haruyuki knew only their names.

"…?" Suddenly, he felt like he could hear the sound of water flowing somewhere in the distance. But when he glanced over, the faucet in the kitchen was, of course, clearly off, so he brought his awareness back to Kuroyukihime's story. As he did, a meager doubt he hadn't noticed before popped up in his mind.

"Um, Kuroyukihime. I understand why you went to take down Red Rider. But why were the other four you were going for those four?" He asked it timidly, but then suddenly answered himself: "Oh, right. The other person was the one who told you about the Incarnate gun, right? So you didn't target her. Um, the kings are seven colors, so that king's color..."

The instant Haruyuki had made it this far, Kuroyukihime shuddered violently, like she'd been bathed in electric current. She sat up on the sofa, almost as if she were being repelled by it, and long hair swinging, she whirled around and slammed her face into Haruyuki's chest.

"Huh?! K-Kuroyukihime?!" Haruyuki's hoarse voice was drowned out by Kuroyukihime's tense cry.

"I...I was a fool!!" She pressed her face into his left shoulder, and her hands gripped both his shoulders tightly. The Black King let out an even more anguished cry. "The one I should have defeated wasn't Knight or Thorn or Radio or Grandé...or even Rider! I—I should have targeted her alone! It was my first and last chance...It took me far too long...to realize that!"

Even as he was stunned by the unexpected outburst, Haruyuki instinctively placed a hand gently on Kuroyukihime's back. When he did so, her stiff body relaxed slightly. Haruyuki summoned his resolve and asked the small ear next to his mouth, "So, this 'her'—you mean the last person, the White King, right?"

After a few seconds, the face pressed up against him nodded sharply. "Yes. The White King showed me the gun Rider made and razed a stage with it...I knew she had absolutely no physical attack power, be it long range or short, so I believed without question that the incredible power of the Incarnate bullets was the ability of the gun itself. But...even the White King, perfect in all ways, made just one careless mistake."

"Mistake?"

"Mmm. She overlooked the possibility that when I brought Red Rider to total loss, the Enhanced Armament he had would be transferred to my storage."

"Enhanced Armament...S-so you mean—?!" Haruyuki's eyes flew open.

"Yes, the gun in question." Kuroyukihime nodded slightly. "After the fall of Nega Nebulus, having lost everything, not only did I cut myself off from the global net—for a long time, I didn't even accelerate. But one winter night months after the incident, I suddenly opened the Brain Burst console. And I noticed there was a Rider-made gun in my storage. I—as if guided by it, I dived into the Unlimited Neutral Field and made the gun into an object. It was indeed the exact same gun the White King had test-fired for me the day before the meeting of the Seven Kings. The safety was off. I held the gun, turned it on my own home in the Accelerated World, and pulled the trigger. However."

In a voice containing pain and regret and hatred, Kuroyuki-hime announced, *"No bullet came out.* Not the Incarnate bullets that had blown away the stage that day, not even a regular bullet. Even though there were bullets in the cylinder. As I pulled the trigger over and over again, I finally understood. That the gun... wasn't about destruction...but rather a symbol of peace. Rider had created them with the intention of gifting all the Kings with a gun that did not shoot bullets as proof of peace and friendship after the mutual nonaggression pact was concluded."

"B-but when the White King fired it, you said bullets definitely came out." After he gave voice to this, dumbfounded, Haruyuki realized something. Bullets had been launched from a gun that could not fire. There was only one logic that would make that possible.

"Exactly. The bullets that so totally destroyed the Demon City stage that day...were the overwrite of the White King herself. And what was launched from the gun was a destructive Incarnate. As for the reason why she alone would have had the gun early...Most likely, Rider had discussed things with her. The design, the name of the gun."

"What...was the name of it?"

"Seven Roads. A revolver with seven bullets. I took all the bullets out of the cylinder. They shone in the seven colors of red, blue, purple, yellow, green, white, and black."

"Seven lords, seven roads," Haruyuki murmured.

"The seven color trajectories reaching out from the single gun barrel did not cross, but had the same starting point. And the same end point. When I felt that this was the intent Rider had put into the gun, I understood that I had been manipulated. I had been made to believe that a gun of peace was a gun of destruction. I had been made to be afraid of a nonexistent threat. And in the end, I had been made to stain these hands with the blood of a friend. This manipulation wasn't just pushing Rider to total loss. For a long time before that, possibly from immediately after I became a Burst Linker, she had made me dance however she pleased, for so many years."

Haruyuki could say nothing further to this sorrowful soliloquy. He put all the feelings into the hand that gently stroked Kuroyukihime's back, but her slender body stayed stiff, shaking. And he was able to hazard a guess as to the reason for this, albeit a hazy one.

The story wasn't finished yet.

He had been invited to Kuroyukihime's house in a corner of Asagaya Jutaku the previous week. The town house she lived in by herself was clean and simple and was filled with quiet and sadness. She had explained that she was living by herself as a junior high student because of an attack in the real on a certain Burst Linker. In which case, the object of this attack was the very White King who had deceived Kuroyukihime, manipulated her, and made her take the Red King's head.

Squeezing Haruyuki's shoulders so hard it hurt, Kuroyukihime pushed an even more strained voice from the depths of her throat. "When I returned to the real world from the nearest portal...I was still in half disbelief. Or rather, I wanted to believe—she would never betray me, trick me like that. Because... the White King, Transient Eternity, White Cosmos—in the Accelerated World she is my parent, and in the real world...my sister, older by a year."

Ever since he had become a Burst Linker, Haruyuki had sometimes thought, from the extremely one-sided information he had been given: What if Kuroyukihime had a special relationship with one of the kings? And that king was a person very close to her in the real as well?

It had been nearly six months before that Haruyuki had asked about Kuroyukihime's parent, and she had only replied with these mysterious words:

That person was once...the person closest to me. I believed this Linker would shine brightly forever at the center of my world and keep all kinds of darkness and cold at bay.

However, one day...one incident, one instant, I realized that this was an ephemeral illusion. Now you could go so far as to say that, for me, this person is my archenemy. So much so that I could almost believe that this inexhaustible hatred existed inside me from the moment we first met.

The "instant" in this recollection—it was none other than the moment when she realized that her parent and older sister the White King had manipulated her and made her push Red Rider into total loss.

"I'm not trying to say that all the sin of taking Rider's head should be forced onto the White King or anything like that," Kuroyukihime noted into his ear, almost as if she had read his thoughts.

"Even if she hadn't shown me that gun, I would have resisted Rider's proposal to the very end, and it was me myself who fully believed the words of the White King and not a single word from the Red King...However, at the time, when I ran from my own room to my sister's, still half in disbelief, and she acknowledged everything while smiling gently, I was seized by an intense rage, like nothing I'd ever felt before. I decided that the fact that Rider had lost Brain Burst, the fact that I had lost Nega Nebulus, was all her fault. Before I knew it, I was holding the letter opener on her desk."

Having told this much of her story, Kuroyukihime pursed her lips together for a moment, and whether he wanted to see it or not, a visual sprang up in the back of Haruyuki's mind.

A girl with black hair clutching a small knife in both hands, tears spilling endlessly down shuddering pale cheeks, anger and hatred swirling in her obsidian eyes, almost eclipsed by an even greater sadness. With the knife turned on a girl only slightly taller than herself, the girl closes the distance between them by one step, another. But even with the sharp tip of the blade before her, the smile on the lips of the other girl does not disappear.

"I said to my sister, 'Push the knife in. Direct duel with me right here.' I said I'd offer her the same fate as Rider. And her smile didn't so much as twitch as she answered me." At the same time as Kuroyukihime spoke, the lips of the girl in the screen of his imagination moved. "'Don't say that. I don't want to take even Brain Burst from you.' In other words, if my sister and I, both at level nine, fought, she would beat me and make me lose all my points by the sudden-death rule—that's what she meant. And despite the fact that I had never once fought my sister seriously, I knew that was certainly what would happen. I stood there frozen, and she tried to take the knife from me. The tip of the blade cut her palm."

The long story appeared to be coming to an end. All the tension suddenly drained out of Kuroyukihime, and she leaned heavily against Haruyuki as she continued haltingly, "You know the rest. The fact that I turned a knife on my sister was caught on the cameras of our home net, and I was expelled from the family home in Minato Ward under the pretext of mental health treatment. And thus I lost not only my Legion but also my actual family—although I never had any real attachment to them. And that is the whole of the story of me; the first Red King, Red Rider; and the White King, White Cosmos."

After a pause, Kuroyukihime continued in a slightly different tone. "So? Are you shocked? Or perhaps contemptuous, Haruyuki? For the sake of my objective, I might someday sacrifice even you."

The moment he heard this, Haruyuki used the hands that had been stroking Kuroyukihime's back to pull her toward him. At the same time, he replied in a voice filled with every emotion in his heart, "If there are higher levels, it's only natural to aim for them. I mean, that's the reason Brain Burst exists."

This exchange was indeed the same as the one he had had with her at the coffee shop the day after he became a Burst Linker. Eight months had passed since then, but he felt the need to assure her that his own feelings hadn't changed a bit.

"The things you've lost," he continued, "you can get them back again—no, you can rebuild. Right now, Nega Nebulus's still a Legion with just six people, but I'm sure the remaining Elements will be back any day now. And we'll recruit new Linkers, too, so it'll be even bigger than it was before. And then this time for sure, as a Burst Linker, you'll fight the White King fair and square and settle this. I'm always right by your side. Right up until you reach level ten."

Even after Haruyuki closed his mouth, Kuroyukihime stayed silent for a while. Normally, this would be when he got anxious that he may have accidentally said the wrong thing, but at just this moment, the thought didn't even cross his mind. He simply continued to put his strength in his hands.

Finally, the faintest sensation on his left shoulder. One small drop, then two fell and soaked into the fabric of his shirt, reaching his skin. "Thank you, Haruyuki. My decision was not mistaken, after all. From the bottom of my heart, I'm so glad I chose you."

These words, too, were essentially the same thing she had said eight months earlier. However, at the time, Haruyuki had pulled back his clenched fist and hung his head deeply. Now, however, he squeezed her even more tightly. "Me too. From the bottom of my heart, I'm glad you chose me."

"...Thank you." Her murmured voice was deep and damp. Her faint sobs continued then for nearly two minutes, but Haruyuki didn't pull his hands away; he simply accepted wordlessly the tears that fell.

What broke the warm, gentle silence was the announcement telling all students still on campus to return home.

Kuroyukihime slowly sat up. "Wait a moment," she said, heading into the kitchen. He heard the sound of water, which then quickly stopped. When the vice president returned, her face had essentially regained its usual cool composure, although there was still a little redness, particularly around her eyes.

They left the student council office together, walked to their separate lockers to change shoes, and met up again in the front yard. Once they stepped through the school gates, the in-school local net was cut off, and in its place, the icon for the global-net connection flashed.

Since the condo building Haruyuki lived in and the Asagaya residence where Kuroyukihime's town house was were in opposite directions, with Umesato in the middle, normally, this was where they would part, going off to the right and the left. But Kuroyukihime stopped at the side of the gate and didn't make a move.

"Haruyuki." The look on her face was serious.

"Y-yes?" He naturally snapped to attention.

Kuroyukihime cleared her throat lightly before continuing. "When I really think about it, it was all fine and good to call you to the student council office, but don't you feel like we didn't talk about the really important thing?"

"Huh? The important thing? What do you mean?" Haruyuki replied.

She brought her face in close. "The matter of the crest inscribed on the cards you brought back."

"Oh!" Now that she mentioned it, that was true. The reason she had called him to the student council office in the first place was supposedly because, for some reason, the crossed guns emblem of the first Red King was on the cards that sealed the ISS kits, but that matter was still shrouded in mystery.

If Kuroyukihime had some kind of theory, he wanted to hear it right then and there, but they couldn't exactly stand and talk like that at the school gates. Haruyuki checked the time display and thought quickly. His original plan had been to head to Nakano Area No. 2 after he left school, just like he had the previous day, and duel Wolfram Cerberus for the third time. Cerberus was also wrapped in all kinds of mysteries, but if Haruyuki kept exchanging blows with him, he had the feeling that he would arrive at the truth of Cerberus at some point. But, regrettably, at that moment, he had a mission that had to take priority.

This was, of course, the destruction of the ISS kits. Magenta Scissor wouldn't stop at taking down one school in Shimokitazawa. Before she spread the kits any farther, they had to cut out the root of the dark power. But the annoying thing was that it was, of course, impossible for Haruyuki to go on his own and attack Tokyo Midtown Tower, where the kit main body was enshrined, and it was too dangerous for even the six members of Nega Nebulus to attempt. Even if they did manage to dispose of the guardian, the Archangel Metatron, they had no way of knowing what was waiting inside the tower. Just as had been decided at the last meeting of the Seven Kings, a joint operation with all seven of the major Legions was essential.

Once his thoughts had reached this point, Haruyuki gasped with sudden realization. "Uh, um, Kuroyukihime?"

"Hmm? If we're going to talk about the crest, we should go somewhere quiet."

"N-no, this is something else. Right now, the Midtown Tower attack is the top priority, right?"

"Whoa, whoa! It's too dangerous to talk about that in a public space with real voices. Even if someone unconnected overheard us, we could be suspected of being terrorists, you know." Kuroyukihime grinned wryly, but when she noticed that the look on Haruyuki's face was serious, she blinked once, then nodded as if to say *Hold on* and reached into her bag. She pulled out a meter-and-a-half-long XSB cable, and without giving Haruyuki the time to say anything, she offered him one end while plugging the other into her Neurolinker.

After all this time, there was no point in being embarrassed about directing, so Haruyuki kept his serious face on—although a light sweat did break out on his back—and accepted the plug, connecting it to his neck.

"It's been a while since I directed with you in town." Immediately, Kuroyukihime's neurospeak voice echoed in his mind. *"You do seem entirely used to it, though."*

"I-I'm not used to it at all. Totally not!"

"Hmm, I suppose you're not, then."

"Oh...s-sorry, I just..." Feeling ashamed, this time he replied in neurospeak.

Kuroyukihime laughed. *"How about we walk a bit? The rain's finally lifted and all."*

Just as she said, the rain clouds that had departed toward the east before lunch showed no signs of returning now, and the rain forecast on his virtual desktop showed numbers in the 10 percent range until evening.

"Okay. Just hold on a minute. I'll turn off automatic viewing," Haruyuki said briefly, and he quickly opened the Brain Burst console. When automatic viewing mode was on, if a duel started between Burst Linkers registered on his viewing list in their current location of Suginami Area No. 1, he would accelerate without warning in the middle of a conversation.

"Um, you're not going to turn it off, too, Kuroyukihime?" Haruyuki asked her casually as he switched the mode to "off."

"No need. Apologies to the other Legion members, but the only one registered on my viewing list is you," she replied as if it were the most natural thing in the world.

He was surprised to hear this, but then Kuroyukihime peeked at his face and winked lightly, so his heart leapt even higher in his chest. Heart pounding and gaze frozen in place, he hit the ok button of the confirmation dialog window and fumbled to close the console. He felt like he heard some kind of unfamiliar sound effect, but his brain had its hands full carefully weighing how exactly to respond to her statement. Eventually, what came from not his mouth but his mind was *"Th-that's an honor."*

It was a simple, inoffensive statement, and Kuroyukihime nodded, still smiling.

"Well then, shall we go?" She turned her feet north.

The everyday road that continued just under a hundred meters from the school gates was deserted, but the instant they stepped out onto the sidewalk of Oume Highway, housewives carrying bags of groceries and office workers headed for the station filled Haruyuki's field of view. Naturally, mixed among them were students from nearby schools, and a variety of expressions popped up onto their faces upon seeing Haruyuki and Kuroyukihime with their Neurolinkers connected by a thin cord as they passed by.

I'll never get used to this, Haruyuki complained to himself, but he kept it as a thought deep enough not to be output as a voice.

"Now then," Kuroyukihime said coolly as they waited for the red light to change. *"About your question concerning the priority of the Midtown Tower attack that you started to ask before, the answer is, at any rate, yes."*

"Huh? Oh, y-yes. Right." Haruyuki rewound his thoughts by several minutes and bobbed his head up and down. *"Um, the thing that was bugging me...For the Tower attack, the seven Legions will be working together, but then that means we'll be taking a cooperative stance with the White Legion, but for you, I mean, the White King..."*

"*...Is that it? Sorry to make you worry about that.*" At the same time as Kuroyukihime lowered her eyes slightly, the light changed to green. The time remaining for the green light displayed in the navigation window in his view had dropped three seconds before her black loafers finally moved forward. "*It's true that the hatred I have for my sister—for White Cosmos—has not faded in the slightest since that night. To the point where if I were to face her without any mental preparation, I don't know what I'd do. However, even so, I have a reason for attending the last meeting and the meeting before that of the Seven Kings, and for accepting this shared mission.*"

"*Reason? What sort of reason?*"

"*The White King does not show herself before Burst Linkers of other Legions as a general rule. In the very early days of the Accelerated World, naturally, she also dueled, but even then, whether by ability or the power of an Enhanced Armament, most of the time, her form was wrapped in a light that dazzled the eyes and so couldn't be seen. And since she reached level nine, I suppose basically the only ones who have seen her are the other kings and the senior members of the White Legion Oscillatory Universe. Well, until I met you, that was me; so I can't really talk,*" she added as they finished crossing the road, and without the slightest hesitation, she turned them toward the shopping street ahead. They continued to walk north, farther and farther from Kuroyukihime's house, but because of the short cable directly connecting them, Haruyuki had no choice but to follow.

"*In other words, although this is pathetic, I was able to attend the meetings precisely because I was certain she would not be there. The shared mission is the same. The location is also the Unlimited Neutral Field, and hypothetically, even if the kings were asked to participate in the operation, she would simply send her representative, as she has up to now. What I hate is not Oscillatory Universe, but White Cosmos alone, so it doesn't make sense to reject the joint mission with my hatred as a reason.*"

Kuroyukihime stopped there and slid the fingers of her left hand along the XSB cable swinging between the two of them. Almost as if it were the physical manifestation of the connection between Haruyuki and Kuroyukihime, she held it tight in her palm.

"But it would be a lie to say I have no misgivings or anxiety whatsoever. I was counting on you to get the Theoretical Mirror ability, and even if the name is different, I have faith that the Optical Conduction ability you did learn will play a wonderful role. But even so, my uneasiness—no, my fear—hasn't gone away since the moment the meeting ended on Sunday."

"What...is that fear of?"

This time, it took a while for an answer to come back to him. The pedestrian-only shopping street was more crowded than Oume Highway, so they were forced up against each other as they walked. Kuroyukihime's arm brushed against Haruyuki's, and she was cool to the touch.

"She's a terrifying person."

Suddenly, these words echoed in Haruyuki's brain. As she continued, the strained thought would have been barely a whisper if it were communicated in a real voice.

"She sees through to the wounds in the hearts of all people, prescribes the appropriate words and attitudes, and heals them. But on the underside of this, she controls the hearts of those other people and manipulates them. The reason I haven't said anything to you before about the White King is because I was afraid that by hearing about her, that terrifying ability to manipulate might affect even you indirectly."

"Th-that's— I wouldn't be manipulated!" Haruyuki replied reflexively.

"Yes, of course, I believe that." Kuroyukihime nodded. *"I spoke frankly with you about my relationship with the White King today because...I realized that being afraid of losing you was the same thing as doubting you."*

Here, her feet stopped abruptly, and she placed her hands on Haruyuki's shoulders and moved the two of them to the side of a large sign so they weren't in the way of the people passing by. Still, it wasn't as though they were now far removed from their surroundings, so the flickering glances of passersby were still turned on them.

Normally, Haruyuki would be painfully aware of those glances, but at the moment, he couldn't take his eyes off Kuroyukihime's serious face. She closed in until their noses were about twenty centimeters apart, and then Kuroyukihime moved her lips to say in both thought and real voice, "Haruyuki, I have one other thing that I must tell you."

"O-okay."

"That—"

However, he didn't hear the rest of it. Because at the moment when Kuroyukihime took a deep breath, a familiar sound slammed into his auditory nerves. *Skreeee!* Cold, dry thunder. The sound of acceleration.

Wh-why?! Haruyuki was stunned. Neither he nor Kuroyukihime had given the acceleration command, and their present location was Nega Nebulus territory, so duels should have been blocked. And he had definitely turned automatic viewing mode off. There should have been no reason for him to accelerate.

This surprise was doubled the instant he saw that message that flamed up in the center of his now-dark field of view. It wasn't the HERE COMES... from when he was challenged, nor was it the REGISTERED DUEL... when automatic viewing was activated.

A BATTLE ROYALE IS BEGINNING!!

9

It was only after Silver Crow's feet touched down on the white ground of the duel stage that he was able to digest the meaning of that line of text.

The fighting game Brain Burst had single match, a tag-team match, and following that, a third type of match: Battle Royale mode. The procedure for starting a Battle Royale was easy: Simply accelerate with the normal Burst Link command, open the matching list, and select BATTLE ROYALE from the submenu. However, that said, it wasn't the case that this pulled everyone on the list into the duel stage. Given that the system was such that only Burst Linkers who had Battle Royale standby on in the console screen settings could be summoned, everyone normally had that standby turned to off. Haruyuki, naturally, was no exception.

So why am I in a Battle Royale?! He started to panic before finally figuring it out: Because he'd been operating his virtual desktop without looking carefully at the screen when he turned automatic viewing mode off earlier, he must've accidentally touched Battle Royale standby in the same tab and turned it on.

"Why am I such a klutz...," he muttered to himself dejectedly, dropping his shoulders.

"I see," came from immediately beside him. "You're not a hero with BR mode always on. This is instead the result of mistaken operation?" The voice sounded exasperated.

Jumping slightly, he turned his gaze and found a dazzling and majestic duel avatar, body wrapped in jet-black semitransparent armor, the sharp swords of her four limbs glittering. Naturally, it was none other than the Black King, Black Lotus.

"Huh?! Wh-why?! You can't have Battle Royale—?!" Haruyuki cried out in a hoarse voice.

"Unfortunately, I am not the hero that you are." The amethyst semi-mirrored goggles popped from side to side. "I was called here not as a dueler but as the Gallery because I automatically view you."

"Oh. M-makes sense. Good." He relaxed slightly. The probability was extremely low, but if another king—i.e., another level niner—had also been summoned to this battlefield, it would have been the abrupt start to a sudden-death final battle. With that in mind, he took a look at his surroundings and found the silhouettes of other members of the Gallery—albeit few of them—on the roofs of the buildings of the pale, frozen Ice stage.

Normally, the Gallery couldn't come within ten meters of the duelers, but parent and child were the exception to that rule. Kuroyukihime brought her face mask close to Haruyuki's face. "Even if the reason you were pulled into the Battle Royale space is simple carelessness, the issue at hand is the person who pulled you in. It's essentially not possible to start a BR through an accident of operation. In other words, this person is either so brave that they don't fear the fact that this could be a battle of many against one in the territory of another Legion, or...they have *reason* to believe that they can win even in that situation."

"......! N-no way. An ISS kit user...?"

"It's possible. And if that's the case, you must avoid close combat to the best of your abilities. The enemy's objective might not be simply to win the duel but to spread the kit infection."

"R-right..." After Haruyuki nodded, he glanced up toward the left of his field of view. If this had been a normal duel, the enemy's health gauge and name would have been displayed there, but it was blank now. In Battle Royale mode, you couldn't see the enemy's gauge until you came into contact with that enemy.

The sole piece of information he had was the guide cursor that popped up in the lower part of the center of his field of view, but that only told him the direction of his nearest enemy. It was currently pointing toward the southeast—the direction of Oume Highway—and was changing direction toward the south at a fair speed.

"S-so fast! There's no hesitation in that movement. That's probably the starter. They're coming this way." Together with Kuroyukihime, Haruyuki turned his eyes toward the south of the shopping street. But a loosely curving wall of ice blocked their view, and they couldn't see through to the narrow lane beyond.

"It'd be better to make contact in a bigger space than here. I'm going back to Oume Highway," Haruyuki said.

"Mmm." Kuroyukihime quickly nodded. "Understood. I can't come close once the duel starts, so make sure you take care and stay on guard against any ISS kits."

"Roger! Okay, I'm off, then!" Haruyuki shouted and, whirling around, he started to run, kicking at the snow piled up on the ground.

Large icicles fell occasionally from the ice walls that had once been shops lining either side of the road. Each time he came across one of these, he kicked it to destroy it. They didn't begin to compare with the crystals of the Sacred Ground stage, but even so, his special-attack gauge was charged little by little. These sorts of little acts often decided battles.

Racing along with Silver Crow's speed, he was through the road he'd walked down while directing with Kuroyukihime in a fraction of the time it had taken them to come. He slipped through the large ice arch that had been the commercial district's sign and came out onto Oume Highway to find a pure, snowy field spreading out to the east and west. It would be an endless delight to use one end of the stage to the other and create an enormous snowman, but that would have to be his fun for next time. Right now, he used a boost jump to get to the top of the lump of ice rising up on the northeast corner of the intersection.

Building entry in an Ice stage was impossible—or rather, because the buildings were all transformed into lumps of ice, a special power was required to ascend higher terrain. Since it seemed that his closest enemy was approaching straight down Oume Highway, if he hid here, he would be able to get a look at his opponent first. Haruyuki held his breath and stared hard at the tip of the guide cursor.

However, announcing the true identity of his enemy was not a shadow on the horizon, but a sound. The deep, throaty rumbling that came to him on the wind was more than familiar. It was the sound of what was probably the sole Enhanced Armament in the Accelerated World equipped with an internal combustion engine, a sound he had had so thoroughly beaten into his ears that very morning—the sound of a motorcycle engine.

"H-huh?!" Unconsciously, this slipped out of Haruyuki's mouth, and he jerked his body up from its prone position on the ice wall. At the same time, a yellow headlight shone and glittered in the distance on the white road.

"Wh-what's going on?" Muttering, he flew down to the road surface again, and as if the rider of the American motorcycle had noticed this movement, the bike sped up slightly as it approached. The machine grew larger before his eyes and brake-drifted in, the rear tire kicking up massive amounts of snow. On the parked bike, a familiar skull face snapped the index fingers of both hands at him.

"Hey heeeeeeeey! I know you triple-heart, überlove mighty me, but maybe a surprise duel in Bat-Ro mode is a little too much, yeah?!"

The voice, gesture, and style were definitely those of the Century End rider, aka Ash Roller. And they had made contact, so a gauge with his name inscribed near it appeared in Haruyuki's view. But the words that came out of Ash's mouth didn't make sense to Haruyuki in a number of ways.

"N-no, I don't actually triple-heart, überlove you— Wait, wasn't it *you* who dragged *me* into this battle?!" Haruyuki hurriedly hissed back.

"Whacha talkin'?" A large question mark popped up above the skull helmet. "Me and my magnificent self were just cruuuuising along Loop Seven, geddit? You seriously for real not the starter?"

The way Ash talked made it sound like he had been running down Kannana Street on the motorcycle, but Haruyuki knew that Ash in the real, Rin Kusakabe, was actually on her way home from school in a bus. However, retorting with that here would have been mean-spirited, so he set it aside and spread out his hands.

"Y-yeah, it wasn't me. But then does that mean you always have BR standby on, Ash?"

"*Naturalmente!* Come at me with a battle; I'm buying in!"

"O-of course you would…But, wait—then who started this?"

"Figured you were all up in the works, living in fire town to settle this morning's draw, you know?" Ash sat on the seat of the bike with his arms neatly crossed, and Haruyuki took on the same pose.

"Well, you know, a draw twice in a row is kind of an incomplete burn, though." He shrugged. "But this morning, you charged in while I was in sleepytown."

"No choice at all there. I mean, you with my sis doing that indirect—" Ash had gotten this far in the most casual of tones when suddenly, red flames sprang up in his eye sockets. From the horizontal slit at his mouth, thin puffs of white steam rose up. "And now I rememberrred…That I gotta press you niiiiiiice and flat, Crow."

"I—I—I didn't do anything with Rin, direct or indirect!"

"D-d-direct?! Y-you're no blue! So why you suddenly talkin' 'bout up-close-and-personal?!"

"I'm telling you I didn't do anything! Anyway, Ash, the issue right now is who started this battle! I mean, whoever it was knew that you and me were on the matching list when they pushed the START button, which means they decided that they could win against one of us—or two against one if things went south." Haruyuki earnestly blathered on and on, and "Protective Big Brother" Ash's attention seemed to pull back to the current situation; the steam coming out of his mouth stopped.

But Haruyuki's relief was fleeting. Now it wasn't just steam but also orange exhaust flames gushing out.

"My mighty mega self is tera-burniiiiiiiiing!! This guy thinks he can beat Ash here and the damned crow solo?! Who's this filthy little brat?!"

"I-I'm telling you I want to know that, too! If our luck's bad, it might be like a high ranker, level seven or something—"

"Tch! Your level plus mine makes ten! You think I'd be driving down Kannana shaking in my boots over a level seven?!"

"Th-that's not the point." Haruyuki wanted to cradle his head in his hands.

Suddenly, the north side of an ice wall ten meters to the east exploded with a roar. Worried that it was a red-type long-distance bombardment, Haruyuki started to look up at the sky, but then realized that wasn't it. The thick wall of ice hadn't been destroyed from the outside, but been blown out from the inside.

In other words, one of the people who had dived into this battlefield was reluctant to waste the time it would take to follow the terrain and come out on Oume Highway and had moved in a direct line from the northeast—from the direction of Nakano Station. But the ice walls of the Ice stage were hard—maybe not as hard as objects in a Demon City or Steel stage, but still hard. To destroy one while moving forward, you'd have to be a Burst Linker with flame-type attack power or have some kind of armor that was so strong that ice was not even a thing—

The instant his thoughts reached this point, Haruyuki moaned, "No. Way."

Springing to life in the back of his mind was a scene from the duel in Nakano Area No. 2 after school on Tuesday. Haruyuki had leaned back against the thick wall of the Steel stage and devised a strategy of lying in wait for an enemy who had to approach from either the left or the right. But his enemy had taken him with a surprise attack from a direction he never even imagined—by smashing through the steel wall behind him.

That Burst Linker had super-hard tungsten armor, a level one cloaked in many mysteries. Manganese Blade, a senior member of the Blue Legion, had assessed this young man as a genius, and he had the ability Physical Immune, which repelled all kinds of non-energy attacks.

"Wolfram...Cerberus..." At the same time as Haruyuki uttered the name, a sharply edged silhouette appeared from within the icy fog hanging in the air.

A right foot wrapped in gray metal armor trod heavily through the snow piled up on the road. The system determined that contact had been made, and a second health gauge appeared in the upper right of his field of view. The name displayed there was indeed that of Cerberus. The visor, reminiscent of a wolf's maw, was open about three centimeters, with dark goggles exposed. Haruyuki couldn't see the eye lenses, but he was keenly aware of the strong, focused gaze going right through him.

Stepping over the edge of the large hole in the ice wall onto Oume Highway, Cerberus walked straight toward them, his feet crunching in the snow. He stopped a mere two meters away from Haruyuki and Ash and bowed his head lightly.

"Hey, heeey. Don't know this face. You may be the sta—"

"Was it you who started this, Cerberus?" Haruyuki asked, interrupting Ash.

"Yes, it was me, Crow." The face mask with its sharp design moved up and down once more, and his clear, young boy's voice continued, "I'm glad to see you. I felt certain that *you* would have BR mode on."

Haruyuki couldn't immediately respond. Because the reason

he had Battle Royale standby on was the result of an extremely careless mistake. But this wasn't the time to be worrying about that.

Just like the Cerberus of his avatar name, Wolfram Cerberus had more than two—probably three—personalities in his body. From his attitude, tone, and the fact that his original head was functioning, the one Haruyuki was currently speaking with was the one he had first fought, Cerberus I. This boy was very neat in his language and extremely polite.

When his head visor closed completely and the armor of his left shoulder opened, his personality changed to Cerberus II. That boy was not so fastidious with language, and his tone was fairly rough. But the biggest change was that even the abilities he used switched. The Physical Immune that Cerberus I had was plenty nonstandard, but II's Wolf Down was even more terrifying. Just as the name indicated, this was the power to eat a duel avatar's ability; II had even reproduced Silver Crow's flying ability, albeit for a short time.

Both I and II were fearfully powerful enemies, but in terms of conversation partners, he couldn't help but still be nervous with Cerberus I. Thus, Haruyuki didn't dare correct Cerberus's misunderstanding—and a part of him did indeed want to come off looking good—so he asked another question. "But if your goal was to see me, why go to the trouble of a Battle Royale? I was planning to head over to Naka-Two again tomorrow after school."

"That..." Cerberus trailed off, which was unusual for him, but then he replied, head hanging slightly, "I absolutely had to see—no, fight you today. I waited in Nakano, but it didn't seem that I would get the chance to see you there today, so I moved to Suginami. But this is Nega Nebulus territory, so I can't challenge you here. So I had no choice but a Battle Royale."

"Oh. S-sorry. I actually was planning to go over to Nakano right after school today, but some stuff happened." Haruyuki automatically apologized before cocking his head for the third time. "But you said you *had* to fight me. Why? I mean, I could understand if you *wanted* to fight me…"

"…Please excuse me, Crow. I can't tell you the reason right now. I apologize for my selfishness, but I beg you, please fight me!" He took a step forward. His voice was a shout, one that sounded the tiniest bit cornered.

Vrrrrrrron! But there, the large displacement V-twin engine roared. Silent up to that point, Ash Roller slammed his right hand down on the throttle.

"Whoa, whoaiiiing! You. Totes no clue about you, but your little chitchat, blah-blah here says neeeewb, Level One. You know who we are?! Gotta respect it! Get it? My mighty self's already got a date with this crow here! You wanna fight, you get in line!"

Um, Ash, that—you're assuming you'll beat me, aren't you?

Before Haruyuki could snap out this sharp retort, Cerberus said in a low voice, eyes still fixed straight ahead, "Excuse me, but please don't get in the way. The only one I want to fight is Crow. I don't know who you are, but I have no business with you."

Instantly, clouds of angry white steam puffed out from Ash Roller's mouth once more. "Y-you braaaaat! Now you've gone and done it, yeah?! So pretty please sorry, I'm not the Gallery. This here's Bat-Ro. Lemme giga burn that into your peewee braaaain!"

Before Haruyuki had time to stop him, Ash had kicked at the shift pedal and was accelerating full throttle. Snow spun up, and the front tire he yanked up high charged toward Cerberus's head.

Ka-klank! The sound of impact roared through the stage, and a spray of snow danced up like smoke. With hands half-raised, Haruyuki waited for his field of view to clear. The sight that finally appeared was—surprising.

The small Cerberus had caught the front tire of the motorcycle with his crossed arms. He had dropped his hips down low, but his knees weren't touching the ground. If Haruyuki had tried the same thing, he would definitely have been unable to support the heavy weight—easily exceeding two hundred kilograms—and he would have been pushed backward, sparks shooting from every joint on his body. When he had once lifted the rear wheel of the bike a mere ten centimeters, he had taken more than a little damage to both arms.

"Ah! Wha—?! You— Damned brat!" Ash Roller stood up from his seat and pushed the weight of his body hard against the handlebars, but Cerberus did not sink down. The visor on his head was still open, so Physical Immune wouldn't have been activated, and beyond that, it was unclear as to whether or not that ability was effective against pressure damage.

In short, Cerberus wasn't just hard, he was also tough. Now that Haruyuki thought about it, when Cerberus had collided head-on with the heavyweight Frost Horn, instead of being knocked back, he had braced his feet and stopped the onslaught. That wasn't something you could do without some serious load-bearing capacity and impact resistance. In other words, locking techniques probably wouldn't work on Cerberus, either. Haruyuki added another line to the list in his head.

"Tera suuuuuuuucks!" Ash shouted in exasperation. "I am gonna seriously crush yooooooou!" Still standing on the pegs, he twisted the accelerator in his right hand, so Haruyuki made a big X with both arms.

"I-it's no use, Ash! If you open the throttle there—"

But it was already too late. The rear tire in contact with the ground spun fiercely, and inevitably, the motorcycle brought the front wheel up once again.

"Unh...aaaaah!" Without missing his chance, Cerberus howled sharply, as he stretched out his arms like a stiff spring. Its front wheel thrust up from below, the motorcycle moved into a basically vertical position, and the vehicle body wobbled in all directions.

"No—no?! Noooooooo!!" Ash tried desperately to bring down the bike in front, clutching the handlebars all the while, but the vehicle body instead slowly inclined to the rear and finally flipped over into the snow, engine racing emptily. There was a cry of "Hnrrk!" from beneath the massive engine block, accompanied by red damage light, and Ash's health gauge displayed in the upper right of Haruyuki's field of view dropped to around 10 percent.

Fortunately, the snow below him was deep, and he managed to escape any further pressure damage. But Ash was apparently unable to lift the bike off himself. Cursing like a sailor, the century-end rider kicked and flailed.

"H-hold on, Ash." Haruyuki started to hurry over to him. "I'll get the bike—"

However, a sharply edged silhouette blocked his way. Wolfram Cerberus, of course, but he seemed somehow different from before. A powerful wave of brooding torment came drifting out from the gap in his wolflike visor.

"Crow. I'll ask you again. Please...fight me." The clear, high-pitched voice of the young boy reminded Haruyuki for some reason of metal under pressure, on the verge of shattering.

He stopped and looked hard at his opponent's eyes hidden beneath goggles. "I asked you this before, too, but why are you in such a rush to fight? I get that you'd want a revenge match for yesterday. But you totally crushed me the time before that and all. If today couldn't happen, then wouldn't tomorrow be just fine?"

"That will be too late!" Cerberus suddenly howled, and Haruyuki swallowed hard. The gray-metal avatar clenched his hands into tight fists and continued, almost forcing the words out. "I—I have to keep winning! If I don't keep winning, I won't be me anymore!"

"Wh-what are you talking about, Cerberus?! Sometimes you win duels, sometimes you lose, right?! That's the way everyone gets stronger, bit by bit—"

"I don't have that kind of time!!" The shout that interrupted Haruyuki sounded more like a scream. "I—I have to prove I'm worthy of being Wolfram Cerberus! For that...my only choice is to win against you right now, Silver Crow!!"

The words dispersed through the stage with a physical pressure and violently shook the diamond dust hanging in the sky. As if to say the conversation was over, Cerberus brandished his fists high and brought them out to his sides before slamming them together in front of his chest. Receiving the motion command to activate his ability, the visor patterned after the maw of a beast slammed shut. He had shifted into the Physical Immune state.

"So I guess we'll say the rest with our fists, then," Haruyuki murmured. "Got it. We'll fight. We are Burst Linkers, after all."

The instant he heard these words, Cerberus's slender body shook slightly, but he quickly nodded.

"Sorry, Ash. Hold on a minute!" The man in question was still kicking and struggling beneath the bike. Haruyuki jumped back; glancing at the time, he saw there were still just under 1,200 seconds left. A fight with Cerberus, whose fighting style resembled his own, was likely to be resolved in a short time, so that was plenty of time to decide this. Haruyuki lowered his stance in the center of broad Oume Highway, readied his hands in front of him, and shouted, "Come!!"

A voice came in response immediately. "On my way!"

A massive amount of snow rolled up from Cerberus's feet with a *whump*. Haruyuki focused all five of his senses on the figure charging at him in a straight line. His dash power was, as before, explosive, but the snow piled up on the ground hindered him, and his speed was slower—albeit only slightly—than in the Storm stage of the previous day.

You won't beat me with the same strategy! Haruyuki shouted in his heart, and pulled his left foot in leisurely.

Cerberus spun his body around and launched a right mid-kick. Crushing even the atoms of ice dancing in the air, the kick closed in on Haruyuki. He caught it gently with the palm of his right hand and turned his own body suddenly to the left, pulling in the direction of the spin's momentum, and grabbed Cerberus's ankle with his left hand.

"Sheeah!" With a short battle cry, he went for a throw to leap on Cerberus and crush him. Just like the day before, Cerberus's direct, rigid technique was caught by Haruyuki's Guard Reversal, and his head met the ground—

Whud! The instant clouds of snow flew up with a wet sound, Haruyuki finally realized that this development was not Cerberus's strategic failure, but his own.

The lone source of damage for Wolfram Cerberus in Physical Immune state was throwing techniques, but in an Ice stage, the effect of those throws was halved because the snow covering the ground acted as a cushion. Cerberus's health gauge dropped by just under 10 percent after being thrown, and he wasn't stunned like he had been the previous day, and he wrapped his arms and legs around Haruyuki from below.

"Nngh!" Haruyuki desperately tried to break away, but the sharply tapered edges of Cerberus's armor caught him like thorns. The wolf avatar was glued to his front, his arms around Haruyuki's chest, and his legs around his waist, holding him fast.

"This is one other method of using Physical Immune."

Immediately after he heard this whispered voice in his ear, an incredible pressure assaulted his chest and stomach. Crow's metal armor creaked eerily, abnormally, and orange sparks shot off in all directions. The gauge in the upper left of his field of view was mercilessly shaved away.

Although the majority of Burst Linkers had mouths, they had no need to breathe. Thus, underwater or in outer space, or when their throats or chests were being constricted, there was no suffocation damage. The reason Haruyuki's gauge was nevertheless decreasing was because he was taking physical pressure damage. The bare-handed restraint technique was something Haruyuki's metal armor would have been able to resist, had the overwhelming strength of Cerberus's armor not brought it up into the land of special attack.

Of. Course. Even as he suffered through this crushing of his body, Haruyuki seriously admired Cerberus.

"Assume the techniques you showed Cerberus in the duel

yesterday won't work on him today," Kuroyukihime had said during the special training with Haruyuki the day before at lunch together with Fuko. Thus, Haruyuki had made free use of the Guard Reversal he hadn't used initially and won. But Cerberus was already responding to those techniques in the span of a single day.

"You're strong, Cerberus. Really strong." Haruyuki pushed the words out from his constricted chest, as he endured the pain. He had said only moments before that they'd talk with their fists, but he simply could not go without asking. "So. What is making you panic like this? You said you'll stop being yourself if you don't keep winning...What does that mean?"

He didn't think he'd get an answer. But in a surprise twist, an extremely quiet voice came once more from the face before his eyes.

"That...is because, just like number two, who you fought yesterday...I, number one, am also nothing more than a spare."

"A-a spare?"

"Yes. Number two and myself are only permitted to be Cerberus during the time we are performing our respective roles. And my role...is to win duels. A tool to simply win and stock up points."

Haruyuki forgot for a moment what a desperate situation he was in and set his brain to work at full power. Cerberus II, appearing at the end of the duel the previous day, had said he was "number two," living in the avatar's left shoulder. "Because I was tuned for a certain purpose." And: "Equip that thing that you sealed off somewhere."

Haruyuki assumed "that thing" indicated the cursed Enhanced Armament the Disaster. If the role of II was to control the Armor of Catastrophe, then the role of I was to build up Burst Points. Was that it?

"So is that the reason you're still at level one? To increase the number of Burst Points when you win a duel," Haruyuki murmured.

"That's right." The head stuck to him nodded slightly. "Therefore, I have to continue to win. I have to win…and continue to prove that I am a useful tool."

The instant he heard these words through the armor pressed up against him, something burst into red flames deep inside Haruyuki. He remembered how he had told his parent Kuroyukihime something similar back when he first became a Burst Linker. Saying that she knew that he was actually just a disposable pawn, a tool to simply be given orders, like it was the appropriate way to treat someone like him. Hearing this, Kuroyukihime had slapped his cheek, and tears had welled up in her eyes. It was likely in that moment that Haruyuki had become a true Burst Linker.

"Prove you're a useful tool? To whom? Your parent? Comrades? Or maybe your Legion Master?" Cerberus didn't make a move to answer this interrogation from Haruyuki, whose rage was bleeding into the questions. Regardless, however, Haruyuki continued to shout, choking up as he did: "That kind of proof, there's no value in that! The only thing a Burst Linker has to prove is the strength of their heart! And the one they prove that to is always and only their own self!"

"Then…please prove that right now!" Now Cerberus shouted, his voice burning with several kinds of emotion. "For you, this duel is nothing more than one fight among hundreds! So even if you lose, no one will abandon you! But it's different for me! *I* have to win every duel! If you're saying that my proof is a fake, and yours is the real thing, then prove it right now! Please win against me here and now, Silver Crow!!"

As the shriek grew louder, the pressure of the bear hug increased. His physical strength itself didn't match that of a large blue-type avatar, but his armor, boasting an absolute hardness, was a weapon in and of itself. Crow's silver armor grew dented, holes gouged out by Cerberus's edges.

Haruyuki had just under 30 percent left in his health gauge. At this rate, he wouldn't last another minute before being blasted away. Even so, Haruyuki nodded his helmet firmly. "Understood. I'll prove it."

He had no sooner made this brief statement than he was placing both hands on Cerberus's head and trying with all his strength to tear him off. This was normally the place where he would attack with blows if his hands were free, but punches and elbows wouldn't work on Cerberus while Physical Immune was activated.

"Nngh…aaah!" A groan slipping out of him, he strained his arms desperately, but even when their two masks were fifty centimeters apart, the arms Cerberus had wrapped around his back showed absolutely no sign of releasing him. In fact, the pressure damage increased due to Haruyuki's efforts, and the speed of his gauge's decrease accelerated.

"It's no use, Crow. I've been shown a vault's worth of material on you. You have no means of turning a situation like this around." The voice that came from the visor pinning him down had regained its quiet.

Those words were definitely not a boast. His special-attack gauge was fully charged, so he could have flown up to a high altitude with Cerberus still hanging on to him and slammed into the ground with a sudden drop to do damage, but Haruyuki's back—the part that deployed his silver wings—was currently held fast. If he tried to force them open, he might actually damage his wings instead.

So the reason Cerberus had used his restraint technique on Haruyuki's chest rather than his more fragile head was because he was aiming to render his flying ability useless. He really had somehow looked into Silver Crow's weak points. Haruyuki was curious about who exactly had prepared those materials, but he had more important things to deal with at the moment.

"Then those materials were apparently…not complete," he said with a groan, and he mustered up every ounce of strength he had to stretch his arms out all the way. Sparks scattered not only from his constricted chest but also from his shoulders and elbows. Their two masks were nearly a meter apart, but even still, Cerberus's arms would not let go. However, that was not Haruyuki's aim.

A mere meter. To create this distance, he had accelerated the loss of his already negligible gauge.

"Unh…aaaaaaah!!" Shouting, Haruyuki released his arms and quickly crossed them before his eyes.

Rrrk! The air shook, and a pure white light gushed from Silver Crow's mirrored visor.

"Wha…?" Cerberus gasped, hoarse.

Haruyuki glared at the goggles, which had narrowed to centimeter-long slits, before flinging his arms open and shouting the technique name.

"Head…buuuuuuuuuutt!!"

Drawing out a trail of light like a comet, the round helmet charged downward diagonally at an incredible speed. Instantly, his head crossed the meter between them and slammed into Cerberus's face. The impact, enough to make the stage shudder, radiated outward and sent the piles of snow around them flying off into the distance.

If this had been an ordinary head butt, it would, of course, not have broken the protection of Physical Immune; it would, in fact, have shattered Crow's visor. But what Haruyuki launched was Silver Crow's level-one special-attack Head Butt. Its range was small, and the pre-motion was long, so normally, even when he did bring it out, it didn't make contact. In fact, the first time he had deployed it, a moment that should have been commemorated, he'd been shamefully crushed by Ash Roller's motorcycle before it activated, so he had basically gone entirely without using it ever since.

Thus, the majority of Burst Linkers wouldn't even know of the existence of this technique, and the reference materials Cerberus had seen would be no exception to that. And even if in the unlikely case that it was noted there, the detailed characteristics of the technique would absolutely not have been.

The damage characteristics for Head Butt were half-physical/striking and half-energy/light. A light energy attack had the exact opposite characteristics as the nihilistic energy attack best represented by Dark Blow and was falsely similar to a laser attack. With no heat, it pierced essentially any armor and gave a pure impact with no directionality. In other words, even if half of the Head Butt power was repelled by Cerberus's Physical Immune, the other half would reach him.

And there was one more thing. The majority of close-range special attacks canceled out any reaction damage, no matter what the target of the attack. Attacking with a normal head butt would have carved away Haruyuki's own gauge, but right now—

"*Nngah!*" Cerberus cried out, showered in the entirely unexpected, extremely close-range impact, while at the same time, he released the hold of his arms. This one instant knocked him onto his back on the exposed white road. Just like the day before, throwing damage was applied, and the health gauge that had dropped more than 30 percent in the initial impact decreased another 30 percent.

Half-embedded in the hard road by the impact, Cerberus boldly attempted an immediate counterattack. He reached out once more and attempted to grab ahold of Crow, who dropped down a moment later.

But Haruyuki's own hands flashed out lightning quick to seize Cerberus's arms instead, and the metallic wings on his back, now free, were deployed to the fullest.

"Ah...Aaaaaah!" The battle cry pouring out of him, he peeled the heavy metal avatar off the road surface and ascended vertically upward at top speed. In the blink of an eye, he had reached an altitude of nearly a hundred meters.

Hazy sunlight pushed through the clouds high up in the distance to make the Ice stage glitter beautifully, the pure white of snow and the pale blue of ice. With Cerberus dangling from his hands, Haruyuki went into hovering mode, and the two avatars were also wrapped in the spectacular silver light.

Wolfram Cerberus didn't so much as twitch. Haruyuki thought that maybe the personality switch had happened again, but that didn't seem to be the case. The visor covering the original face opened with a *clack*.

Cerberus looked around at the icy world that continued to the far-off horizon with the exposed black goggles. "I had no idea… So you can see this far even in a normal duel stage, hmm?"

"Yeah. This world's infinite," Haruyuki replied, and then continued after a brief pause. "There's still a ton of things you don't know about the Accelerated World, Cerberus. It's the same for me, though. Sometimes, I think that even the wins and losses of the duels are really nothing more than one element of this world."

"One…element," Cerberus murmured in a voice that was almost inaudible.

"Yeah." Haruyuki nodded deeply. "A long time ago, in that hospital you can see over there"—as he spoke, he fine-tuned the direction of his body to make it so that the large hospital soaring up to the northeast of Asagaya Station would enter Cerberus's field of view—"I fought a close friend. It ended up with me dangling him just like this. He was on the verge of total point loss, and I was about to drop him to the ground."

"…"

"…But I couldn't. And not because he was my friend. It wasn't because I felt sorry for him, either. It was because I realized that what decides the meaning of the duel isn't the BB system; it's us. We fight to get Burst Points, go up levels, and get stronger. But that's not everything. I'm sure there's something bigger that we win and lose in the duels."

"And…what is that?"

"I still don't know. But I think if I fight—no, live in this world with my friends, someday I'll find out."

"…"

Shifting his gaze from the hospital in the distance to Wolfram Cerberus, silent once more, Haruyuki gasped and opened his eyes wide.

Because he saw glittering droplets of ice falling from the edges of the goggles he could spy beyond the visor patterned after a wolf's maw. It wasn't that the diamond dust dancing about the stage had gotten stuck there. They were frozen tears.

"…I, too." His voice trembling, Cerberus moved his hands and grabbed onto Haruyuki's arms from below, his own wrists clasped by Haruyuki's hands. "I, too…would like…to know that. If there is something in this world…more important than winning fights…I would like to…see it."

"You'll get to," Haruyuki said, pushing back whatever it was welling up inside him, and then took a deep breath, about to continue with "Come with me" in a firm voice. But he didn't get to utter those words.

A pale-purple light reaching up from somewhere on the ground quickly pierced his left wing. A little after that, *bwwan!* He heard the high-pitched sound of vibration.

"Ngah?!" Haruyuki cried out in surprise.

"Aaah!" A shriek slipped out of Cerberus as well. He sounded almost like he knew the true form of the light, but before Haruyuki had time to check, he was plunging to the ground in a tailspin.

He tried desperately to get his body under control with just his right wing, but he couldn't manage it with the heavy Cerberus dangling from his hands. To at least not have damage for a fall from up high applied to him, he forced a reverse thrust as they were on the verge of slamming into the ground and somehow managed a soft landing.

The place where they came down, kicking up snow, was about fifty meters to the west of the original intersection. Having finally gotten out from under the bike in the intersection, Ash Roller was for some reason pointing the index fingers of both hands intently to somewhere on the west side.

Pulled in, Haruyuki looked in that direction.

Bwwwan! He heard the sound again. A purple light shone on the roof of a five-story building, and at almost the same time, an incredible heat pierced his right shoulder. Combined with the previous blow, it brought the remainder of his health gauge down to less than 10 percent.

"Ngaaah!" Haruyuki collapsed with a moan.

In front of him, a figure blocked the way, arms spread out. Cerberus.

"Wh-why?! It's supposed to be my role to fight Silver Crow!!" Once more, a shout that was a shriek. These words made it clear that he knew the attacker behind the purple laser.

Pressing on the injured area of his right shoulder with his left hand, Haruyuki stared intently at the roof of the building. It appeared that someone was standing there, but they were back-lit; he could only make out a silhouette. Slender body, dispropor-tionately large head. This figure raised the right hand that had been on its hip, popped up one finger, and lightly waved it.

"Not like I wanna be doin' this sorta thug stuff, Onesie." A girl's smiling voice.

He had heard that Kansai accent before. More than heard it—knew it. It was the voice he had heard by his side when he had been made to stand on the witness stand at the meeting of the Seven Kings a mere four days earlier.

"Argon Array." The instant Haruyuki called the name in a trembling voice, the sunlight was blocked by the clouds again, and the silhouette took on color.

Pale-purple armor covered her entire body. She wore a large hat, and the upper half of her face was hidden by large goggles with round lenses. On the front of the hat, two lenses even larger than the goggles were embedded; one was covered by a shutter, while the other was exposed.

Argon Array—also known as the Quad Eyes Analyst—had the unique ability of being able to see the status of other Burst Linkers. Thus, she was given her nickname, or put another way, Haruyuki had been convinced this meant she was a type with no remarkable abilities, but...

"So then why are you interrupt—?" Cerberus started to say in a hoarse voice, and purple light flashed.

The source of the light was the lenses on Argon Array's hat.

Rather than targeting Haruyuki this time, the thin laser that reached out from there, with an audible vibration, passed beside Cerberus's head and dug deep into the ice wall behind them.

"Interrupt? You're awful, Onesie. I was jus' helpin' you. Now quit messin' around and take the boyo's points already. Otherwise"—she was nearly thirty meters away, but even so, Haruyuki could see the cheerful and yet freezing chill-inducing grin that popped up on her face—"this time fer sure, Threezie'll come out?"

This statement was meaningless to Haruyuki, but as soon as he heard it, Cerberus shuddered noticeably. The angle of the arms raised to protect Haruyuki dropped slightly. However, his gray hands were clenched into tight fists. The small level-one Burst Linker looked directly at Argon, already at level eight.

"I...I don't want to fight only to earn points anymore!" he shouted. "Crow taught me something! That there's something in this world...more important that points, than winning and losing—"

Bwaaaan!

The fourth laser shot hit Cerberus's left side. The beam of light, narrowed down to the diameter of a needle, easily pierced the super-hard tungsten armor and its absolute resistance to all physical attacks, and the health gauge with over 30 percent left in it was instantly whittled down to less than 10 percent.

Cerberus staggered and almost fell backward, but Haruyuki caught him with outstretched arms. However, with no strength in his body, he dropped to his knees in the snow.

"Tut-tut, Onesie!" Argon said in a voice that even now did not lose its sunshine, even as she looked down on the two crouched helplessly on the ground. "No talkin' back to me now. Your job's to get loads of points, yeah? You don't need to think about nothin' else. I mean—"

Her speech was interrupted by the sudden roar of an engine. Followed by a voice shouting even louder.

"Tera suuuuuuuuucks!"

Haruyuki shifted his gaze and saw that, having gotten back on his motorcycle again in the intersection off to the east, Ash Roller's eyes burned with flames of unprecedented rage.

"Hey! Four-Eyed Violet up there! Quit yer smaaack taaaalk! Mighty Me! Is gonna give you a lesson! Time to mean the dueeeeeeel!" Red exhaust flames jetted out of the double muffler, and the longhorn motorcycle charged in a straight line toward the building upon which Argon stood.

"A-Ash!" Haruyuki shouted desperately. "No! Run—"

The laser that shot forth cruelly punched out the headlight of the bike and apparently kept going to pierce and ignite the gas tank. The bike was enveloped in hot, red flames struck through with black smoke.

Even as it burned, momentum propelled it forward for a while, but eventually, the bike fell over on its side, and Ash staggered a few steps away from it before pitching forward and collapsing. Perhaps stunned from the serious explosion damage, he showed no signs of getting to his feet again. His health gauge was, like Haruyuki and Cerberus's, down to 10 percent.

"Ah…Aah…"

This was not the Unlimited Neutral Field, but rather the Battle Royale variation of the regular duel space. Thus, even if Haruyuki's gauge did drop to zero, the number of his battle losses would go up by one, and his points would drop by however much, and with that, he could escape from the stage. Even still, a cry of anguish slipped out of his mouth, and tears filled his eyes.

The exchange of Burst Points was not the end-all for the duel. There was surely something bigger that they were winning and losing. Haruyuki had said that to Cerberus earlier. Argon Array's merciless and overwhelming attack was taking something precious away from Haruyuki, Ash, and Cerberus. His tears were for that. Although he wanted to take that something back, to stand and face her, his body wouldn't move. Still holding Cerberus, Haruyuki looked up at Argon, who stood atop the building.

"That's that, then." The Analyst smiled again. "Guess we'll have to call it a day here. Lucky, huh, boyo? Gettin' killed by me, you won't lose too many points. Rest easy."

A purple light was lodged in the hat lens targeting Haruyuki. Before his eyes, it grew brighter and stronger, and finally focused on one point—

Glint!

What shone was not the laser. A blue glimmer flew in from somewhere and scraped Argon's left shoulder. A second shot, and a third. Pouring down one shot after the next were not lasers, but ice. Ice lances with sharp tips like needles.

Interrupting her own shot to dodge the others, Argon was pushed to the edge of the roof before the barrage of lances finally stopped.

The smile gone from her face, Argon shot a glare outward, and Haruyuki absently followed her gaze. There was a building about the same height on the north side, with Oume Highway in between them. A fifth Burst Linker stood on the southeast corner of that building, clad in an aqua blue even more transparent than the lances.

It was indeed a female type, but the form wavered unsteadily because her entire body was covered in a clear, flowing liquid— water. Perhaps due to the chill of the Ice stage, particles of ice were mixed in with the water, and these made the avatar's entire body glitter like diamonds.

The eyes that shone with a pale light in the flowing lines of the face mask locked on Argon Array, and the mysterious water avatar spoke in a quiet yet powerful voice.

"You're the one who's going to be crushed by a level one and lose a lot of points."

Somewhere deep, deep in Haruyuki's memory, he could hear the babbling of flowing water.

To be continued.

AFTERWORD

Reki Kawahara here bringing you *Accel World 12: The Red Crest*.

I'm sure all of you kind enough to read the novel now understand the meaning of the title, but in this volume, I finally was able to clarify the details of the incident in which the total point loss of first Red King was brought about by the Black King, an incident which has been teased out endlessly since volume one.

I have the bad habit of adding one thing after another to premises in the story, but unusually for me, this incident is just as I initially conceived of it. Her appearance is finally…well, not yet, but her name's out there now. (lol) I hope you will wait for the next book to see how Kuroyukihime and Haruyuki face the White King, White Cosmos! Please! In other words, I've continued to expand the story again this time, and I am sorry!

Now then, additionally in this volume, we have the appearance of Chocolat Puppeteer, one of the duel avatars I adopted from the Accel World Avatar Contest that I informed you of in the last afterword. She ended up having a more critical role than I was expecting, and I, too, am both delighted and surprised by this. But what was even more unexpected was that my editor, Miki, is quite attached to little Chocolat. (lol) To the instruction of "More licking scenes," I replied, "But this is an avatar!" In response, I got, "So it's fine, then!" *I see! Yes, of course!* I thought, so I put in lots of licking. Nagomi Kiya, designer of this avatar, I am so sorry! And thank you very much!

With regard to the avatar contest, I will announce another three of the works entered in the second round for use as avatars in the novels. They'll also appear in turn (although the space each gets will likely be different…), so look forward to that!

Around the time this volume comes out, I believe the TV anime will be reaching its climax. Meanwhile, Aqua Current, one of the Four Elements and a character appearing in episodes six and seven of the anime (in Volume 10 of the novels), has finally managed to reappear in this volume. I intend for her to be a regular starting with the next volume, but this means that there will be yet another girl around Haruyuki, which does fill one with trepidation, doesn't it!

To my illustrator, HIMA, who drew amazing and adorable looks for all the new characters appearing one after another in this volume, including Aqua Current; and to my beleaguered editor, Miki, to whom I gave an entirely different manuscript from the meeting we had in advance—thank you so much.

Volume 13 is scheduled to come out a little later than usual, but the next book for sure should finish this stage, so I hope you'll join me again!

Reki Kawahara
On a certain day in June 2012

SKY-BLUE WINGS

ⅡⅡⅡⅡワ: ▢▶ⅡⅡ◰ⅡⅡ▶ⅡⅡⅡⅡⅡⅡ千」
━ⅡⅡⅡⅡⅡ匚ⅡⅡⅡ屮ⅡⅡⅡⅡⅡⅡ◀」: ▼
千ⅡⅡⅡⅡ▪ⅡⅡⅡⅡⅡ力▪ⅡⅡⅡ▪」。

1

The world was spinning. He was profoundly dizzy, like he'd been hit with Silly-Go-Round, Yellow Radio's special attack, but that was impossible. Because this was the real world—the Arita living room, on the twenty-third floor of a high-rise condo in northern Koenji.

What made Haruyuki stagger, his body pitch back and forth, and his field of view spin back and forth, around and around, was definitely not fever or alcohol or some strange mushroom. The VR space Kuroyukihime had created—code name: ZG01—he had just dived into was having an intense effect on his sense of balance even after he linked out.

"Unh…Ooep…" Finally, a curious noise slipped out of his mouth, and Haruyuki hurriedly pressed his hands against his belly. But the sensation of his stomach trying to turn itself inside out would not leave him.

"W-we can handle it…Be strong, Haruyuki!"

When he somehow managed to turn his gaze in the direction of this voice, he saw Kuroyukihime sitting on the sofa immediately to one side, her pale head bobbing. He couldn't exactly have a full reverse of the spaghetti with cod roe that his beloved swordmaster had personally cooked for him an hour earlier, not right before her eyes. Maybe it was the standing that was making him dizzy; he took a step back to sit down himself.

But his body lurched once more, knocking him off his intended course by about thirty degrees to the left and back. There was no way he'd be able to correct his trajectory now. Half falling, he set his backside down heavily.

Instead of the harder elasticity of the leather sofa, an extremely enticing sensation, soft and gentle, enveloped him from his bottom up to his back. At the same time, a kind voice remarked in his ear, "Oh my! Are you all right, Corvus?"

After struggling to make his spinning head understand what had happened, he finally figured it out. Apparently, he had somehow sat down not on the sofa, but on the lap of the third person in the room.

"Eeah! Whah! S-s-s-s-sorry!" He hurriedly tried to stand up, but before he could, supple arms reached out from behind him and squeezed his chest.

"It's fine. See? Bad feelings, fly away!"

As the owner of the voice spoke, she caressed his chest, and his nausea did actually recede, leaving him totally dumbfounded. Still on the lap of Fuko Kurasaki, who apparently could use de-buff abilities in the real world, he marveled that the distinct drunkenness of just a moment earlier could vanish just like that.

"Exactly how long are you going to be held like that, you?!" Having recovered from her dizziness seemingly under her own power, Kuroyukihime had no sooner picked up a tea cake from the glass table than she was shooting it at Haruyuki's forehead.

Five minutes later.

"I know you went to the trouble of making that VR space, Kuroyukihime," Haruyuki said with a sigh as he rubbed his forehead, his senses having at last returned to normal. "But it's a little too rough. My eyes were spinning while we were inside, too, but I can't believe it made us this sick even after dropping out."

"Mmm. I also didn't believe it would be to this extent. But, Fuko, why are you the only one here who's fine?!"

The sudden focus of both Haruyuki and Kuroyukihime's eyes, Fuko brought her glass of iced tea to her lips with a composed look and smiled brightly. "I've never been the type to get motion sick. I'm completely fine in cars and 2-D racing games."

Her "2-D" here meant the type of game that opened up in a game window in a flat screen on her virtual desktop, rather than a full-dive type. In other words, the player's five senses continued as they were in the real world, so that the G changes due to acceleration and cornering of the vehicle were not in the slightest agreement with the other car behavior within the racing game.

Haruyuki suppressed the urge to "ooep" again just picturing it and brought a lifeless smile to his lips. "Th-that's amazing. I thought I was pretty tough when it came to car sickness, too, but with this today, I give up."

"Hee-hee-hee! You just have to get used to it little by little, Corvus. The evening is still young, after all."

"Y-you plan to keep going?" he asked, the smile frozen on his face.

"Of course." Fuko nodded as if it were the most obvious thing in the world and turned her eyes on Kuroyukihime, who was sunk into the sofa across from her. "Sacchi went to all the trouble and hard work of making it, that completely zero-gravity VR space. Normally, it's impossible to activate something like that."

True enough. Kuroyukihime's nickname for the handmade ZG01 was short for Zero Gravity No. 1. Until a few minutes earlier, the three Burst Linkers had been on a full dive into a virtual world where the sensation of gravity was completely canceled out. The loading of such worlds, however, was prohibited by every Neurolinker company in a voluntary restraint.

Naturally, this app was completely unconnected with Brain Burst, so the time they'd dived was a mere fifteen minutes. Even so, Haruyuki's sense of balance had been completely paralyzed, and the instant they returned to reality, he had been assaulted by an intense gravity sickness. The reason Kuroyukihime had taken such pains to create a 0G space—a space that had pretty much convinced him that this *was* something manufacturers should regulate—however, was directly related to Brain Burst.

Because, currently, the Accelerated World was afire with a single rumor: that exactly one month after the Hermes' Cord race, on the upcoming July 5, a new stage would be supplied for normal duels—and that this stage would be the completely weightless environment of the Space stage.

"If that rumor's true, then it'll make a huge difference if we're used to the sensation of zero G, after all." When Haruyuki said this half to himself, he clenched both hands tight and then continued, "I'll keep trying. At the very least, I'll get so that I don't get sick! Kuroyukihime, let's go again!"

But Kuroyukihime did not immediately respond to this forceful declaration. Looking like she was about to slide off the sofa onto the floor at any moment, she remained silent, her eyes still closed. Normally, this was the sort of situation where she would immediately come back with something like "Mmm, that's the spirit!" so he wasn't sure what was going on, and he watched over her hesitantly.

A few seconds later her eyelids finally lifted, and her black eyes stared at the ceiling, a little sluggishly. Through barely parted lips, a single word fell out into the world. "...Bath."

"Wh-what?"

"I'm taking a bath." Kuroyukihime stood up, her upper body wobbling unsteadily, still in her uniform because she had come to the Arita house directly from school. Fuko supposedly stopped at home on her way, but for some reason, she too was wearing her high school uniform.

Kuroyukihime staggered to a corner of the living room and hoisted up a large sports bag that apparently held a change of clothes, and Fuko stood as well, with a smile that was almost fondly exasperated.

"Excuse us, Corvus. We'll be getting in the bath first. I'm just going to go and take care of Sacchi. In that condition, she's likely to drown in the tub."

"Y-yuh?" Still frozen solid, Haruyuki thought for a moment and finally understood that Fuko was basically saying, "I'm going to take a bath with Kuroyukihime." The bath had been run, but he'd thought they were going to use it after their weight-lessness training was over, so this was a bit of a surprise attack; his thoughts couldn't keep up.

"Y-yuh! Please, t-t-t-t-take your time!" Even so, he somehow shifted to vertical mode on the sofa and tried to see the two girls off.

Supporting the still-staggering Kuroyukihime with her right hand, Fuko opened the living room door with her left hand. But then she turned around slowly. "What do you think? Since we're all here, perhaps you'd like to jaeen—"

The last word fell apart thanks to Kuroyukihime's fingers flashing out lightning fast to grab Fuko's cheek.

"Hauch, hauch, Sacchi!" Fuko cried out lightly with a smile as Kuroyukihime dragged her in the opposite direction and disappeared into the hallway. When Fuko's left hand, waving merrily in his direction, pulled back and shut the door with a bang, Haruyuki exhaled all at once the breath he had been holding.

Slithering down deep into the sofa, he looked at the analogue clock on the wall. The two hands were indicating that eight o'clock had finally rolled around. He wasn't sure if it was because this was the last Friday in June, but he had gotten an e-mail from his mother to the effect that she wouldn't be home that day, which meant the night was still young.

At any rate, the purpose of this gathering was Space-stage special training, so when it came down to it, the other three members of Nega Nebulus—Takumu, Chiyuri, and Utai—should have had every right to be there, too. But there was a reason why only Kuroyukihime and Fuko were taking part, and why they had both come prepared with sleepover kits.

On the night before the Hermes' Cord race approximately one month earlier, heavy rain, followed by thunder and lightning, had triggered network outages—so Kuroyukihime had stayed over at Haruyuki's for the first time. And the next morning, Fuko had arrived at the Arita house, the base of their race sortie, a fair bit earlier than the set time and had clearly witnessed a pajama-clad Kuroyukihime coming out of Haruyuki's room and disappearing with a yawn into the washroom.

Haruyuki and Kuroyukihime took turns explaining, and after acknowledging at any rate the inevitability of the situation, Fuko had declared, Raker Smile fully deployed, "Please invite me to a sleepover as well sometime this month. Under that condition, I would be delighted to keep this quiet."

For Haruyuki, he was certain it was at best a joke, or in the event that it wasn't, that she would forget over the course of the month. But. When he saw her in the Accelerated World the other day, Fuko had smiled gently and—with the utterance, "June's almost over, you know? ♥"—had made him aware that her declaration had neither been a joke nor faded away into obscurity. After discussing it with the other concerned party (Kuroyukihime) and shaking all the while, this and that had happened to lead to the present situation. In other words, what was supposedly a session of weightlessness training for the three of them was also a stormy sleepover.

Naturally, it absolutely was not the case that he was unhappy his beloved Legion Master and Submaster had come over to hang out. However, that said, he didn't have the mental leeway to simply have fun. Because Kuroyukihime and Fuko (and this was also something he was glad for, but) both had the powerful conceit of being Silver Crow's teacher, and when they were together, they had a tendency to try to drill him, with a strange rivalry sparking between them. If they ended up saying something about a little instruction in the Accelerated World while they were at it once the 0G training was over—actually, yeah, that would almost certainly happen.

"I wonder what'd happen if I ran away to Chiyu's place right now," Haruyuki murmured, pulling his body back into the sofa.

Chiyuri Kurashima, who lived two floors down, was likely to cover for him, grumbling about it as she did so, but he probably couldn't escape the super-sensitive radars of Kuroyukihime and Fuko at that distance. In which case, Takumu's house in the neighboring building— No, wait, what about Utai Shinomiya's house on the southern side of Suginami Ward, or the cake shop occupied by the Red Legion Prominence in even more far-off Sakuradai in Nerima Ward...?

Then, at that moment: *klink-a-ring!* Together with the light sound effect, a window opened to fill Haruyuki's virtual desktop. A live call through the Arita home server. This was the image communication system using the security cameras set up in every room, which meant—

"Wh-whoa?!" Haruyuki threw his head back fiercely at the white (steam and foam from the call location) and light pink (the bare skin of the caller) that was deployed in his field of view. The momentum sent him tumbling off the sofa, but of course, the window did not disappear.

"Hey, Fuko, what are you looking up at the ceiling for?"

"I forgot to give a warning about one little thing."

"Warning? To whom?"

This back-and-forth held the unique echo of the bathroom and filled Haruyuki's hearing. There was no room for doubt that the owners of the voices—which equaled the owners of the bare skin—were Kuroyukihime and Fuko.

I can't look! He squeezed his eyes shut, and even pressed both hands over his eyelids, but the window was displayed on his virtual desktop—it was actually inside his head, so it wouldn't disappear with these sorts of actions. In fact, closing his eyes cut off the bright light of the living room, making the live video window even more vivid.

In the center of this window, Fuko Kurasaki, foam like whipped cream strategically positioned on her body, smiled brightly as she looked directly up at the camera. "Corvus, I'll say this just in case. If you should happen to run out while we're in the bath, you know verrrrry well what will happen, okay? ♥"

Y-y-y-y-yes, o-o-of course, I know! But before Haruyuki could answer—

"Wh-wh-whaaaaaat?!" A cry that closely resembled a rival character from the shonen comics of the last century rang out on the other side of the camera. "F-F-F-F-F-Fuko, you didn't actually connect a live circuit with Haruyuki, did you?!"

"Now, now, it's all right, Sacchi. I'm protected with carefully calculated angles and obstacles. ♪"

Just as she said, due to the foam from the body soap and the angle of her body, only Fuko's left arm and back were shown on the right side of the window.

However, in front of her, Kuroyukihime had apparently been having her hair washed by Fuko and was, befittingly for the Black King who poured all her potential into attack power, without defense or maybe taking a no-guard battle strategy.

"A-a-and what about me?!" Shouting, she wrapped her arms around her own body, but this action only further weakened her thin foam armor.

No, Kuroyukihime! We're still in junior high! Haruyuki cried out in his mind as he tried to turn his face away. But, naturally, the window chased after it, so the effort was in vain. And he couldn't even remember the simple fact that all he had to do was disconnect the circuit or minimize the window with the hands currently covering his eyes.

"Sheeah!" Suddenly, Kuroyukihime's arm flashed out in a move like one of Black Lotus's thrusting techniques, and the lump of foam she launched covered the camera on the ceiling of the bath in a thick layer.

Haruyuki stared with a mental *Ah!* at the window dyed a single shade of white, and in his ears, he heard the voice of his Legion Master.

"Haruyuki."

"Y-yes?" he replied ever so timidly.

"While we're in the bath, get three direct cables ready at the emergency disconnection hub," she said in a tone that could even be considered kind. "It seems tonight's special training is going to go long."

Getting the emergency disconnection ready meant they were diving not into the normal duel field but rather the Unlimited Neutral Field. In that case, the words "go long" held a truly terrifying nuance. Like someone saying *"This is going to be a long trip..."* in some sci-fi space movie as the crew, from a faster-than-light-speed ship, gazes at their home star.

"L-long? Like how long...?" Haruyuki asked, not knowing when to give up.

Kuroyukihime's response was crisp. "Long enough that you'll completely forget this video feed."

2

Rubbing her hair with a towel as she returned to the living room, Kuroyukihime looked in turn at the three XSB cables and the small hub set out on the glass table, then at the glass of mineral water Haruyuki reverently held out to her, and nodded. "Mmm."

She accepted the glass and drank the water down, the ice lightly clinking. Standing at attention before her, Haruyuki sent glances at his Legion Master, fresh from the bath.

Her warm, gray pajamas were the ones she had bought at the shopping mall attached to the condo on the day of her unexpected sleepover a month earlier. At the time, she had grumbled that they didn't have black, but she had actually brought them with her today. The top was short-sleeved, while the bottoms were knee-length, so her flushed pink skin offered a vivid contrast with the gray of the fabric.

Perhaps this thought was a trigger; in that instant, the live video from earlier started to puff up and start playing in his head. Kuroyukihime pressed the glass, now with nothing but ice in it, up against his cheek.

"Heeyaaah?!" Leaping up, Haruyuki then faced a direct hit from the special attack Super Chilly Kuroyukihime Smile.

"If you don't hurry and forget the things you should forget, the time we dive in the Unlimited Neutral Field will only get longer, you know, Haruyuki."

"Uh, um, we're not doing the zero G training anymore?"

"That'll make us sick—I mean, I don't like the background texture, so we'll do it next time. Or are you saying that you'd like to try and firm up your memories in a weightless space?"

"N-noofcoursenotridiculous! I'll forget everything—I've already forgotten! I've completely forgotten!" he shouted, moving his hands and head from side to side on a horizontal.

"Oh my, is that so, Corvus? So then, are you telling me you've forgotten my heartfelt warning?" Now it was Fuko's voice echoing in the living room, and Haruyuki's entire body snapped to a stop, frozen.

He turned toward her, emerging slightly behind Kuroyukihime, with her Vacuum Smashing Raker Smile, and protested vehemently, "N-n-n-no, I didn't forget! I remember! I completely remember!"

"What? Those words are going to extend your special training by a month, you know?"

"N-n-n-no, I don't remem— No, I forg— Wait, um…" Flapping his hands, he displayed his powerful Mega Stunned Haruyuki Panic.

The two older girls suddenly let out small giggles and then began to laugh out loud in earnest. Unable to react any further, Haruyuki could only freeze in place.

Five minutes later.

In a state of total lethargy in reaction to the too-great mental load, Haruyuki stared vacantly from a ways off on the carpet at Fuko's handling of the blow dryer she held to Kuroyukihime's hair.

In contrast with the simple gray pajamas that were Kuroyukihime's sleepwear, Fuko's was a pale-blue, fluttering negligee. Since she was sitting on the sofa with her legs out to one side, about 65 percent of her shapely legs were exposed beneath the lacy hem. Normally, he very much wouldn't be able to turn his gaze in that direction, but he was currently in a state of mental shutdown, so thinking it had to be okay, he took in this sight, more beautiful than anything.

"Ah!" A small cry of realization fell from his mouth. Now, he did hurriedly look away. And then hung his head deeply. It wasn't that he had seen something he shouldn't have; just the opposite. When he looked at Fuko, something that normally would definitely have entered his view did not now: her trademark over-the-knee socks.

"It's all right, Corvus," she said, suddenly.

A shudder ran through his body. But he couldn't lift his face. "B-but…" Head still hanging, he managed to get this out.

"Right from the start today, I wanted you to see, Corvus," came her immediate, gentle response. "So, go on then, please lift your face."

"……"

After hesitating another few seconds, Haruyuki nervously started to move his gaze. His eyes traced out the striped pattern on the carpet, reached the angle of the sofa, and went left. Finally, his field of view captured two snowy white, bare legs. The nails shining brilliantly at the ends of the toes and the line of the metatarsals popping up slightly were entirely without uncanniness, but the construction of these legs was different from Kuroyukihime's or Haruyuki's. They were artificial, made of metal and biocompatible nanopolymers—prosthetic legs.

Going back from the legs to the negligee, Haruyuki finally met Fuko's eyes again, and she greeted him with a smile more gentle than anything.

"Please come closer, hmm?"

Kuroyukihime, having her hair brushed by Fuko, also encouraged Haruyuki with an unusually warm smile.

Steeling his resolve, he lifted himself up from the carpet and crawled over to the girls on all fours. When he plopped down on the floor again, Fuko's hand stopped, and she sat up straight on the sofa. At the same time, the noise of a motor so faint Haruyuki normally didn't notice it reached his ears.

"About eighty percent of the output is covered by artificial muscle fibers, but fine control is difficult with just that, so I still need servo motors in the joints." Her fingertip traced the knee area.

When he looked closely, a faint line ran around the leg, about five centimeters wide, at the kneecap. Other than that, it was really impossible to tell the leg apart from a biological one. This line, normally covered by her over-the-knee socks, was probably the connection between her real leg and the prosthetic, but the precision with skin color, the continuity of faint shadows was such that it was thoroughly impossible to believe that the area above the line was flesh and the area below it machine.

"It's. Amazing. It's like…a work of art. Um, if they're this beautiful, I wonder…if you really need to wear socks," Haruyuki murmured.

Fuko giggled and ran her fingers from the connection line up to the thigh above. "The reason I wear the knee socks isn't to hide my prosthetic legs, but to protect the artificial skin. In fact, from this line until about fifteen centimeters up is, strictly speaking, not biological."

"Huh?"

"The attachment socket is covered in nanopolymer skin and wraps up my own legs. They're fused on the skin cell level, so I can't take off the attachment part by myself anymore."

"Your own…legs," Haruyuki repeated in a quiet voice.

"I talked to you a little about this before." Fuko started to nod slowly. "My legs aren't missing because of an accident or an illness, but because of a hereditary genetic defect. So the fetal defect would have been reported to my parents fairly early on in the pregnancy."

The expression on the face of the older girl as she told this story didn't seem to be at all different from her usual look, but the end of her sentence trembled just for the hint of a second. Sitting alongside her, Kuroyukihime moved about ten centimeters to the side to bring her body up against Fuko's. She placed her hand on her friend's knee.

As if encouraged by this contact, Fuko began anew: "Normally, with a defect like missing legs, the parents would think about aborting. There was a real possibility that I wouldn't get life in this world...At the time, actually, my parents apparently really struggled with it. Considering that, I should be grateful they allowed me to be born. But...ever since I was little, until this year, when I turned sixteen, this feeling of resentment toward my parents has stabbed into my heart like a small thorn. Why...why did they give birth to me...?"

"..."

Unable to immediately think of something to say, Haruyuki clenched his hands tight, still sitting on his knees on the carpet.

All Burst Linkers carried in a place deep in their hearts their own individual wounds. The Brain Burst program used these wounds as a forge to produce the duel avatar, so an avatar's appearance and abilities inevitably reflected the state of these wounds, although the degree to which they did so varied.

The most significant characteristic of Fuko's other self, Sky Raker, was not the beautiful female-type duel avatar itself, but the Enhanced Armament it had been born with, Gale Thruster. A streamlined rocket booster equipped on her back, although its firing time was short, the thrust surpassed even Silver Crow's flying ability.

Fuko had once described Gale Thruster as "incomplete wings"— that her feeling of being afraid of reaching the sky even as she sought it produced its absolute maximum altitude of three hundred meters. However, that was not the case. Haruyuki and Fuko had learned this in the final stage of the Hermes' Cord race, at the pinnacle of the orbital elevator they reached together. Gale Thruster—no, the duel avatar Sky Raker—hadn't been born to fly, instead bound to the surface of the earth by gravity.

"But, you know, that thorn, Corvus...You pulled it out for me."

Sunk into thought as he was, these words reached Haruyuki's ears in a cloud.

The servo motors made a slight operation noise, and Fuko got down off the sofa and dropped to her knees in front of Haruyuki. She shifted to a more formal kneeling position with such a smooth motion, it was no different from biological legs, then reached out her left hand. Her soft palm gently wrapped around Haruyuki's clenched fist.

"What you said to me at the end of the Hermes' Cord race, 'You've always been a duel avatar meant to fight in space'...these words made me finally realize what's important. That...maybe there's meaning even in being born with legs that are only less than half as long as a healthy person's."

"Meaning..."

"Yes." Fuko nodded and took her hand away from Haruyuki's fist, which had loosened at some point, and touched her own leg with her palm. "In the bottom of my heart, somewhere so deep that even I can't see it, I'm sure I've wanted it all this time. A world that's natural with these legs. That's..."

"A weightless environment?" Unconsciously, Haruyuki finished Fuko's sentence for her.

The gentle smile before his eyes moved slowly up and down. "I'd forgotten for a long time, but when I was still in the lower grades of elementary school, before I became a Burst Linker, I read this small paper media book at the library nearby. It was science fiction for adults, so the kanji characters and terminology were difficult, and I struggled with them, but I used the AR *furigana* reading function in my Neurolinker and pushed myself to keep reading. Because that book was about children who were given arms instead of legs through genetic engineering to be more adapted to a weightless environment. It was almost like I was one of them. I was totally captivated."

Here, Fuko's smile changed into something a little sadder.

"The book was incredibly old, published in the last century, so there wasn't a rating chip embedded in it. Which was why

I could read it; it was actually designated as fifteen or older. So halfway through, the librarian found me and took it away. I just *had* to read it to the end, so I tried to get my parents to buy me the digital media version, but there wasn't one. The PM version was removed from the library before too long, and I never did get to finish it."

She moved pale fingers gently on her knees as though tracing them across a paper page.

In Haruyuki's brain, novels, manga, and anime were things scattered around as data on the network. It was hard for him to imagine a book you could lose and never read again, but even so, for some reason, he felt like he could understand Fuko's sad bittersweetness.

"Of course, I was very sad." Lifting her face, Fuko continued, "But I was a child, so eventually, I forgot about the book, and now I can't even remember the title or the author's name. But…I suppose that desire, me also wanting to go to a weightless world, remained somewhere in my heart all this time. After that, when I became a Burst Linker, the program took the mold of this wound and desire that even I had forgotten and produced Sky Raker and Gale Thruster."

She stopped there and looked back at their Legion Master, who was still on the sofa. The pajama-clad Kuroyukihime looked at her friend with a tranquil expression and then finally, soundlessly, stood up and sat down so that she was on Fuko's left side.

Fuko's mouth stayed shut for a while before she started again in a slightly softer tone. "But because I forgot my true wish, I set my sights on something stunted in the Accelerated World. If I had realized sooner that the place my avatar symbolized was not the sky, but space beyond that; if I could have believed in the existence of a Space stage that would someday come and had waited for it—I wouldn't have made Sacchi so sad, I wouldn't have created the trigger for the destruction of the Legion—"

"You're wrong, Fuko." Kuroyukihime reached out both hands abruptly and wrapped her arms around the girl to cut her off. "If we're going to talk about blame, then it also lies with me and all our Legion members for not trying to understand the strength of the feelings you were holding back all that time. You reached level eight to be freed of the yoke of gravity, and still you were not permitted to touch the sky. I should have understood and accepted you, the fact that you were willing to cast aside even your avatar's legs. But rather than doing so, I chastised you. I was so reluctant to lose your combat abilities. I was the one pushing my desire to become level ten on everyone in the Legion, an act of ultimate self-righteousness."

At that time, Haruyuki hadn't been a member of Nega Nebulus—he hadn't even been a Burst Linker—so he could only guess at the details of the situation. But from the bits and pieces of information he had gained so far, he thought he had grasped the facts at least.

Two and a half years earlier, in the winter of 2044, the first Nega Nebulus had been destroyed. The sequence of events leading up to this tragedy was tangled and complex. The fact that Kuroyukihime accepted Fuko's request and amputated Sky Raker's legs with her own sword. The fact that at the meeting of the Seven Kings immediately after that, she had taken the head of the first Red King Red Rider, who was insisting on the necessity of a mutual nonaggression pact. And the fact that even later, everyone in the Legion had taken on the challenge of attacking the Castle and the utterly impenetrable guard of the Four Gods. These were not all unrelated incidents.

Most likely because of her perception that she had been the initial trigger, Fuko's avatar had remained without legs until a little while after she came back to the second Nega Nebulus. Normally, damage from missing parts was healed the instant the duel ended, and what had made it permanent in this case was Fuko's "negative will," convinced as she was that she did not deserve to get her legs back. Put another way, it was basically a curse she had cast on herself.

However, in the Hermes' Cord race, when she flew with Gale

Thruster in the sea of stars that she finally reached, she got her legs back. The curse that had bound her for over two years—several times that, when time spent in the Accelerated World was included—had been released.

"You can just get back the things you've lost bit by bit," Haruyuki murmured suddenly, abstractedly.

With Fuko and Kuroyukihime's eyes on him, he would normally shrink into himself and be unable to say anything further, but at that moment, he earnestly put his thoughts into words.

"You get lost, you lose, you make mistakes…But if you just go back a little, I'm sure you can find the things you've lost again. And then you can just start walking from there. I mean, you, Master, and Shinomiya did actually come back to the Legion. I'm sure the other two members of the Elements, and the rest of the Legion members, too—they'll come back to you soon enough, Kuroyukihime. That's what I think…"

It definitely wasn't a long speech, but here his vanishingly small speech engine overheated, and Haruyuki hung his head, closing his mouth. But even after waiting a few seconds, there was no reaction from the other two, and he started to think that maybe he'd made some kind of terrible mistake and that maybe he should use a So-Sorry Dash and escape to the washroom.

"Honestly, Corvus. Here you are, the younger one, making us ladies tear up. It's not fair."

Hearing this, he got flustered—"*ladies*"?!—as he gingerly lifted his eyes. It was just when Fuko lowered the finger she had up at the corner of her eye. Before he knew it, the look on her face had returned to the usual Raker Smile, and the legs she had tucked neatly underneath her slid out to one side inexplicably—until she stretched them out in front of Haruyuki.

"As a reward, you're allowed to touch them, just a little. ♥" The paleness of the legs stretching out from the hem of the negligee, and the super-destructive force of this line easily smashed Haruyuki's mental powers.

Not noticing the unnaturalness of the situation or Kuroyuki-hime's hard eyes on him, he said, "O…kay," and gradually advanced the fingers of his right hand.

The instant his fingertips made the contact with her surprisingly thin ankle, Haruyuki gasped. The nanopolymer had an overwhelmingly smooth texture, and the faint warmth surprised him. When he thought about it, it was probably only natural that the electricity of the battery inside was continually converted into heat, but this "body temperature" definitely didn't seem like that of a prosthetic leg. He finally moved his fingers up. The elasticity produced by the artificial muscle fibers covered by the polymer skin was indeed natural and had a suppleness of trained muscles that was far from the pudginess of his own legs. The connection area from the shin to the knee was apparently a combination of many motors, gears, and dampers, so here alone was a slightly mechanical feel.

The instant his fingers moved around to the back of the knee, an "Mmm!" slipped out of Fuko, and her leg moved slightly.

"Uh, um, you can feel that?" Haruyuki asked in surprise, hoarsely.

"Yes. Well, it's just on the level of a rough sense of pressure. The skin sensation sensor elements are still under development. But when they're touched gently like that, I feel a little tickle."

"I-I'm sorry," he hurriedly apologized, and he started to pull his hand away.

But Fuko pushed on his hand and grinned. "It's all right. I want you to really know my legs, Corvus. Please, continue."

"…O-okay…" As he was told, Haruyuki returned his fingers to the artificial skin. He moved around from the back of the knee to the top of the round kneecap and arrived at the faint connection line. From there down was completely prosthetic, but from what Fuko said, the top was also the connection attachment and socket, and on top of that, the nanopolymer skin and her own skin were fused at the cellular level. But he couldn't tell at all at a glance how far the polymer went. Admiring the high level of cutting-edge cybernetics technology, he slowly traced his fingers along the slender thigh. He advanced five, ten, fifteen centimeters above the connection line, and the instant he was fairly near the hem of the negligee—

"Ah!" With a faint voice, her whole leg twitched back again.

"Fr-from that area, it's my own skin. Original human sensors are indeed amazing, hmm? The sensation of touch is totally different."

"Huh? Th-this is the border? I totally can't tell from the feel or the look of it. They really are fused, huh?"

"Mmm! C-Corvus! If you touch me like that, it tickle—"

Gnyaaaaang! There was a sudden assault on his left cheek, and Haruyuki took his fingers off Fuko's leg and flew up.

"O-owhowhowhowhahaha!"

"Just. How. Long. Are you going to do that?!" The one shouting was, naturally, Kuroyukihime, yanking as hard as she could on Haruyuki's cheek with her right hand. "Normally, a person pokes a little and stops! And you, Fuko! You! Why would touching your leg be a reward?!"

"Goodness! It's just that Pard from Promi told me that Corvus was apparently quite weak to legs."

"What?" Kuroyukihime's voice held a dangerous edge.

"Wh—N-no!" Haruyuki jumped a little, left cheek still pinched. "I definitely don't have a leg fetish or anyshing!"

"Setting aside the veracity of the information, why would Blood Leopard know something like that?!"

"I—I—I don't hnow! I jush rode behind her on the motorshaicle and on her avatar's back!" he protested, totally absorbed in his defense, and now it wasn't only Kuroyukihime, but also Fuko's eyes that suddenly grew cold. Without even the time to think, *Crap*—

"That reminds me, Fuko. There's still something we have to do, hmm?"

"That's right, Sacchi. We forgot our responsibility to give Corvus special training in the Unlimited Neutral Field, didn't we?"

Held tight on either side, Haruyuki was dragged over to the glass table.

"Uh, um, it's late already, and we have school tomorrow."

"Not a problem. We took care of homework a while ago, didn't we?"

"B-but we have to do the Space-stage training, too."

"Don't worry. We can do as much of that as we want later."

"B-but it's getting to be time to go to bed…"

"It's fine, Haruyuki. The night is long in the Unlimited Neutral Field." Kuroyukihime had no sooner said that than she was inserting a cable into his Neurolinker. The other two cables were quickly connected to each of the girl's Linkers, and three indicator lights flashed on the hub on the table.

"All right then, we'll go on the count of five. Corvus, for each minute you're late, the special training menu will go up a level, hmm? ♥" Fuko announced this with a smile even kinder than the one she had flashed him earlier, and there was no way he could not shout the command and just run away somewhere instead.

Sweat oozing down his forehead, Haruyuki was still secured on both sides as his Legion Master and Submaster began the countdown together.

"Five, four, three, two, one…"

""""Unlimited Burst!""""

Shouting in unison with the girls, Haruyuki thought, *It'd be great if the Space stage happened soon. Then I could tag-team with Master, and we'd win all over the place with the combo of Gale Thrust's propulsion and Crow's maneuverability. I won't ever let anyone call Master "Icarus" again. I mean, Master's—Sky Raker's— wings have finally arrived, glittering sky-blue.*

In the world of the stars—that world she's wanted more than anyone else…

END

ACCEL WORLD, Volume 12
REKI KAWAHARA

Translation by Jocelyne Allen
Cover art by HIMA

ACCEL WORLD
© REKI KAWAHARA 2012
All rights reserved.
Edited by ASCII MEDIA WORKS
First published in 2012 by KADOKAWA CORPORATION, Tokyo.
English translation rights arranged with KADOKAWA CORPORATION, Tokyo, through Tuttle-Mori Agency, Inc., Tokyo.

English translation © 2017 by Yen Press, LLC

Yen On
1290 Avenue of the Americas
New York, NY 10104

Visit us at yenpress.com
facebook.com/yenpress
twitter.com/yenpress
yenpress.tumblr.com
instagram.com/yenpress

First Yen On Edition: December 2017

Yen On is an imprint of Yen Press, LLC.
The Yen On name and logo are trademarks of Yen Press, LLC.

Library of Congress Cataloging-in-Publication Data
Names: Kawahara, Reki, author. | HIMA (Comic book artist), illustrator. | Beepee, designer. | Allen, Jocelyne, 1974– translator.
Title: Accel world / Reki Kawahara ; illustrations, HIMA ; design, bee-pee; translation by Jocelyne Allen.
Description: First Yen On edition. | New York, NY : Yen On, 2014–
Identifiers: LCCN 2014025099 | ISBN 9780316376730 (v. 1 : pbk.) | ISBN 9780316296366 (v. 2 : pbk.) | ISBN 9780316296373 (v. 3 : pbk.) | ISBN 9780316296380 (v. 4 : pbk.) | ISBN 9780316296397 (v. 5 : pbk.) | ISBN 9780316296403 (v. 6 : pbk.) | ISBN 9780316358194 (v. 7 : pbk.) | ISBN 9780316317610 (v. 8 : pbk.) | ISBN 9780316502702 (v. 9 : pbk.) | ISBN 9780316466059 (v. 10 : pbk.) | ISBN 9780316466066 (v. 11 : pbk.) | ISBN 9780316466073 (v. 12 : pbk.)
Subjects: | CYAC: Science fiction. | Virtual reality—Fiction. | Fantasy.
Classification: LCC PZ7.K1755Kaw 2014 | DDC [Fic]—dc23
LC record available at https://lccn.loc.gov/2014025099

ISBNs: 978-0-316-46607-3 (paperback)
        978-1-9753-0093-7 (ebook)

10 9 8 7 6 5 4 3 2 1

LSC-C

Printed in the United States of America